I0639067

FOOL'S BETRAYAL

TIM FORD

ISBN: 978-1-989506-64-6

© 2022 Tim Ford

All rights reserved. No parts of this publication may be
reproduced or transmitted in any form or by any means,
electronically or mechanically, including photocopying
recording, or any information storage or retrieval system
without either prior permission of the author.

Published in Canada by Pandamonium Publishing House™.
www.pandamoniumpublishing.com

Cover Design: Alex Goubar
alexgoubar.com

CONTENTS

1 1
2 11
3 16
4 22
5 25
6 32
7 35
8 37
9 42
10 45
11 48
12 50
13 52
14 57
15 59
16 61
17 67
18 69
19 74
20 76
21 103
22 127
23 133
24 143
25 153

26 162

27 166

28 169

29 173

30 189

31 190

32 191

33 192

34 196

35 206

36 211

1

When we landed in Reno, Sean called Nyah and gave her a specific time to meet us at the airport. He never mentioned anything about his injury. With this, and Chuck's death, it once again proves nothing good comes from Mexico. Fuck, even their weed now sucks, screw them and the burrito loving donkey they rode in on.

Once we landed, Sean looked at us in angst, and actually asked for our help. Sean said he would be fine, a minor wound. Donnie told him if gangrene sets in, he will not be fine. That poison could take his life. Donnie reminded Sean that emergency room docs know a gunshot wound from, say, dumping a motorcycle and ripping the shit out of your leg. So, make sure he has a solid cover story.

The pig-headed Sean finally agreed with us. He will say he was hunting, and his gun accidentally went off. One of the guys in the hunt camp was a medic, performing triage until he could see a real doctor. Donnie told him to keep repeating this story as more than likely the cops get called for every gunshot wound that ends up in Emergency.

Donnie took one side of Sean, and I took the other side.

"Jesus Christ, Sean! Quit drinking so much beer. Fuck, I am going to join you in the hospital as I think I now have a hernia." He growled at me.

We saw Nyah pull up and we continued walking towards her. You could see the shock in her face as she now started running towards us.

"Daddy, daddy what happened?"

"I am all right, little one. My gun accidentally went off. After you drop the boys off, I should maybe get a doctor to look at it."

She teared up and asked to see it, Sean told her it was all bandaged up. This shook her so badly, she couldn't even drive. So, after we loaded up the vehicle with all our weapons, I drove Nyah and Sean to the hospital. I told Nyah to call me once they are done and I will come and pick them up. I dropped off Donnie and said let's do beers tomorrow, he said sounds good. Then I drove Oscar and I back to my place.

Pamdora's was closed so I put the weapons in there for now through the alley side door, still to light out to be bringing them upstairs.

As soon as we went upstairs, I headed for the fridge and a beer as Oscar sat down and rolled a king joint. Both the beer and joint complimented each other quite well. I checked the answering machine, and the only calls were from Rachel, Ella, and surprisingly Herschel who asked me to call him. Still nothing from Charlene. *Where the hell are you, girl?* Yeah, I didn't feel like talking to anyone, but if I stunk as half bad as Oscar, not even a fly would land on me.

So, I jumped in the shower and had so many things racing through my mind. Then it hit me why this death hit me so hard.

When Jake was murdered, Rachel was all alone. I was ten thousand miles away in the jungles of Southeast Asia. The pain on Candice's face must have mirrored the pain on Rachel's face.

As soon as I got out and dried off, I called Rachel, I got her voice mail but told her I am home safe and sound, and that I loved her.

Oscar in the meantime had passed out on the couch. Even the phone ringing didn't wake him. I was excited expecting it to be Rachel, but it was Nyah, she said she and Sean are ready to be picked up. I couldn't wake him, so I made sure I had extra cash to grab a taxi home, in case Nyah still wasn't able to drive me.

I pulled up out front, and both were outside waiting for me. Sean now had a pair of crutches. He had this goofy look on his face, they must have given him a shot of morphine.

I helped him in the car and then opened the door for Nyah.

Nyah said yes, they did give him a shot of morphine, boy do I know my drug induced smiles. They gave him prescription painkillers and antibiotics. She said the doctors cut him open and cleaned the wound properly. And yes, the coppers showed up. Uniformed ones at that.

They took down his name, and his cover story.

Once at the Quinn household, I helped Sean up the stairs to the front door which Nyah had opened. We helped him inside and for the first time I met Sean's wife, and Nyah's mom. You could see this is where Nyah gets her looks from, a very pretty lady. Mrs. Quinn thanked me. I said the big lug is a good guy deep down, of course I was going to help in whatever they needed. This was the biggest smile Nyah ever shot me. They asked me to stay for dinner and you know what, I did, especially after Sean insisted. He was even smiling at me; I knew he liked me as a son figure all along. Mrs. Quinn asked if I had ever had jerk chicken before. Can't say I had. That's what we had for dinner.

After dinner, Nyah said she would drive me home seeing how she had to go and pick up Dad's meds. We didn't even get out of the driveway when she reached over and held my hand. We pulled up in front of the drugstore and necked for at least ten minutes before both going inside.

As we stood at the pharmacy, I heard this girl at the dispensary call the pharmacist over. She told him it was Doctor Mattina on the phone.

Ella, my sweet blonde friend doctor Ella Mattina. Did I feel guilty standing there holding hands with Nyah? Fuck no, as of right now Ella and I are friends and not even lovers yet. Even then I am not sure I want to get serious with anyone for a while. The ghost of Charlene is still pulling on my heart strings.

After the prescription was filled, we pulled up to my place. I asked Nyah if she wanted to come up for a toke.

"Only if I can suck your cock afterwards, Mitch."

I leaned in, kissed her, and said of course she can. We went upstairs, Oscar was still passed out on the couch. So, I grabbed the bag of weed, a couple beers out of the fridge and we went into my bedroom.

Nyah loved the freedom of not wearing clothes, I didn't even have to try and undress her as she was naked within a millisecond.

She sat on the floor with her legs crossed while she lit up the bong pipe. After a couple tokes she looked at me all stoned and started to giggle. I asked what was so funny.

"My Dad actually thought you were decent tonight. He calls you a man whore, most of the time."

I started to laugh, "If only dear old Dad could see us now, baby."

We smoked about a nickel worth the weed. With Nyah the more

stoned she was, the better a lover she was.

She rocked the shit out of me, what a great rider she is, full thrusts. when you thought the head of your cock would slide out of her pussy, she grinded back the other way, amazing lover.

We did it twice before the two of us jumped in the shower, and she headed home. I told her to call me, so I know she made it home safe.

Nyah's phone call woke the living dead aka Oscar. I thanked her for a great night.

Oscar was almost in a state of shock, he didn't have a clue what time it was and why was Nyah calling. I told him and then said I am off to bed. He looked at the clock and asked if it was 2 in the afternoon, or morning.

"No sun out, talk in the morning."

It was funny how out of sorts he was. Perhaps me making fun of Oscar came back to bite me in the ass as when I woke up twelve hours later, I did the same thing as him, no idea what time of day it was or even what day it was.

Oscar had vacated the couch and he was not in his room. I walked to the kitchen and saw a newspaper on the table. Today is Tuesday, I look outside, and it is quite sunny, so it is afternoon. So, I scratched my balls, made a pot of coffee and had a bowl of cereal. I finished cleaning up when the phone rang, it was Ella.

"Hey, I have been worried sick about you. When did you get back?"

"Late last night, I actually got up, sorry Ella I was too bagged."

"Are you too bagged for dinner and cocktails later tonight?"

"Never too tired for you, hon."

"Glad to hear Mitch, I want to make it up for you as I was not a perfect first date."

"You were great, hon."

"You are too sweet, Mitchell. How about I swing by and pick you up around eight?"

I said that would be great, looking forward to it. After I hung up the phone, I had this flash of Candice's face full of pain over the loss of her brother. So, I called Rachel at home and left a voicemail. I said let's do something this weekend. I then jumped on my bike and headed to Popeye's for a workout. Came home and took a long hot shower. I rolled a couple joints for Ella and myself, and before I knew it, I heard a knock at the door. It was Ella all dressed up real spiffy. I was in jeans and a Levi's jean shirt.

I could tell by Ella's look and the way she eyed my outfit up and down that my attire is not suitable for the restaurant she had in mind.

Well, I haven't got in her pants yet, so if it means putting on dress pants and a nice shirt, well worth it.

"If this restaurant has a dress code I can change, that is not a problem, Ella."

Ella then had this huge smile come to her blushing face.

She took off her glasses and said, "How about we stay in and order pizza instead?"

I passed her a joint and said this will help us get nice and hungry. I asked if she wanted a beer, she said yes. We didn't finish the joint or beers when I found myself necking and then picking up Ella and carrying her to my bedroom. You could tell she was a bit nervous as her body was covered in goosebumps. We are lying on the bed as I am starting to undo her top while kissing away. Much to my surprise she was not wearing a bra. At first, I started to squeeze, and play with her breasts.

Her hands are still around my neck, so I move her arm down lower and put her hand on the bulge of my jeans. She gives it a squeeze and then giggles. I then have this horrifying thought come to me, is she still a virgin? It is like I have to orchestrate everything for her. Fuck it, so I now start to suck her breasts, small B cup by the way, really dark nipples as I rub her crotch through her dress which is radiating a lot of heat. She now lays her head back on the pillow and is totally into what I am doing.

I then slide my hand up her dress and start to run her clit through her panties, man you can feel the moisture seeping through. Let's see what the good doctor tastes like. I got on my knees, reached up and started to pull her panties off.

You know that look you get before you go on a roller coaster ride for the first time? Well, that was the look Ella was giving me.

I was gentle taking them off. I lifted up her dress and then my tongue went on a mission.

Good thing Nyah took care of me last night as I would be a little pissed, she is not playing with me, but for now, time to give her multiple orgasms, never let it be said that I am a selfish lover.

I started to do the alphabet on her with my tongue while reaching up and playing her breasts. Ella wasn't a loud moaner, she was a soft and gentle moaner, subtle enough that I knew I was doing a damn good job. After about twenty minutes my head was drenched in sweat and my tongue was done.

So, time to get down and dirty. My cock needs to get into her pussy. I stood up, wiped the sweat from my face and took my clothes off.

Ella stared at me with a smile.

"Take your dress fully off, baby."

"Before we start, Mitchell," said Ella. Fuck here we go; *do I love her*, or *I am a virgin* speech is about to happen.

"Yes, Ella?"

"I am not saying you are not a clean person. But right now, there is an epidemic of sexually transmitted diseases in the Bay area. Do you have any condoms?"

That was not the conversation I was expecting, I am pretty damn sure I don't have any condoms.

"Let me have a look around."

I knew better then to look in my room, so I headed right to Oscar's room, and sure as fuck right on the nightstand table was a whack of condoms. I walked back in the room still hard and saw a naked Ella grinning ear to ear and giggling. She told me to give her a condom package and come closer. She tore open the package with her teeth. Rolled the condom backwards and then rolled it onto my cock.

"Nice cock, mister Strongbow," said Ella with a serious, yet sexy voice.

Once the condom was fully on, she started to lick my cock. This was a first. She then laid on her back, spread her legs and pulled me on top of her. I once again started to neck with her while fingering her pussy, it was wet, no make that soaked, but still really tight.

After a couple minutes I stopped the kissing and looked at her and asked if she was ready, she giggled and said yes.

My cock wouldn't slide in on its own, damn she is tight. I had to hold onto my cock as I was penetrating her pussy. By far the tightest pussy I had ever been in.

It took me a couple minutes to be fully inside of her. If I didn't know better, I would think I was going in her ass. My knees were spinning on the bed like car tires on ice. They were starting to burn from the friction.

I could tell after a few failed full thrusts Ella was not enjoying this.

So, I pulled my cock out of her pussy and said to hang on. Top shelf was a jar of Vaseline, last used on Charlene's ass. I told her to take some and gently rub it on the condom as I put some my two fingers and rubbed it on the inside of her pussy

"This will be better, baby."

She smiled, and said she trusted me. I still glided my cock into her, but I could tell the less friction made it more comfortable for her.

I could tell after the first ten thrusts Ella was not a virgin which made me happy. If anything, wearing the condom gave me extra stamina. And my little doctor was able to take a good hard pounding, those little supple moans became more intense the harder and faster I was fucking her.

All was good onto she moaned out for fuck me harder, she was close to cumming. That angelic voice begging for it made me jump on the orgasm wave and I tried my best to make sure I rode that wave to the orgasm shore for my woman.

I stared at her as I was now starting to cum, fuck she was beautiful.

I kept my hips moving even though my cock was soaked in my own juices and getting really sensitive. I eventually collapsed on top of her. Caught my breath and then rolled onto my back. Ella threw both of her arms around my shoulder and was kissing me and telling me that I am amazing.

"Thanks, did you cum?"

"Holy smokes, Mitch; I lost track of how many times I climaxed. You are amazing, wow!"

About now, my head grew three times its normal size.

"You are amazing yourself, Ella."

The glow in her face and smile I knew she was telling me the truth.

I peeled the condom off, asked if she wanted a beer. She said she needs something. So, I walked in the kitchen to grab a beer and throw my condom in the garbage. In the kitchen is Oscar and some blonde doing hash tokes by the gas stove.

"How long have you guys been here?" I said to them.

They were both pretty fucking stoned as Oscar said, "Like throwing a full-grown sow down a groundhog hole."

He and the blonde started to laugh. I was not amused and told them to shut the fuck up. I grabbed the beers and headed back to the bedroom. And yes I let her know that Oscar and some chick came home.

Right away she had this worried look come to her face as she pulled the sheets up to her neck, that kind of made me chuckle.

"He gets his own place next weekend; all good, baby."

"Speaking of weekends," Ella said. "There is a fundraiser for the San Francisco philharmonic orchestra, and I need a date, would you be willing to go with me?" She could tell this was not my cup of tea, but she promised she would make it up to me.

So, I said sure, why not, it could even be interesting. After a couple more beers she opened up about her past sexual experiences.

I was only the third guy to get inside of her and the first

circumcised cock in her. Her high school sweetheart took her cherry on prom night. After that was a doctor in med school with her, that was a five-year relationship. She then asked about my sexual history with a grin and raised eyebrow. I delayed as I smiled at her, and she told me to spill the beans.

"There have been a lot."

"I could tell the way your tongue worked, like more than ten?"

So, do I tell her the truth? Fuck, she will want me to double bag my beast if I do.

Add humor to it, "Ten, or ten thousand?"

She smacked me on the arm, and I said I was being silly.

"You are my first doctor if that means anything?"

Ella liked hearing that. We had sex one more time, missionary once again. I feel I am obligated to help open up her sexual world seeing at how so many doctors have taken care of me over the decades. Lord knows how many times I should have died, if not for their work. We grabbed a nice long shower and then we fell asleep in each other's arms.

The alarm went off at seven, what an awful hour. But Ella had to go home and get changed before work. And me, well I tried to talk her into a quickie, but to no avail.

So, after she left, I crashed out for a bit before hitting the gym. I dragged Oscar's lazy ass with me. Donnie was there with his two newest hires to his bike shop, Steve, and Rick, or as I know them, Sokol and Ringor, yes, Dafina's brothers. Both are strikers now for the Oakland Hell Hounds.

Now, this was my first time meeting them. Last I heard they were still in Nam. I can only imagine what Dafina or Korab, their dad, said about me. Yeah, things didn't end so well with her.

As Donnie does the introductions, I make sure to make solid eye contact, firm grip, no smile. Let's see them tip their hands first.

There was a little bit of tension at first, but we talked about our tours in Nam. I made sure to tell them I came home pretty fucked, head was not on straight, and made a lot of mistakes. Now this was not me admitting weakness to them. I guess letting them know, I kind of fucked up things with their sister. And yes, I am man enough to admit I have fucked up in the past. All in all, they seem to be decent guys, brothers in arms.

Donnie said he talked to Joseph and said good job. He will be back tomorrow and wants to take us all out for dinner. Spouses and girlfriends included. So, I told Donnie I am sort of seeing this doctor, and she is Mike Battaglia's first cousin.

"Does Mike know you are dating her? Those Italians getting really overprotective when it comes to family."

"He dated Rachel, fuck him. I treat her like gold, fuck I have even committed to going to a SFPO fund raiser with her!"

"You, mister rock and roll? She must really suck mean cock."

Donnie could tell the way I didn't answer and sort of did a face he asked if I was serious.

"I am only the third guy she has been with; in time, man."

After the gym, Oscar and I went and grabbed something to eat. He asked if I remembered Tommy Jovanaski from San Quentin.

"The big Pollock biker from Alaska, right?"

"Yeah, that's him, well he gets out next Monday and he asked if I could fly him home with as much dope as my plane could handle."

"How do you know this? I hope you two haven't been talking over my phone."

"Not at all, Strongbow. That blonde that was here last night is his wife. I have been corresponding with her on the phone, relax Mitch, phone booth and Tommy, via coded letters. I have the oil and you have the weed, Strongbow. Plus, my fee to fly him and his old lady home. I can see us making fifty grand each if not more, what do you think, man?"

"The one thing I don't like is flying into a state where we have zero connections. Almost like us going into Indian territory pardon the pun. Nothing saying as soon as the plane lands we are not ambushed. If we do this, I want to be paid before our wheels are in the air. I want to do a little background check on Tommy, and his gang up there. I want to make sure he is not being released early for setting us up to the cops. How do you know it is his wife?"

"I have saw pictures of her in his cell."

"Curious, you fucking her, Oscar?"

"Of course I am, that is the cost of doing business."

"Albert would know what is up with Tommy J. I have to find someone solid without a criminal record to be allowed to visit Albert, no way am I putting anything in a letter. It will have to be someone I trust, I will see if Donnie's new guys Steve and Rick have criminal records.

I want to sit in on the next set of meetings with Tommy's wife. Him I know, her I don't."

"I am taking her out for drinks tonight, so you can talk to her then or in the morning as she will be sleeping over."

My back went right up. "No, she won't. Grab your own motel room or go back to her motel room. If she is a narc, I don't want her to plant a listening device in my place."

"Look, you're getting all paranoid."

I shook my head and told him not to go there.

"O.K. I promise she will not be allowed at your place until you say so. I am picking her up at six for dinner and then drinks, I will call you and tell you where."

"Make sure it is not at the Drunken Leprechaun either."

"I figured that was coming. You know Strongbow, she is a bit of a kinky bitch. You want a piece of her?"

That made me laugh, "I will pass, I have more than enough pussy to play with right now, but from me and Tommy J, thanks."

2

If Tommy wants a large amount of grass, I will have to call Jerry and see if he can get large amounts with little notice. I phoned around and found out he was at the clubhouse. So, I drove my bike over and asked him if he wanted to go for a ride. He seemed intrigued and said sure. We went down the coast for a beer at this shack beside the ocean.

"How is life, little cousin?"

"Life is interesting. I started to see a doctor who is Mike Battaglia's first cousin. And heard about twenty minutes ago, that one of the guys I did time with in San Quentin is getting released this coming Monday and he wants to head back to Alaska with as much weed as I can score. I am a little nervous, so I am going to do a background check and make sure nothing else is going down. Listen, he is in a motorcycle gang in Juneau called The Disciples of Doom, have you ever heard of them?"

"Can't say that I have. They must be independent. Let me make a few calls and I will tell you what I hear. A doctor! Look at you, moving up in the pussy ladder."

That actually made me laugh. "Thanks, Jerry. She is smoking hot. Listen, if I needed say a hundred pounds, how much notice would you need?"

"A day. I could have it all ready, something that big would come by kilos, so you would need forty-five kilos. When will you know for sure?"

"I am meeting with his wife tonight, asking for half upfront and the other half once we land."

"That Syrian friend of yours I hear has his own plane, is that how you are getting it there?"

"Yeah, and Oscar will charge them extra for that."

Jerry was thinking, then said good stuff.

"How is Rachel doing?"

"All right, playing phone tag with her right now. She is working at a law firm in Sacramento."

"Good for her, she is a good kid, your folks would be proud of her."

"And how is your life and your dad and Val doing?"

"I am doing good, peace between the clubs means lots of money to be made, Popeye's is still the number one gym in the Bay area. Dad is good as is Val."

"Good stuff, every time I see your Dad I think of mine, it's that voice, they sounded so much alike growing up. Hey… Steve and Rick, solid guys?"

"Yeah, I am impressed with them so far, why?"

"I need someone without a criminal record to go to San Quentin and talked to Albert Maganini and see if he has heard anything unusual about Tommy J."

"I know Rick did some time. Steve, as far as I know, is without any criminal convictions."

We finished off our beers and then drove back home. I stopped off at Ella's practice and in between her seeing patients I said my boss is taking us out for dinner tomorrow night and would she be my date.

"That is very sweet of you, Mitch. Of course I'll be your date!"

I thanked her for that and last night. She asked if I had plans tonight as she has tomorrow off and would like to have dinner and see the movie Jaws.

I thought of us meeting Tommy J's wife for drinks, and said I have to move a few things around, but that would not be a problem. I told her to call me later and tell me what time the show was at and we can plan dinner around it. I gave her a kiss goodbye, the one nurse gave Ella and me a look, older chick, jealous?

Went home and told Oscar lets go and see Tommy J's wife now as other plans have come up. He said sure and told me where she was staying. I packed my 9MM and he asked if I was expecting trouble.

"In our line of work, I always expect trouble."

Oscar laughed, then knew I was serious, thought about what I said, and he went and grabbed his 9MM.

We jumped in my Mustang and headed over to see Nicky, aka Mrs. Tommy Jovanaski.

She had a room on the 3rd floor, but we didn't have to make it up there as she was sunbathing by the pool. She was drinking beer with a couple guys. I asked Oscar if he knew these guys, he said no. So, we walked over, and these guys were now eying us.

"Mitchell, you finally got dressed," she said laughing.

"Are these guys friends of Tommy?"

She shook her head no as the one guy asked if there was a problem.

I looked around to see if there was anyone else watching then I pulled out my 9MM and said, "I did two years in prison with her husband. There is going to be a big fucking problem if you don't leave right now."

They both got up and left with their cooler full of beer.

Nicky looked at me and said I was one big party pooper.

"Well, I am not here to party, I am here to do business. Tommy gets out on Monday, correct?"

"Yes, he does; been a long three years."

"And he wants a lot of weed and oil, do you know how much?"

"I am seeing him tomorrow as we have a conjugal visit."

"Tell him I need exact amounts and then I can give you a price on the weed. Now, I will want half down, and half when we arrive in Juneau. That is still the plan for us to fly you guys home, right?"

"Yes, that is what Tommy wants. Oscar said that wouldn't be a problem."

"Nicky, I am a great person to do business with, and I am a nasty nightmare to do business with. I don't fuck around, I don't play games, it is business. I like Tommy, he is a good man. I really hope everything works out good for all of us. Rule number one is no talking over phones. And I want you only talking business with Tommy, and Tommy only. Understood?"

"You sound like Tommy now. I know the drill, Mitch."

"Good glad to hear it, those fucking goofs that were here. I don't want to see them around again."

She nodded her head. I finished my beer and asked Oscar if he was staying or coming back home.

"I will be staying, Strongbow. Don't wait up for me," said Oscar with a smirk.

I looked at Nicky who seemed to be embarrassed by this.

If Rachel ever said Oscar asked her out, he wouldn't even hear the gunshot. I drove home all the time thinking of different scenarios with Tommy J and this deal. It has the potential for me to make a lot of money. If these guys in Alaska really like my product I can see steady runs up there, or them coming down here. I have to think of a way to launder all the cash though. I can do some through Pamdora's. not sure how much. I might have to get another business on the go, a front for this.

Ella called me and said the show starts at nine, does that work?

I said yeah that is good. I said I would be by around six thirty to pick her up and take her to dinner. I went and grabbed a long hot shower; I heard the phone ring, but I was still deep in thought about the deal with Tommy J. If it is important, they will leave a message. I got out, dried my hair and balls, then checked the message.

"Mitch, it is Charlene. I was hoping you were home as I need to talk to you about something important. I will try and contact sometime later this week, hope all is well."

Jesus fucking Christ. My heart skipped a beat and my stomach flipped. If my brain wasn't into overdrive with the upcoming deal, with this message or lack of I am now in the red zone. I sat on the couch for ten minutes, blown mind could be an understatement. My first initial reaction was that she was pregnant and moved away on me, flashbacks to 1967 and Tash all over again. This made the most sense. I can't see the cops having her roll on me and she is now in witness protection, but she really knows jack shit about my criminal life. I am sure the cops have more things to do then lock me up for smoking dope, fuck.

The ringing phone snapped me out of my dreaded state of confusion. Heart palpitations, it is Charlene trying me again. I frantically jump up and answer the phone and say hello.

"Mitchell, it is Jerry. I have that information you were asking about"

His gruff voice was not what I was expecting.

"Cool, I have a date tonight with Ella, what time are you working out tomorrow?"

"Around nine, meet you at the gym."

"Yeah, that works Jerry, thanks."

Fuck. I have to continue getting ready or I am going to be late.

I jumped in the car and smoked a joint on the way over to calm my nerves. As soon as Ella got in the car, she asked if I was using a Cheech and Chong air freshener.

"No, I drove Oscar over to this chick's place and he sparked it up; don't worry, baby, I have lots more for us."

14

At dinner I felt myself drifting back to Charlene's message. Ella asked if everything was all right.

Time to think quickly once again. "One of the guys I did time with in San Quentin is being released on Monday. He asked if Oscar could fly him home, and he asked me to come along and see Alaska. I have never been, you?"

"Can't say I have ever been there." I was picking up something off her.

"So, I have to ask you the same question, everything O.K.?"

She put down her folk, did this kind of forced smile with a bit of a shoulder shrug and said, "After you kissed me today, I was reminded by Nancy, my one nurse, that I can actually lose my medical license for dating a patient. I still want to be dating you, so I need you to see another doctor, Mitch. I hope you are not too upset with me over this?"

"Not upset, that was silly of me, sorry. No, I don't want you losing your license. I will look for another doctor."

"Thank you so much, I was worried to tell you this tonight. Now I did call around and I have three doctor friends that would gladly take you in as a new patient."

"That's cool, do I get to sleep with them as well?"

She laughed and said all three were male doctors.

"Never mind. I will stick to sleeping with you, baby."

She gave me a wink and said good answer.

At the show I leaned in after the shark ate Roy Schrieder and said time for Nurse Nancy to go shark hunting, she couldn't stop giggling at that.

3

After the show we went to a bar around the corner from her place.

It was a little snobby for me. Professionals, doctors, lawyers, high end businessmen All the regulars knew Ella and each one certainly eyed me up and down. Being half native, I am used to it, doesn't mean I don't want to break their jaws, though.

Ella grabbed a table, I asked what she wanted to drink, she said white wine. So, I ordered her a glass, and a pitcher of beer for me. Popcorn makes you thirsty.

Not sure what went down faster, my beer or Ella's wine. Time to order more drinks, nice to see my girl relax and yours truly. Been a rough day mentally.

About an hour later, in walks this guy who stares at Ella, and then shoots me a dirty look.

"Oh shit," said Ella, staring back at him.

"Why oh shit, and who is this guy?"

"That is my ex-fiancé, Roger."

I felt my back go up and the blood started to pump a little harder. This fucker wants trouble or anyone else in this bar, I will knock them all out. I would have no problems running this entire bar.

Roger got himself a wine and then walked towards us.

I was clenching my jaw making eye contact with him the whole time.

"Hello Ella, who is your friend?" he said looking at me.

I didn't give Ella a chance to answer, "I am Mitch Strongbow, her boyfriend."

That certainly spun his head as his jaw opened in shock. His eyes now started to flutter.

"Well, I am Doctor Roger Hughes, Ella's ex fiancé I guess you would say."

He stuck his hand out for a shake, what kind of proper gentleman is he?

"You know doc, you and I have a lot in common other than Ella," I said to him rather sarcastically.

"Humor me, how is that?"

"Well doc, I know there are 206 bones in the body. I break people's bones, and then they come to see you to have them fixed."

He looked over at Ella, she told him I was telling the truth. Roger stood there for another ten seconds before turning around, dropping his glass off at the bar before exiting.

"Oh, Mitch that was awesome. I have never seen him at a loss for words, he is such a know it all, I love you!"

Ella hugged and then kissed me. Now I am the one who is at a loss for words. I can't say the same back to her, maybe it was a fleeting momentary rush, or way too much wine. We stuck around till last call and then I had to help Ella back to her place. She was feeling zero pain.

She was all over me the whole way back to her place. Kissing, groping, and even trying her best to talk dirty.

Once we got up to her apartment, she told me how horny I made her tonight. She said she had a special treat for me. She went into the bedroom and said she needed ten minutes. So, I went out onto her balcony and looked at the city. Very cool view of the bridges, the skyline, and even Alcatraz out in the bay.

After about ten minutes I came back inside and was waiting for her to call me in, I am thinking she bought a new sexy outfit for bed.

I wait another ten minutes and I hear this noise coming from the bedroom, I now get this huge smile. Fuck, Ella must have went out and bought a vibrator, total turn on, thought she was kind of prudish for that to be honest.

I stand up and walk into the bedroom picturing Ella with that bad boy toy in her pussy, but man was I wrong.

Ella passed out cold, and she was snoring. So, I tucked her in. Went back out to the balcony, sparked up a joint and once again enjoyed the view of my city.

I eventually crawled into bed beside a still dead-to-the-world Ella.

Was able to figure out her alarm clock and set it for 07:30, yeah it will be interesting to hear what Jerry says.

I crashed pretty solid and was awoken by the alarm clock. Ella was still half drunk and asked if she slept in for work, I reminded her that it is her day off.

Now, totally confused, she asked why the alarm went off. I told her I have to go and workout with my cousin. She leaned in and hugged me and asked me not to leave.

I promised her I would come back after I am done working out then we can do something for the day. I told her to go back to sleep as I needed a shower. She smiled and then put her head back on the pillow and closed her eyes. I stripped down in the bedroom and saw her eyes open up.

"Mitch, I need to feel you inside of me."

Fuck the shower as I jumped back in bed with a now erotic Ella.

"I don't have any condoms, babe."

She pointed to her top drawer of her nightstand table as she now put a finger in her mouth as she was taking her clothes off.

Glad to see she is relaxing a little bit more around me. Let's see how relaxed I was, as I was really dying to see my cock in her mouth.

So, I smiled, shook my head no and grabbed a hold of my cock and began to rub it all over her body. I was smacking her tits, rubbing my manhood in between them. I would then go down and kiss her for a bit and then start to rub my cock somewhere else. I did start to see a little fear as I started to rub it along her jawline.

I looked at her and said, "Time for me to play doctor, open your mouth and say *ahh*."

She smiled and shook her head no, while almost making sure nothing was going in her mouth.

For now, I will let it go, but if she has any thoughts of being my full-time woman, she better start sucking cock sooner than later, as my lips or tongue will no longer be going near her pussy.

I went to the top drawer and broke out a condom, ripped the package open and slid the condom on all the while looking at Ella who seemed to be relieved. Yep, erect nipples and rosy cheeks are a dead giveaway. I started to finger her to get her nice and moist. Those little Italian moans sound sweet first thing in the morning.

After about five minutes of fingering and, yeah, towards the end I was getting pretty rough I decided to get on top of her. Get ready Ella as you are about two take a good pounding.

I seemed to slide in a little bit easier this time, she was still tight, but not to the point of being frustrated. She wrapped her arms around my neck and brought me in to kiss her. I started nice and slow and enjoyed necking with her, our tongues seemed to be in perfect tune with each other. Like a train going up a long steep hill I took my time, track by track until Ella was totally into it. The deeper her moans got the harder I started to fuck her and by the time I was built up to the point of no routine I was slamming her hard.

My little girlfriend is going to be sore from this.

As I was cumming I bent down and bit her nipple pretty hard. I was surprised I didn't draw blood and I have no reason why I did it, it just kind of happened.

I rolled onto my back as Ella put her hand over her boob, "Fuck that hurt Mitch, please don't do that again."

I said I was sorry, but I really wasn't sorry, once again not sure why. I peeled the condom off and said I need to grab a shower and did she want to join me. Ella said no, she wants to enjoy not having to jump up out of bed.

So, I jumped in the shower to revitalize and to clean myself off, fuck I really hate wearing condoms.

I was a little surprised when I got out and Ella made me some scrambled eggs, fresh juice and a coffee, a nice surprise indeed.

Before I left, I reminded her that Joseph is taking us out to Martin's Steakhouse and reservations are at six and I would be getting her around five thirty. She promised she would be ready by then. I gave her a nice long kiss and said I would see her then.

Jerry's bike was parked out front along with John and Scotty Kantonescu's bikes.

Well, looks like I better bring my "A game" as those boys like to take no prisoners when lifting.

And today was all about legs, and by the time I was done, my legs were shaking like jelly. Not looking forward to tomorrow.

After we were done, Jerry said for me to go home and get my bike as the four of us are heading to San Jose for a ride.

So, the three of them followed me to my place. I switched my car for my bike and off to San Jose we headed.

It was a good day for a ride. All four of us drove like maniacs cutting in and out of traffic on the highway.

Drivers see that Hell Hound patch on the back of three monsters you know they won't honk their horns.

We pulled up to the San Jose clubhouse and were all ushered in.

We parked our bikes and were met by Eric Von Kruder, national chapter president for all the Hell Hound chapters.

"Mitchell Strongbow, Jesus H Christ, look at the size of you now!"

"Thank you, sir, good to see you."

"Eric, not sir, you're not in the army anymore. Mitch, I need a favor."

I told him to go ahead, no way do you tell a man of his power, no.

"This Tommy Jovanaski, I want to meet him. Can you make that happen for me?"

I looked over at Jerry, he smiled at me.

"I am picking him up from San Quentin Monday morning at ten."

"Good bring him to the Oakland clubhouse. I want to have a little chat with him."

A million things are now running through my head and none of them have good endings with Von Kruder asking to see him.

Eric could tell I was not so sure about this. "It's all good, Mitch; I want to discuss some business. There will be no bloodletting, or at least not yet."

Yep, my mind is now racing a thousand miles an hour. Kind of wished Jerry would have given me a bit of a heads up that Von Kruder is now involved.

The four of us had a couple beers, shot some pool, and got caught up with other club members I haven't seen in a while.

Around three, I told the boys I had to get going. Jerry, John, and Scotty stayed at the clubhouse.

Yeah, mind was racing the whole way home.

When I got there, Oscar was hanging on the couch watching soap operas. I asked how things went with Nicky and Tommy J. He said that Tommy wants a hundred pounds of Columbian; he said no one in Alaska has a contact for it. I then asked if he knew who Eric Von Kruder was, Oscar said yes, he knows of him, and why. I told him the whole story and watched the wheels in his head turn. Eventually Oscar said, I could tell Tommy J about the meeting, but he was staying out of it.

Yeah, for sure I would take charge.

I grabbed a shower, got dressed and told Oscar I have to swing by and pick up Ella.

"Strongbow, next week I am car shopping, this throwing me into the back seat while your woman sits up front is becoming annoying."

"Fair enough, I can get you a deal on a bike."

Oscar said he prefers 4 wheels.

I pulled up to Ella's and pushed her apartment buzzer. She said she would be right down. And when she came down, damn, she turned every male's head within a hundred yards.

She was wearing this tight short black mini skirt, a white blouse with no bra and six-inch platform shoes. Her makeup was stunning, and the wind was blowing her straight blonde hair that she was wearing down.

If Oscar wasn't in the back seat, I would have taken Ella in the back and fucked the shit right out of her. I had to tell Oscar to quit staring at her, horny Syrian bastard. She might not be the greatest in bed, but she was by far one the hottest chicks I have ever gone out with, and no doubt about it, the smartest one I have ever dated, or at least book smart.

Driving around in my killer Mustang and seeing my woman's golden locks flow in the air I felt like some famous Hollywood movie star.

4

Martin's was an upscale steak and lobster joint. One of my favorites.

We walked in and the maître d said, "Hello Doctor Mattina. Good to see you again. Sorry, but I don't see anything under your, or your father's name."

This fuck wasn't even looking at Oscar or myself, so I piped up and said, "We have reservations under the name O'Reilly."

snooty fuck looked down at the book, looked up at me and said in a dry dull voice, "yes." He snapped his fingers and this guy popped out of thin air and took us to our seats.

We were the first to arrive. Oscar and I ordered Heineken seeing how Joseph is footing the bill. Vodka on the rocks for my lady.

Joseph and Cathy were the next to arrive. I did the introductions and said, "This is my girlfriend, Ella Mattina."

Ella piped up and said *Doctor* Mattina. Joseph was shocked. The wise ass asked if she was a doctor of psychiatry, as that is what I really need. She hugged me and said I was a good guy, and she was actually a family doctor.

Both girls seemed to hit it off well and Joseph gave me the thumbs up, that doesn't normally happen with girls that I date.

Donnie and Jeanie were next to arrive. Both were wearing full length leather jackets. Ella's eyes got a little big as Donnie is very scary looking. It was nice seeing the smirk on Donnie's face as he checked out Ella and then looked at me.

The final couple is not what I was expecting. It was Sean but instead of his wife, it was Nyah

Sean was still limping and using a cane. Nyah walked in, she looked at me and then lit up with a huge smile and then saw Ella hanging onto my arm. That smile went south really quick and she glared at Ella. I did the introductions, and yeah, no love for Ella from Nyah. Sean was actually kind of funny and asked Ella if she needed to see a doctor for being with me. I have no doubts that Ella picked something off Nyah as she leaned in and kissed me on the cheek and said I am a great guy who keeps her happy.

I can tell when Nyah wiggles her head a certain way her back is up, this is going to be a long and stressful night for me.

During dinner, Cathy said she would like to have us over for dinner next weekend.

Ella said right now she can't commit as training camps for the 49ers open up next week.

Nyah with a glow from the drinks sarcastically asked if Ella played for the 49ers.

"My Dad is the team doctor for the 49ers, and I help out with team physicals, from training camp and right up till the end of preseason."

"You must have seen a lot of cock in your time little lady, do any stand out?"

Everyone was totally shocked by that including Sean.

"Nyah Patricia Quinn, that is enough filth talk coming from your mouth. There will be no more of that, you hear me young lady?"

Sean was pissed and embarrassed. Nyah rolled her eyes and muttered something under her breath.

At one point, Nyah said she had to go to the bathroom. On the way there she gave the look motioned with her head for me to come over.

So, I excused myself and said I would be right back, Sean was the only person to make eye contact with me. His face now had this dark look come over him. I gave him a nod, no facial expression and headed to the Nyah and the washroom.

As soon as I got out of eyesight of everyone Nyah said, "Your girlfriend reminds me of a stuck up Italian cunt."

"She is good people Nyah, please don't be jealous."

Nyah grabbed my cock and asked if Ella is a better lover than her.

"No, she isn't, look your dad gave me the eye when I got up, if you wanna talk shit about Ella, I really don't want to hear it right now."

"Whatever Strongbow, actually I need five pounds of weed and this guy at school Dave Schinn told me I am cutting in on his action. He said if I don't back off, he is going to fuck me up."

My back went up right away. "Who the fuck is the guy?"

"Some piece of shit who thinks he is the big bad ass dealer."

"O.K. Call me tomorrow, nothing on the phone, we will talk more about him and the weed situation in person. Now get your ass back out there before Dad wonders back here."

Nyah smiled, gave me a kiss, which I had to stop.

I went into the washroom and thought of dead kittens, so I didn't come back to the table with a raging hard-on.

Some guy was in there spraying the bowl. My hard-on went away really quick. He leaves and within a minute comes a limping Sean.

I am washing my hands; he takes one sniff and asks what died inside of me.

"That stench wasn't coming from me." I fucking knew he would make his way here.

Eventually, Donnie and I got to talk about the whole Tommy J and Von Kruder situation.

"Thanks for the heads up that Von Kruder wants to meet Tommy J, suppose I were to say no. Not appreciated man."

"It's all good, Strongbow. It will be a friendly meeting. No blood will be spilled; you have my word on it. And listen, I did as you asked, Steve visited Albert, and Tommy is getting out on his regular release date."

For the first time that I can recall I see Donnie a little differently. I actually feel like an outsider around him. Yeah, serious trust issues. The club over me.

Joseph, the Irish silver tongue devil was catching a really good glow as the night went on. He was actually starting to flirt with Ella, Cathy was not impressed.

Nyah would then try and play footsies with me. While Donnie and Jeannie seemed to be in a foul mood with each other. This is one fucked up night. And because of this we were the first ones to leave. Ella certainly had her drunk on, this girl likes her booze.

Once we got back to my place, I had to help her up the stairs and into the bedroom where she said she was horny, but once again passed right out on me, this was starting to get on my nerves.

I tucked Ella in and then sat in the living room, smoked a bowl or ten trying to make logical sense of Tommy J and the Von Kruder situation. I passed out on the couch, nothing sensible that I could recall did come to mind.

5

The smell of bacon cooking woke me up the next morning. I opened up my eyes to see a smiling Ella with a coffee mug in her hand.

"Morning baby, breakfast will be ready for you in ten minutes."

I took a sip of coffee as my brain needed that jolt for the jump start. Ella seemed to be all happy and energetic.

"Mitchell, silly question, do you own a tuxedo at all?"

Took a big gulp of coffee as I have no idea why she is asking this.

"Nope, no reason to... why?"

"We have the fundraiser tonight for the San Francisco Orchestra, remember, silly?"

I downed what was left in the coffee mug and sort of remembered her asking me about this.

"Tonight, really?"

"Yes silly, tonight. So, let's get some food into you and then we can go to Sil's tux shop. He is a friend of the family. He will take care of you."

I smiled an evil smile, grabbed my cock, and asked if she had any plans to take care of me. She blushed and said her period arrived while we were out last night.

"You know there are other things we can do."

Like a deer in the headlights. "Well, let's see how we are for time after we get you a tux."

I smiled and realized that Ella is anything but a sexual being. Well,

I can accept this, which won't ever happen. Or I can try and corrupt her or keep her as an eye candy hot girlfriend and have someone on the side. Oh Charlene, where are you?

So, I ate, had a shower, and jerked off thinking about the madness at Herschel's wedding and Charlene getting fucked and sucked by several guys and girls.

Then we headed to Sil's. As soon as I walked in, I knew I should have smoked a joint beforehand.

Sil himself was obnoxious as fuck. I made sure to give him a little growl as he was measuring around my dick. I left with a tux rental and drove Ella home. She told me to come and pick her up around four.

I drove home, raced upstairs with my tux, hung it up and then grabbed my bike keys. I really need to go for a ride and clear my head.

I drove about an hour north up the coast. At times I kicked it down and needed that rush. At one point I pulled over and looked to the west, all I saw was water, but I know there is a continent out there that almost killed me. I looked to the east and over the horizon was a prison that tried to break my soul and take my life.

And now I have a hot doctor as my steady. I smoked a joint and had an epiphany. I am trying to corrupt Ella and bring out this sexual beast in her. I wonder if she is trying to tame the beast in me? You know, make me something I can never be?

Who fucking knows, I guess it will boil down to who has more will power or goddamn stubborn enough not to change. I truly believe like every battle I have endured in life that I will win.

I checked out my watch and took a big breath and realized I better get back home and get in that monkey suit I rented.

When I got home, Oscar was chilling on the couch. He said Charlene Borden called for me. My heart skipped a beat and my stomach flipped.

"Did she leave a number for me to call her back?"

"No said she would try again later on this week."

"Fuck, did she say anything else?"

"Said she really needs to talk to you and she asked how you were doing. I said nothing about Ella."

I thanked him, and then got dressed. The whole time I can't shake Charlene from my head. Same thing with the drive over, all my thoughts were Charlene. A couple times I even missed my gear shift and grinded gears.

I have to say, this whole mystery is really fucking my head up. Did she sense I was jerking off to her earlier on? Yeah, I can never decide who was more of a nymph, her or Lucy.

I fucking love and miss her. These chicks that allow myself to actually open up my heart fully always go away in the end. Tash, Lucy and now Charlene. No more being hurt, fuck that.

When I pulled up to Ella's building, I even contemplated heading home. Look at me; I am dressed up like some ape in a suit, had to jerk off in the shower for fuck's sake. I started my car and was ready to put the clutch in and head home when I saw Ella looking stunning. She was wearing a powder blue ball gown. Her makeup was bang on, she looked like an angel. She walked towards the car smiling and waving. I got out and said she looked beautiful.

"Mitchell, it is a good thing Carl my door man buzzed me to tell me you were here. I am sorry I was waiting for you to buzz me." She was so happy, so full of life, no way was I going to hurt her and tell her I am heading home.

"Sorry babe, stomach is a little funky, was waiting for a minute."

Never ever bullshit a doctor. Right away she felt my forehead, checked my glands, asked me to stick out my tongue and said the obvious, "You appear fine. I am thinking you might be eating too much red meat. It is really hard on the digestive system. Maybe add more chicken and fish into your diet and I can't really recall seeing you eat any green veggies." She laughed and said smoking green veggies doesn't count.

"Having said that, do you have any weed on you?"

"Have I ever let you down, baby?"

"No, you haven't, you treat me so good."

So, we smoked a joint on the way over and yes I did relax a bit, enough that I will try and have a good time.

As we pulled up, I handed the car keys to this young kid. I told him to be careful with her. He smiled and said of all the cars tonight mine is the baddest one of them all.

As we walked in, I truly felt out of my element. All guys were wearing tuxedos. All females dressed in long flowing ball gowns, many of them wearing stoles around their neck and the weirdest looking fucking hats I have ever seen.

And the jewelry, god damn I want to give Joseph a call and tell him we should think about robbing this even next year. That was until I saw the police commissioner and several deputy chiefs who were shocked to see me.

Suddenly, they all came together and held a little crisis conference. The one deputy chief left after a quick talk, as the commissioner and another deputy chief headed over to Ella and I. Funny at how their wives didn't tag along. Oh, this ought to be fun.

"Doctor Mattina how are you doing this evening?" said the commissioner with one eye on her and the other eye on me.

"I am having a wonderful time so far, commissioner Gordon."

"I am glad to hear this, your date looks kind of familiar."

"This would be my boyfriend, Mitchell Strongbow."

He didn't stick his hand out as a sign of good will nor would I, in fact, fuck him.

"It's all right, Ella; Gordon and deputy chief Berry know exactly who I am. Don't play games, not appreciated."

"Well Strongbow, you are the last person I would expect to see her as a guest. Doctor Mattina, has your dad had the pleasure of meeting Strongbow yet?"

"No, he hasn't but he will soon. Let's find our table, Mitchell."

I said sure and eyed the two fuck heads as we walked away.

As we found our table, I explained to Ella about me suing the cops for police brutality, and ever since then I have become a bit of a target.

She said that was horrible and said they might back off now that I am her full-time boyfriend.

The tables held eight chairs, I was hoping none of them included cops, or any city officials. My blood is still boiling. Lucky for me or us the rest of the table was filled up with old stuffy shirts. All businesspeople. I certainly stuck out, that was for sure.

Speaking of sticking out, there was this stunning blonde sitting halfway across the room. A couple times I caught her looking at me. Huge blue eyes, a perfect smile, she was showing tons of cleavage. I was certainly captivated. I would say early thirties, she had this sexual magnetism that I felt myself drawn to. She sort of stuck out much like me being here tonight.

After dinner, which tasted like rubber chicken, and left me starving, I see this guy and his girl headed towards us. He nods his head and smiles.

They stop at our table, and he says, "Your name is Mitch, correct?" with an English accent.

"Yeah, that's correct, you look familiar."

"We met at Herschel's wedding. I am Basil Thomas, and do you remember my wife, Lynn?"

She shoots me this smile and I flashback to actually fucking her as she was going down on Charlene. Yeah, she shoots porn, fucking right I remember her.

"Yes, I remember you both now." As I say this Ella gives me this little tap on the foot.

"Sorry, this is my girlfriend Ella Mattina"

Ella once again jumps in and corrects me by saying, *Doctor* Ella Mattina. My back doesn't go up too far tonight as she put Gordon and Berry in their place.

"Listen mate, I asked Herschel to call you as I wanted to discuss some business with you, did he call you?"

"I apologize, he did call me. I haven't had the chance to call him back yet, I was out of town a fair amount lately. Let's go for a walk and talk, shall we?"

I ask Ella if she doesn't mind, she says go ahead.

So, I tell Basil let's go outside and talk. On the way out he says he has to go to the washroom so I said I would meet him out front.

On the way out, I see the blonde who has been teasing me sitting with a bunch of guys about fifty feet away smoking a cigar with a glass of what looks like whiskey on the rocks. She hoists her glass to me, and I give her a nod and smile back.

I am not even outside thirty seconds when Berry steps outside and asks us if I have a light for his cigarette.

"Don't smoke," was my stoic reply.

A minute or two later Basil comes out. I tell Basil let's go for a walk. As soon as we are far enough away, I tell him that asshole standing by us is the deputy pig here in town.

I tell Basil let's talk when the fuzz is not going to be eavesdropping.

So, he hands me a business card and says to call him on Monday, and we can have a business lunch.

"Monday, I leave out of town for a couple days, but I will call you once I get back into town."

Basil shakes my hand and says good stuff. He asks what happened to the girl I brought to Herschel's wedding. Not telling a stranger my Scooby Doo secrets.

"Not seeing her anymore and by the way, Ella knows nothing of her, or me swinging, or whatever other illegal activities I may partake in."

"Fair enough, Mitch. Herschel speaks highly of you; says you are the man here in the bay area. I hope we can do business together/ "

I look at his card once again and it says SOL records.

"I am positive things will be good for both of us."

We go back in together, of course, Berry is ten steps behind us. As much as it pisses me off, I believe I have ruined Berry's night with him keeping an eye on me. I am sure his wife is pissed at him and commissioner Gordon.

The sexy blonde is nowhere to be found, too bad as I was going to try and strike up a conversation with her. As we go back to my table, I see we have other guests and no they are not cops, they are Italians. Mike Battaglia and some Stella looking broad.

I can tell by Mike's body language he is pissed. Ella seems to be a bit concerned. I stick out my hand to shake Mike's and he says, "Let's go for a walk, Strongbow."

I look at Ella and she shrugs her shoulders.

As Mike and I are walking outside I tell him the cops have been watching me all night. Mike doesn't answer and as soon as we are outside, he starts.

"What the fuck are you doing going out with my cousin for?"

I really don't care how much power Mike has in this city. I will not be belittled by him or anyone else.

"Why is that a problem? Is it because I am not an olive skinned Italian?"

"First, you said you needed a doctor, not a girlfriend."

"So, tell me why you have problems with this."

"Your fucking track record isn't the greatest. I swear to God Mitch if you hurt her you will have to answer to me."

"Fuck you Mike, you own a strip club, and did I bust your balls about going out with Rachel? I told you as long as you treat her with respect, I will be happy"

"That's different," said a flustered and pissed off Mike.

"Why the fuck is this different. Look at what the fuck I am wearing, look where I am. Do you not see happiness in Ella's eyes?"

Mike did eye me up and down, I saw a little smile come to his face.

"You look like Magilla Gorilla in that tux Mitch. Look, I wish you would have told me about the two of you. My Dad adores Ella, he is her Godfather. Don't hurt her man or you will have to deal with him, even I won't be able to save you."

"I didn't see this coming, honestly, she pursued me. Mike, look at me. I have zero intentions of hurting her, she is a classy chick."

Mike then stuck out his hand and I shook it.

Then we both gave Berry the middle finger and laughed at him as we walked by him.

On the way back to the table I gave Ella the thumbs up. She smiled, stood up and came over and hugged me and then hugged Mike. We had a drink together before we were told the concert was ready to begin. Mike suggested we meet after the show at Charango's for drinks.

I looked at Ella and she said that works.

As we took our seats, I noticed in a private box was the mysterious blonde who was flirting with me the whole time. She was beside an older guy, he looked rather stuffy, and she looked totally bored.

That was until she spotted me. Once again, another big smile. How could I not smile back? She then started to run her fingers around the rim of her glass as she stared at me.

Ella picked up on this and asked if I knew her. "I know her from somewhere, not exactly sure where."

Ella then looked up at the blonde and pulled my arm closer to her as she now rested her head on my shoulder. I knew better than to turn my head towards the mysterious blonde, but my eyes were still able to make contact. I have no doubts in my mind, I intrigue her as much as she intrigues me. Even when the show started, I caught her looking over from time to time.

And by the way, classical music with singers, like opera shit, fuck give me a fix of heroin to survive. The Sound of Music was the production. This will be two hours of my life I will never get back. Maybe the German in me should jump up on stage and take out the whole Von Trapp family.

At the end of the first set, I looked up and my cock teasing blonde was gone.

The second set started, and she still wasn't back. I was disappointed as this little flirting game we had going on was the only reason I am still in my seat.

At the end of the concert Ella asked what I thought. "I am here for you, baby."

"You are such a music lover, Mitch; I thought for sure you would have liked it."

"To be brutally honest, I was hoping the Nazi's would have caught up to and killed the Von Trapp family so this musical was never made."

She laughed and smacked me on the arm and said I was awful. Yeah, couldn't get out of there fast enough and the only reason I didn't spark up a joint was the cop situation, fucking pigs.

6

Mike and Nancy, his date, were already at Charango's. As we walked in Mike took one look at my face and started to laugh.

"What's so funny, man?"

"Well Strongbow, you proved how much you cared for Ella as Nancy, and I split after twenty minutes."

I called him a bastard and then ordered drinks for Ella and myself. All in all, it was a good night. Ella drank at least two bottles of wine by herself. I had a nice buzz, but with me being a heat score pissing off the cops tonight, I knew better. She was slurring and telling me how much she loves me once again. I had to help her up the stairs to my apartment. Help her out of her gown and like last night, she passed out on me again. I smoked a bowl, had a cold beer while the cock teasing blonde was racing through my head.

The next morning, I was woken by a frantic Ella saying I have to take her back to her place right away. I looked at the clock in the living room and it was after eight. I was totally confused and asked what was so urgent.

"I have to meet my family at eleven o'clock mass."

Fuck. This Columbian weed must keep you stoned even when you are sleeping as I asked her to repeat what she said. She did and it still didn't make sense at all.

"And will they ground you if you miss mass Ella, seriously, let's get it on baby, super horny for you right now."

She laughed but had this real serious look on her face, "Mitch, it is the Sabbath, I can't have sex today."

I was waiting for the punchline, but she was dead serious. So, I threw some water in my face and started to drive Ella home. On the drive, over she said her dad hosts the whole family and their spouses over for dinner and she would really like me to join her today.

Last night's insanity is clearly filtering into today. I am in no hurry to meet anyone's family. She grabbed my cock and promised she will make it worth my while.

"How much is my worth?"
She put her tongue into her cheek and moved it around.

"But Ella it is the Sabbath, you even said no can do."

"You meet my family, and I will say ten hail Mary's and go to confession next week. If Mike talks to my folks and tells them all about you before I get a chance, my dad will guilt the hell out of me. I told them some minor stuff about you."

My cock will be the death of me, that is for sure. So, I reluctantly agreed, Ella said she would be by around five to pick me up. She told me to get dressed up.

I said, "define *dressed up*."

"Nice pants, long sleeve shirt with a tie, and a dress jacket."

I took a long deep breath, looked at her and asked if she was serious.

"Yes, daddy is impressionable, and first impressions are lasting impressions. Please? For me, Mitch."

I almost said only if I get to fuck you in the ass, but took another big breath and said, "Fine. But I am no artsy-fartsy type of guy. I do have my limitations, Ella, and I will not be embarrassed. What do they know about me?"

"I told them you are a hard-working guy who keeps their daughter very happy, and I would never embarrass you Mitchell, you truly keep me so happy."

Fuck it, I agreed, gave her nipple a little twist, and said I will try my best. I drove home with a gnawing feeling in my gut, not sure this is a good idea with Ella. She seems to be more into me then I am into her.

Within five minutes of being home my thought process proved me right.

Nyah called me and asked if she could drop by. How ironic was it that I said sure and asked what she was wearing?

"No panties, no bra and I am horny as hell. You going to fuck me, Mitch or are you now loyal to your doctor girlfriend?"

"I guess you will find out once you are here, won't you?"

In the meantime, I called Herschel and asked if he was going to be home today. He said yes and for me to drop by. Perfect as I will ask him all about Basil.

7

Nyah came to the door wearing a halter top and shorts, and I mean *short* shorts. I got a hard-on right way, she smiled and grabbed my cock and said, "I guess we will soon see how loyal you are…wanna fuck?"

I pulled down her halter top and started to suck on those big brown nipples and was playing with her pussy through her shorts right on the stairs. I couldn't handle her moans any longer and grabbed her by the hand and raced upstairs with her.

Within ten seconds of being in my bedroom, we were both naked and I had Nyah's legs in the air with me already inside her wet and throbbing pussy. So nice to feel the inside walls of her snatch without wearing a condom. What was even better was blowing my load inside a hot pussy rather than a condom.

I actually started to laugh after the last drop of cum was out of me.

Nyah asked what was so funny. I couldn't tell her why; I said something I heard last night on T.V. Nyah started to tell me about this fuck head from school. He had threatened to hurt her physically and to hurt her family.

Once again, another secret I couldn't or dare tell Nyah was that her dad scares me, and I don't fear many people.

"Tell you what. Give me his name and where to find him. I will tune him, but you can't tell your dad."

Nyah thanked me and promised to say nothing to her dad. She said she needed five pounds of weed and can she pay me at the end of the week.

"I am going out of town for a couple days, so giving you the weed and waiting for payment is cool. Then I will handle Dave for you."

I could tell something else was bothering her, so I asked her to be honest with me.

"I know you told me that you and I could never be a couple, it bothers me when I see that other girls can be your girlfriend."

"It hurts me seeing you like this, Nyah. I am sorry."

I pulled her in close and kissed her and then had a thought, "I have to go up the coast and see this guy; wanna go for a ride on the bike with me?"

Her face lit up and said she would love it.

"The guy's name is Herschel. I did time with him in San Quentin, great guy, what he does for a living might bother you, so I better forewarn you."

Nyah had this look on her face with one eyebrow raised and as she asked what Hershel does for work.

"He is in the porn industry."

Nyah burst out laughing and asked if I was serious.

"Dead serious, hon."

"Like he is a porn star… maybe my next boyfriend," said a laughing Nyah.

"No, he writes, directs, and produces porn. His wife stars in a lot of his movies actually."

"What? That is some fucked up shit, who wants to see their woman fucked by other men?"

I didn't dare tell her me, or at least with Lucy and Charlene.

Nyah said she was fine with heading there. So, I grabbed her a bike helmet and away we went on the bike and headed to Hershel's ranch.

Like when she rides me, Nyah had no issues on the bike.

8

We pulled into Herschel's ranch and Nyah was blown away.

"So, you are telling me, him filming what every adult does behind closed doors paid for all of this?"

"One hundred percent correct."

Herschel came out and met us in the driveway and asked who the beautiful young lady was. I did the introductions and within two minutes Herschel asked if Nyah ever thought of a career in acting.

"Herschel, I agree Nyah is absolutely breathtaking, but her dad would take your last breath, seriously he scares me. So, the answer for all of us will be no."

Herschel grabbed Nyah's hand and said if she ever changes her mind, I can get a hold of him.

"Herschel, I need to talk to you for a couple minutes; Nyah would you excuse us please?"

Herschel told her to go inside and there is a pool outback, bathing suits are in a dresser before you go out back, or you can go buck naked if you wish.

Nyah smiled and went into the house as I asked Herschel to tell me all about Basil Thomas.

"Basil made it large in Los Angeles as a record producer. He had a huge blow up with the record label he was working for as they wanted to invest more money in disco and less in rock. So, Basil, with the financial help of Marvin Matheson, is opening a whole new record company here in San Francisco. They have built a huge recording studio. A lot of big-name artists whose contracts are up with his old label are following Basil to SOL records."

I asked Herschel what he would need me for.

"I told Basil that you can get whatever he needs in the Bay area right from muscle, dope and knowledge of how the Bay area works."

The biggest question I needed answer was is he solid

"Mitch, this guy is as solid as they come. He has worked with the Stones, Deep Purple, and Jeff Beck. He is legendary in the music industry. I trust him one hundred and ten percent."

That is all I needed to hear. I fully trust Herschel so I will at least have a sit down with Basil and see what all he needs from me.

I looked at my watch and it was after one. I better grab Nyah and head back.

As we go out to the pool, there is Nyah laying there fully nude sunbathing.

Herschel turns to me and says, "her dad is that scary?"

"Ex IRA, one of Joseph's main enforcers, I saw him use a blowtorch on a guy's nuts."

"That is very scary. What a waste of beautiful talent. You fucking her, Mitch?"

I nodded yes and then Herschel asked what happened to Charlene.

"Vanished into thin air; not sure, man."

"Too bad, she seemed like a fun girl to play with. I heard she took on five guys at once at my wedding. She is a legend you know."

"Yeah, she did."

I felt myself getting hard flashing back to that scene, "Oh well, shit happens right? I am playing with Nyah and this doctor who actually is pretty damn boring in bed to be honest. But I am trying my best to corrupt her."

"At least you have Nyah to please you Mitch, you sly dog!"

We both walked over to Nyah who didn't seem phased that Herschel was seeing her buck naked.

"I have to head back, baby; as much as I hate saying this, get dressed."

Nyah smiled seductively at me and asked if I was sure.

I still had Charlene's gang bang in my mind, Nyah looks amazing naked opening and closing her legs showing me her pink meat, so I asked Herschel if he had any cameras out there.

"Security cameras."

"Herschel, go back inside and turn off those cameras. When we are done, I will let you know."

He smiled, slapped me on the back and told me to have fun. One trait I learned being a career criminal is knowing when you are being watched, you know I am not so sure it is a trait or a gift.

So, I leaned down beside Nyah and said, "I will fuck you, but not here. I don't want your dad sitting in a toss off theater seeing his daughter getting slammed by me."

"But Herschel said he would shut off the cameras."

"Herschel said he would shut off the security cameras, not all the cameras. Trust me, baby."

Nyah is naive at times, not a lot of street smarts. Surprising knowing who her dad is. When I get into Katrina's life. I will school her.

So, I stood in front of Nyah in case old Hershey Squirts was at a window with a video camera.

Yeah, something was up as he came back outside as soon as Nyah was fully dressed, bastard, I knew it.

I thanked him for the info and then Nyah and I jumped on the bike. Before we hit the main highway back to town I did as promised.

I pulled over to a secluded area. Walked hand in hand with her and then we both got naked, some kissing, stroking, fingering and next thing I knew Nyah was on top riding me hard.

It has been a while since I pulled over on my bike and had sex, you forget certain things including blowing your load inside someone. Normally not an issue, but considering Nyah wasn't wearing underwear. She was going to drip the whole way home. Better make sure to clean my seat off as soon as I get home.

On the drive back, Nyah said she had to pull over as her legs had a steady flow of cum rolling down her legs. We were about an hour outside San Fran, so I pulled over to this beach side restaurant for Nyah to get cleaned up.

With it being a Sunday, the lot was full so I pulled right up on the sidewalk beside some picnic tables.

As Nyah got off the bike, she nervously said two tables away was Dave Schinn and two of his buddies. I had her tell me which one exactly is Schinn as all three were wearing Grateful Dead t-shirts.

Schinn was wearing a Wake of the Flood tour t-shirt. His pain threshold will be awake as a flood of blood will be coming from his body in a couple seconds.

I felt the adrenaline flowing as soon as she said it. I didn't have any weapons on me but none of the three appeared to be of a serious threat.

I told Nyah to take off her helmet and we will walk hand in hand to the bathroom.

I did let her know if shit goes down stay out of my way, and number two, so many witnesses here, I may sound like a pussy, but it is all part of a bigger picture.

As we started walking to the bathroom, Schinn tapped his two buddies and mouthed *there's Nyah Quinn.*

All of them had a quick look at her, stood up and then they looked at me. Yeah, they are not sure what to make of me.

We got about ten feet away when Schinn with a real smart-ass look said, "Well, if it isn't the cunt Nyah Quinn, and I am not sure what the fuck kind of inbred you are…"

Let's see if my years being interviewed by the cops, and my lawyers have taught me anything.

All three start walking toward us, I know this walk all too well, intimidation through numbers, and course with three against one, they are fearless, even cocky. Time to get schooled, Strongbow style.

I make sure to speak loud enough for all to hear, "We are not looking for any trouble. Please leave us alone, you guys hurt us enough already, when will it end?"

"When that fucking bitch leaves school and you give us the keys to your motorcycle."

Hook-Line-Sinker. Time to have some fun. I waited for them to get close enough so only they heard what I was about to say.

"Nyah told me that you three take turns sucking each others' dicks."

It was nice seeing the rage come to all their faces, but what was even better, seeing the pain and suffering wipe away the rage, that will turn to fear.

Schinn threw an overhand punch off his back foot, fucking rookie. I grabbed his wrist with my right hand and with my left forearm I went full force strike into his right elbow. Sounded like a branch breaking off a tree in a freezing rainstorm.

I then did a complete spin around backfist and nailed his buddy right on his nose. Blood sprayed everywhere as his legs now gave out on him. He looked so cute dazed on the ground, I had to give him a kick right into his jaw. When I thought he couldn't look any cuter, I knock him out cold. He looks so angelic.

Now, the third guy decides to pull a switchblade on me. Schinn is yelling at him to cut me to pieces.

Nyah now screams my name as she is scared, I tell her to give me her motorcycle helmet. Like Fred Flintstone, strike, and that strike meant I nailed him right in the nuts.

A part of me wants to pickup the switchblade that is now on the ground and slice his throat. Too many witnesses and I have these fucks exactly where I want them. I kick the knife away and land a hammer fist punch right between this fucker's shoulder blades; always nice hearing someone gasp for air not knowing if they will ever catch their breath or not.

Now, where was I? Schinn, yes Schinn must pay the highest bill, and that bill is more pain than the others. I give him a little thumb punch in the windpipe. He falls to his knees; fuck I didn't ask him to pray. I pull him up by his hair. Look him in the eyes and whisper that I am the devil, and I am here to take his life and claim his soul. I throw a overhand right and land it flush on his orbital bone. He went flying backwards like a drunken gymnast coming off the parallel bars. I slowly walk towards him and can see the whole one side of his face is starting to swell up.

Time to fuck up the other side of his face. While still holding onto Schinn by the hair, I looked up and saw two cops with their pistols out and pointed right at me. I look at the cops, let go of Schinn's hair, and let his face hit the ground again.

The cops now tell me to put my hands on top of my head.

Nyah is freaking out I tell her, "all is good, baby."

The one cop stands with his gun pointed at me while the other cop comes around and tells me to put my hands behind my back. Within two seconds I hear the ever so familiar clicking sound of handcuffs being locked.

The cop takes me to the back of his cop car as he tells his dispatcher one in custody but will need a couple ambulances. He then asks me what happened. Before I answer I actually smile, not too often will you see me smile and breathe a sigh of relief.

"Me and my girl pull off to use the washroom, we walk past these three guys, one calls her a cunt and me an inbred. I said pardon me and the guy on the ground pulled me onto the table, he swung at me but missed. I did my best to protect myself and my girlfriend."

"Do you know these three guys?"

"I don't know them personally; the one goes to school with Nyah. I think they are Nazi's. Always intimidating her, calling her a cunt and stuff."

So, he asks me my name, birth date, and if I had any previous criminal convictions. I give him all the info; he runs me to see if there

9

As soon as we got home, I gave Nyah her weed, told her to pay me whenever. She asked did I really have to go see Ella as she will make it worth my while to stay with her.

Fuck it. I told her she better grab a shower before heading back home, and yes, I joined her and yes, you would be correct if you asked if we fucked in there.

Then Nyah headed home. I put on my one and only suit and headed to Ella's parents' house. Way too early to be meeting them in this relationship, but her call, not mine.

On the way over I smoked a joint to get mellow, yeah fucking mellow; I have already had a stressful enough day. Snob Hill is where they lived. This is where all the rich snobby fucks called home.

The Mattina house was a mansion. I had to get out of the car and push a buzzer as the front entrance was gated.

The person who answered the buzzer said can I help you in a very stoic voice.

I said it was Mitch Strongbow, no verbal response, the sound of the gate being electronically unlocked. Oh, this is going to be a blast and a half.

I parked Emma and was greeted by Ella. I hugged her and went to give her a kiss when she said no signs of affection in front of her parents. What the fuck is she? Thirteen? I gave her the *are you fucking serious* look. She apologized and said she will make it up to me when we are alone.

As I walked in the house, it had a really cold feeling. I could smell cigars, this house really needed to smell of grass.

Ella said they have eaten already, and Mommy and Daddy are in the rose garden having a cocktail.

By the look of Ella's eyes, it appears she too has had a few cocktails. So, we went out to the rose garden where her parents were. Dad was smoking a cigar while her mom was having a cigarette.

Yep, within a millisecond I was eyed up and down. Yeah, they were not impressed, could they tell this was my one and only suit? Could they tell I felt like a prisoner of war in it?

The dad got up and introduced himself as Doctor Anthony Mattina. He at least stuck his hand out. I shook it and he commented on the size and strength of my hands. He said maybe I should be trying out for the 49ers.

The mom sat in her chair and stuck her hand out for me to shake, it was weak and sloppy. Her dad asked me what my poison was. Anything but Scotch was my answer. Grey Goose on the rocks he asked, I said that works fine for me.

He walked over to the bar on the patio, I gave Ella a wink which turned her face red. The mom was three quarters in the bag and looked at Ella, looked at me and shrugged her shoulders, that showed her view of the two of us dating.

The dad handed me my drink and said cheers. I echoed what he said and smiled at Ella, yeah, the old man is at least trying. I took a drink and by the time the vodka hit my gut the questions started.

"So, Mitch, Ella tells me you served in Vietnam. I served in World War two and was called back during the Korean conflict. Who did you serve with?"

"506th infantry, 101st Airborne, 75 LRRP."

"Very impressive, young man. And Ella says that is where you met Mike?"

"Yes, that's correct"

"I heard you saved Mike's life after he was shot down."

"Yes, Mike saved my life by flying into hot LZs, it all evens out."

"The one tour?"

"No sir, I was in my fourth tour when my slick crashed causing me some pretty extensive injuries, enough I was giving a medical discharge."

"And what do you do for a living now?"

Stick to the cover Mitch, "I am a bounty hunter and I own a custom t-shirt store in Haight Ashbury."

The mom finally piped up and sarcastically said, "Are there enough criminals and t-shirts sold for you to eat, Mister Strongbow?"

I looked at Ella who rolled her eyes and then looked straight at her dad. He took a big breath and re-asked the mom's question with more couth.

"We get anywhere from ten to twenty five percent of the bail, so say a fifty thousand dollar bail I would make twelve thousand five hundred dollars. And as far as the t-shirts, I employ one full time girl and two part time students. Yes, decent money."

Ella then piped up and said I owned a Harley Davidson motorcycle, a mustang car, a pickup truck and a building.

The dad seemed impressed; the mom, I stopped looking at.

"So, Mitch…49ers or Raiders?" asked her dad.

"No disrespect sir, but I am a Raider fan all the way."

"Sorry Mitch I can't let my daughter date a Raider fan."

Ella smiled and shook her head before her dad started to laugh.

"Well, if the 49ers start off slow, I can see lots of player changes happening, I can see a complete rebuild to be honest."

The dad seemed like a decent guy, not sure what kind of guy or how would I act if Katrina brought someone home like me.

The mom was a drunk, but she was Sonny Battaglia's sister. I see where Ella gets her drinking from. I am not being a hypocrite but drinking every night till you pass out, not cool. And yes, I have been there, done it. Still do it from time to time. I am sure Ella has demons, maybe I can help her.

By the time we were set to leave, Ella was in no shape to drive. I approached her dad and voiced my concerns about this. Wasn't sure about his reaction, but he totally respected what I said, and he agreed.

He even shook my hand and thanked me for worrying about Ella.

Ella decided to spend the night with her parents with me on standby to head to Alaska. I told her to call me in the morning.

On the drive home I realized even rich people have issues.

10

I opened up the door and two steps in I heard a female moaning hardcore. I didn't recognize it.

So, I went upstairs and saw Oscar's bedroom door closed. So, I grabbed a beer, rolled a joint and put on some Santana, going old school tonight.

By the time the joint was done, out walks Oscar and Nicky Jovanaski. They are both naked heading to the fridge. I am not impressed at all. I shoot Oscar this intimidating look, he has seen this before.

"Mitch, glad you are home. One of Tommy J's guys is landing tonight with the down payment for the dope."

So, right off the bat Oscar broke two rules that are like the Ten Commandments for gangsters; he brought Nicky back here after I said she is not allowed around here and now some stranger is bringing me large amounts of cash. And why is he throwing a fuck into Nicky with Tommy out of prison in less than twelve hours?

Fuck it, he doesn't wanna take my rules serious, I will show him how pissed I am. I told them to stay put and then I walked back into my bedroom and grabbed a 9MM, emptied the clip, made sure the chamber was clear. I walked back out with the weapon in my hand.

"Oscar, what is my rule about me meeting strangers?"

"Are you fucking serious, Strongbow?"

"I am dead serious." I then raised the gun and pointed it at Oscar's face. He has seen me kill in the army, San Quentin, and here on the streets.

Nicky started to get upset, I told her, "This is no fault of yours, you are good. It is Oscar that has a hard time listening."

I glared at Oscar, "Give me one reason not to spray your brains all over the wall."

I certainly succeeded in shaming him and him realizing I have certain rules that must be followed.

"Mitch, I swear this will never happen again. Look, you need me to get the dope up to Alaska and what would Joseph say? I thought we are all one solid crew."

"Joseph said you are on probation. At any point if I feel you are a threat to us, I have been given the green light to take whatever actions I feel fit to rectify any situation. And right now, you are not being solid and this 9MM is mister rectify."

There was now intense fear in his face and voice with yet another promise not to fuck up with my rules. I lowered the gun and told him last fucking chance. I then told Nicky to go for a five minute walk.

"I want you to grab a motel room for this guy and Nicky, grab the cash and come back here without them, understood? I really want no dealings with him, I will only deal with Tommy J and that is all. When we get back from Alaska your apartment will be ready. Black Paul said he has a couple vehicles if you are interested."

Oscar was humbled and he said he will make it up to me.

"Make sure I don't get popped and all will be good."

I gave him the keys to my truck and told him I would see him in a bit, I emphasized the word alone. Nicky came back and then they fucked off.

About an hour later, Scott Kantonescu showed up with my weed for Tommy J. I ordered ten kilos for Black Paul and Tommy the Greek.

Starting to move a lot of weed these days, my bank account is expanding, so far life is good.

Scotty had a beer before leaving with the cash for the dope.

I still have a little gnaw in my gut about this meeting tomorrow. No sense asking Scotty anything as he is a foot soldier. I reloaded my 9MM and then crashed out on the couch.

Oscar showed up a little after two with a gym bag full of cash. It was late but I knew I had to count the cash before I met up with Tommy J in the morning. If we are to do business, I want zero issues right off the bat. Oscar gave me a hand and every dollar was present.

By now it was almost two thirty. I told Oscar we should crash now and do breakfast in the morning. I have a feeling tomorrow is going to be a really long day. The plan was to sleep as I lay in my bed and looked up at the ceiling, yeah, the brain didn't seem to shut off. I saw the sun rise and that was the last thing I remember.

11

I cursed the alarm when it went off, but I am glad I set it. I kicked Oscar a few times to wake him up before jumping in the shower.

As I was showering, the one positive vibe I had going was that Tommy J was going to be a free man in a couple hours. Can't really describe the feeling to be honest, reborn or second chance at life, I guess. Oscar called the hotel that Nicky and Kevin were staying at. He said we would be there by around 9:30.

Before we left, I handed Oscar the keys to the truck. He asked why we were taking two vehicles.

"My cousin won't want you or Nicky at the clubhouse. He might O.K Kevin."

Oscar rolled his eyes and said, "So take Nicky back to the hotel room and not back here, right?"

"Yes, that's correct and NO fucking her, Oscar." That made Oscar laugh.

Before we left, I called Jerry and told him that I was heading out and that I would see him in a bit. I said one of Tommy's boys was here and should he be dropped off or come along. Jerry said he is more than welcome. Interesting to say the least.

During breakfast, we laughed at the antics the three of us pulled in San Quentin. Then we headed over to pick up Nicky and Kevin at the hotel.

Nicky was all dolled up, she looked good. Kevin was a big, solid looking guy. Full beard, long hair you would think he was a Hell

Hound, then again, bikers all seem to look the same. Kevin jumped in with Oscar while Nicky jumped in the front seat with me.

On the drive over, Nicky thanked me once again for helping her.

I said no problems at all. She then asked if I thought she was a bad person. She didn't say why but I know it has to do with her fucking Oscar while Tommy is in the pen.

I had to really think about this one, did she want me to comfort her tortured and her much guilted soul?

"I am pretty sure I was put on this planet not to judge you or others."

She then went out how rough it is being married and not getting any affection.

To me, it didn't matter what she said to justify what she did. She is a whore plain and simple. Another reason why I will never get married.

I started to snicker and pictured me married and having mistresses all over the place. Yeah, I am never getting that serious ever with anyone, no one stays solid or faithful including yours truly.

12

Once we got within sight of San Quentin, it was my time to reflect on life. The place looks evil, that dark hole that took twenty-two months of my life. And how can I not think of Charlene, deep breath and big sigh.

I park the car and walked Nicky up to wear Tommy J will be released. I then walk back to Oscar and Kevin and hang with them; this is Jovanaski's moment, not mine.

Once Tommy came out, Nicky ran towards him. She jumped up and Tommy caught her and spun her around all the while kissing her.

Oscar asked why I couldn't greet him like that when he was released.

"You were my bitch inside, not outside."

Kevin looked at us and didn't know what to think until I said, "Fucking with you, man. I don't swing that way."

After a couple minutes the Laurakowski's walked towards us hand in hand, both with ear-to-ear smiles. Kevin gave him a hug and welcomed him back as did Oscar and I. After I hugged him, I asked him to go for a little walk.

"Listen, I got the weed all ready to go. Your guy Kevin gave me the standard half down and half when we arrive in Alaska. Now my cousin Jerry asked if you could drop by this morning as he wants to have a talk with you at the clubhouse."

"And what does he want to talk to me about?" said a suspicious Tommy.

"No idea, must be club shit."

Tommy eyed me up and down as he pondered what I told him, "He is the chapter president, correct?" I said yes.

"Are you coming along?" Once again, I answered yes and told him that Jerry said he will make it worth his while.

Tommy looked over at Nicky and Kevin and said, "I want Kevin to come along."

"Jerry said that is not a problem, Oscar and Nicky tagging along would be a problem though."

Tommy nodded his head yes and then called Nicky over, he asked for a couple minutes with her.

I headed back to my car and told Kevin to follow me.

You could tell that Nicky was upset but they hugged and walked towards us.

"Mitch, can Oscar and Nicky hang at your place until we get back?"

Oscar had this little smirk; I know it wasn't him sneaking in a quickie into Nicky; it was me and my commandments. "Of course they can." I then squinted my eyes at Oscar.

Tommy gave Nicky one last long hug and kiss before jumping in the Mustang with Kevin and me. Kevin asked where they are going.

"To the Oakland Hell Hound Clubhouse." responded Tommy

"Far out," was Kevin's response.

13

As we pulled up to the fully fortified clubhouse, Tommy said he was impressed.

Scotty Kantonescu was on sentry duty. He unlocked the massive steel gates and let my car in. I did the introductions as Donnie now made his way to us. Donnie shook their hands and asked all of us to follow him to the main building.

As soon as we walked inside, I was totally shocked as it appears most of the Hell Hound California senior ranks were waiting for us including my cousin Val's husband George Townes. Last time I saw George, Lucy and I were full fledged junkies, make that out-of-control junkies. I have no doubts in my mind that if I wasn't a relative of his wife, and her brother Jerry who is the Oakland Chapter President, Lucy and I would have been buried in Texas, along with all the secrets as to who exactly killed Kennedy.

He looked at me and smiled. I walked over and gave him a hug. George said I certainly look better than the last time he saw me. I told him I certainly feel a hell of a lot better as well. This made him laugh. And sure as fuck, I thanked him for everything he did for us in Texas. I apologized for being such a heat score. He said I can make it up for him in time. I asked how Ruby was doing. He said he almost came but didn't need Texas Rangers contacting the FBI saying senior leadership left the state, see where they are going. I told him to make sure to say hi, and thanks to Ruby for his help. George promised he would do that. Hell, he even said I should make a point of spending a couple weeks out his way. I told George that is not a bad idea at all.

Certainly, haven't forgotten what Silverhorn said before I cut his head off that Kevin Thomlinson wanted me murder. Might have to make it a perfect threesome with Silverhorn and Hyde, the headless Hell Hounds of Texas.

Dick Coltrane was present. He is the San Fran president, along with three other chapter presidents and Von Kruder himself.

I did the introductions, and then Scotty told me and Kevin let's shoot some pool.

A couple of the girls who keep the boys happy were in the pool room. They came up to Kevin and asked if we wanted a drink, to get high or get laid.

"Why not all three?" he said before leaving with them.

So, it turned out to be Scotty and I shooting pool. I looked at my watch before the first game and it was 10:35. Forty minutes later a stoned Kevin appeared back with the girls. He was happy.

An hour later Tommy J appeared with the senior executives, all of them were laughing as if they have been friends forever. Jerry took me aside and asked me when we were planning on flying Tommy, Nicky, and Kevin home. I said I was not sure, but Oscar would know.

"Well, there are some things in the works. It would be better if they flew back tomorrow."

Jerry then started to peel off hundred dollar bills. Five for me as promised and three hundred more that is going towards a five star hotel that Jerry rented the presidential suite for Nicky and Tommy. He booked a room in the same hotel for Kevin.

Jerry then asked if I could take them there and drop them off and he would be in contact with me later on.

For five hundred bucks I would carry them over on my back. So, I drove Tommy and Kevin back to my place. As we walked in, I kept thinking *Oscar, please be a good boy.*

Once upstairs, I asked both of them if they would like to try some of the Columbian weed I am selling.

Five of us on the one joint and we all had a nice buzz happening. Tommy and Kevin were totally impressed. Who was not impressed was Oscar when I said our flight has to be put off till tomorrow.

I told him, "After I drop everyone off, I will come back, and we can discuss this matter."

I dropped everyone off, gave Tommy my phone number and said play things by ear. He was pleased with how things were going for him with his first few hours of freedom.

As soon as I walked upstairs Oscar started about the delay in the flight. I reminded him that it is not Jerry who made this decision, but others and those others would not even bat an eye to have Oscar cut up into a million pieces and fed to the sharks in the bay.

He said something in his mother tongue, Oscar was pissed so I told him I have to drop some weed off at Paul's. Let's see what wheels he has for him.

Paul has this used car lot that always has anywhere from fifty to a hundred cars on it. Most are stolen from other states; he changes the VIN on them and makes them all legit. Oscar likes his muscle cars even though there were gas issues all around the states. He found this 1972 GTO that appealed to him. He took it for a spin with Paul while I stayed at the lot.

When they came back the haggling started. I swear it went on for almost an hour. I told Oscar that if he and Paul didn't make a deal soon, I was going home.

Eventually, they came up with a price, but of course, Oscar had no cash on him so I had to pay for the car with the weed, and Oscar would pay me once he gets the cash from the oil we were moving to Alaska.

Paul said he would have everything changed over, plated and into Oscar's name by tomorrow night.

We jumped in my car, looked at each other and said now what?

As stupid as this sound, this sitting around waiting to see what goes down with Tommy J and the flight to Alaska was draining.

Ella was at 49ers camp, Nyah was in school. Didn't feel like working out so I said to Oscar let's go home and get changed and then hit the beach. Oscar liked the sound of that, all that pussy on display.

We headed home and as we were walking in the phone was ringing. I hauled ass up the stairs and answered it. I am hoping it is Jerry and he gives us a takeoff time for tomorrow.

"Mitchell it is Joseph, are you busy right now?"

"Was going to hit the beach for a bit, what's up?"

"Drop by the bar for a coffee, lad."

I told him I would be over in ten. I asked Oscar what he wanted to do. He said he would tag along and then we can hit the beach.

As we walked into the Drunken Leprechaun Joseph looked at us and said what a gruesome twosome we were

He asked what mischief we were up to. Told him a guy we served with got out of San Quentin today and we planned on heading to his home in Alaska for a couple days.

Joseph raised his eyebrow and said that is a long chaperone ride. The man is anything but stupid. But I can hear Donnie's piece of advice saying don't tell Joseph about dealing dope.

"This has been in the planning for years now. First time all 3 of us are free."

He then asked when I planned on being back by. Yeah, he did it in a way I knew he was up to something, so I asked what was up.

"I am meeting some important people from the old country in Chicago. With Sean on the mend, I need some muscle. I plan on unloading Barry's diamonds. They are so hot no one in the whole fucking state wants to touch them. I know people up there who are very interested."

Right now, with me dealing more dope than ever, I need to show Joseph I am still loyal to him.

"I will be there for you, Joseph; that is not a problem. What time do we leave?"

"Flight leaves at eight Friday morning. I was hoping that Oscar could fly us up."

Oscar looked at me, then Joseph, he knows he is on probation with Joseph.

"I am sorry boss. This flight plan, plane maintenance for this long flight has been 3 weeks in the making. All I ask is if we can give me at least 12 hours notice next time."

Yeah, no way is Oscar going to miss out on this cash win.

Joseph nodded at Oscar and said, "In our line of work, emergencies come up without any notice. This time I will let you go, and there will not be 12 hours notice. There will be enough notice for you to either sober up, or kick out of bed whatever whore you are fucking at the time, understood?"

Oscar took a deep breath, I was truly waiting for the Syrian pig-headed bull to lose his temper, but he didn't. He said understood.

Joseph turned to me and started to peel off a couple hundred-dollar bills and said, "Everyone needs more than one suit in life lad. Go to O'Grady's and tell Jack I sent you." That made me snicker; fuck, does everyone know I have one and only one suit?

"I agree, I will head there now before hitting the beach." This actually seemed to shock him.

On the way over to get the suits, Oscar reminded me that, the longer we are delayed leaving, the better the odds of us not getting back in time for me to go to Chicago.

I nodded my head yes at first. "Well, then I will say to Jerry we have a time deadline or are you willing to do the trip alone?"

"Not at all. Me and a whole bike gang? That is how people go missing. Tommy J tells you Alaska has the highest rate of airplane crashes. You think poor Oscar died doing what he loves best? Well, maybe the second favorite thing he likes doing, so that's a great big no."

"Fair enough, man. I will tell Jerry we are under the gun for time. If we are not in the air tomorrow, then Tommy will have to find his own way home."

14

I picked out two suits, one black and one black with pinstripes.

I told Jack I need them by Thursday and asked if that would be an issue.

He said no problem, but he asked what shoes I have to go with them. Yeah, it seems runners or motorcycle boots don't go so well with a nice suit. I drew the line at nose picker shoes, they look like something Aladdin would wear. Eventually I picked out a nice pair. He asked if I ever served, and I said yes so, he threw in some shoe polish and a kiwi cloth. Brings back memories.

By the time we left the suit store, it was starting to rain, so I asked Oscar if he wanted to go and shoot some pool and grab a beer at Tommy the Greek's pool hall. I had eleven kilos of weed for him.

If anything, all my weed will be gone except Tommy Js, and that better be in the air by tomorrow night.

Now, Tommy the Greek bought the same pool hall that I had a dust up with as a teen, in fact the scrap I had was with Natasha's ex David and his drug dealing friends, and yes, the scrap was over me dealing weed…freaky.

As you walked inside it still had the same decor and it seemed to feel like cloth and pool balls as sixty-seven.

Tommy was sitting at the bar with some of his Greek crew. He poured us a shot of Ouzo and asked if we wanted a table. We said yes and he asked if we wanted to play some poker pool. I made sure to tell him when he was away from his boys, I had his weed. When the

Greek smiles at you in this certain way you know he has something else up his sleeve and he is a big solid guy, so those sleeves are pretty big.

"Strongbow, how much do I owe you for the weed?"

"Fifteen thousand, Tommy; you know that."

"Tell you what, how about we play for the weed? A game of snooker. If I win, I get the weed for free. You win, I will pay you thirty thousand." That legendary smile of his came out.

"You know, Tommy, the last time someone offered my people a deal that good, it was blankets containing smallpox. I will take the cash you owe me."

"Strongbow, I can't believe you put me in the same category as the American government."

I shook my head, Tommy smiled and said he has the cash once we are done playing. Nice try, Tommy. We shot three games, each of us winning one but we did do a dinner bet on the next game.

Needless to say, Tommy ran the table, so it was his choice of restaurant, and he chose Martin's steakhouse. I was there last week.

15

As we pulled up there had to be at least a dozen motorcycles out front and many of the bikes I recognized including Jerry's, Donnie's and both Kantonescu brothers'.

As we walked in, the maître d' asked if I was with the Strongbow party. I was totally confused. My birthday was over two months ago. If this is a surprise birthday party, they totally fooled me.

"I am a Strongbow, but I don't think this is for me." I turned around and looked at Tommy and Oscar and they shrugged their shoulders.

So, I asked for a tab, and they sat us. In the back of the restaurant was everyone I saw at the clubhouse today including Tommy J, Nicky, and Kevin.

I was a little hurt to be honest, but I know this must be Hell Hound shit and I have told all, I want to remain a civilian. Donnie looked over and I could tell he felt a bit uncomfortable as he raised his glass to me.

Tommy the Greek asked if that was Tommy J over there.

I said yeah, he got out today. Greek went to get up and go over, but I told him, "Let Tommy J come to us. You might be walking into a wolf's den."

Eventually, Tommy J spotted us and made a bee line for us. He grabbed a seat, and it was the four of us at the same table like being back in San Quentin, except this hooch we were drinking was not made of prunes. Once our food came, Tommy J made his way back to the Hounds.

After we ate, Jerry called me over and asked to talk to me outside in private.

It wasn't so private as George and Donnie joined us.

Jerry started the conversation, "Mitch, Donnie tells me Oscar has a good size plane that is capable of carrying up to sixteen bodies."

I look at Donnie and nod yes.

George then said, "I understand your Syrian is flying Tommy, his wife, and Kevin home?" Once again, I nodded yes.

"I want to rent out several seats on the plane. Talk to him and tell him I will make it worth his while."

I told George I will ask him outside and he can talk to him.

George looked at me and with a very serious look said, "It would be in his best interest if he accepted what I am about to offer him."

George is a no-nonsense type of guy. In fact, I am willing to bet if Oscar gives George attitude or refuses, I will end up with Oscar's brains all over my clothes.

So, I said to hang tight, and I will go in and get him and be right out.

Oscar is hot and pig-headed. How the fuck am I stuck in the middle of this Hell Hound shit? They wonder why I never wanted to strike for the club, bullshit.

I told Oscar to follow me in the bathroom, I made sure no one else was in there and then I told him the story and who we are dealing with.

Oscar shocked me and said no problem, two fifty a body, but we leave tomorrow night at the latest.

So, I said let's go out and talk.

I love the stare up and down when Alpha's meet, especially when you are not part of it.

George said his spiel, Oscar said his price and both parties shook hands. We would leave here tomorrow night at eleven and arrive during daylight, then again Alaska this time of year has eighteen hours of sunlight a day, this should be a trip and a half.

After Oscar agreed to fly the boys, we were invited over to their table, even the Greek was allowed. We ended up back at the clubhouse and partied till the sun was starting to come up.

I grabbed Oscar and said I need him flying sober. So back home for some much-needed sleep.

16

I woke up around dinner time, I grabbed a long shower to clear my head. I had this nervous energy happening and I kept hearing Nazareth's version of "This flight Tonight" and the specific lyrics of *shouldn't have got on this flight tonight*. This bad vibe wanted me to stay in bed. But there was too much money to be made.

I got out of bed, knocked on Oscar's door, and told him to wake up. His room was empty, I hope he didn't fuck off and hook up with some whore on a bender. It won't end well for him. I was totally shocked as he was sitting at the table going over maps. He had a notepad out and was writing down all kinds of stuff. He asked if I had a calculator.

At first, I laughed and asked why I would ever need one. Oscar said for dealing of course. I then asked what he needed it for, we already set a price for the weed and oil. And surely, he can do math for the cost of the Hell Hounds flying with us.

"Strongbow, such a narrow mind. If I don't calculate our fuel consumption, we will be one of those planes that crash in Alaska."

That statement didn't help my anxiety, or I guess *bad vibe*.

I had a shot of Jack for breakfast. Still couldn't shake that vibe and my gut was starting to flip. I hate getting high when anxious, especially doing a large drug deal, and a long flight with a plane full of Hell Hounds.

So, by the time Oscar was done with his shower, I had a nice little buzz happening.

Oscar told me to tell Donnie to head to the airport. We used to head to Mexico with his gang around ten.

So, I jump on my bike and head to Donnie's. Several times I give the bike full throttle, the rush helps to get rid of my anxiety.

Donnie is sitting on the front porch with Jeannie, they are both calm and collected, holding hands with each other. Not sure how he stays so cool and how she says nothing about him going away.

Donnie has never fooled around on her or at least that I have ever saw, and lord knows chicks would suck and fuck him if he snapped his fingers.

I decided to have a beer with them and feed off them. Yeah, they were like teens the way they gazed into each other's eyes. I gave Donnie the message when Jeannie slipped inside. Shook his hand, gave him a hug and told him I would see him at the airport.

On the drive home, I replayed the whole dynamics between the two love birds; Donnie is a total badass killing machine and yet around her he is a totally different person. He has learned to turn it off. I still don't know how, or how to stay loyal to one woman.

Then it sort of hit me; I was loyal to Charlene and yet she went AWOL on me without a reason why. Whatever swinging we did was in mutual agreement. I never forced her to do anything she didn't want to do.

On the drive home I made sure I wasn't being tailed by any cops. The closer I got to my place the more I looked for anything out of the ordinary. Yeah, I was starting to feel more grounded and ready for the flight.

Oscar was upstairs putting ammo in his weapons, he had on his game face. I asked Oscar how long the flight is, he said depending on refueling and head wind, anywhere from six to eight hours. He said the one concern was us needing fuel and having to land in British Columbia. He said the RCMP would be all over us.

"Too bad Walker didn't make it back; he would take care of us hey, Mitchell?"

"Yes, he would, Oscar."

I loaded up the entire weed for Tommy J in the back of my pickup truck and the two of us then headed to the private airport.

Oscar's main job was to look for cops and not the black and white street patrol units. Narcs are the ones who make me nervous. They dress like us, act like us and most of them are Vietnam vets so they have that nasty edge to them where they would do anything for a bust and it would be a huge bust, surely a feather in someone's cap.

Everything looked good, so Oscar went upstairs to the tower and gave them his flight pattern for the trip. I stayed downstairs until I was giving the green light to head to the hangar.

So, you shut off the truck and the music and you do a 360 for any movement at all. And fucking right I had two fully loaded 9MM on me and of course my Fairburn Sykes knife in my boot.

After about twenty minutes, Oscar came down and said we are good to go. We loaded up the plane with the weed. Oscar went and started his inspection while I went out front and parked the truck and then waited for everyone to show up.

I was looking at my watch and at two minutes to twenty-two hundred, five vehicles came down the road. You get the butterflies happening and make sure both pistols are within reach of you.

All five vehicles were Cadillacs, so you know they were not cops but the adrenaline flowing doesn't stop there. You make sure all five guys getting out of these cars are the people you are expecting, no surprises. You make sure they are not followed by the fuzz.

Jerry and George took me aside along with Donnie and asked where Oscar was. I said he was inspecting the plane, why?

Jerry and George said they wanted to talk to him. I knew I wasn't to be part of this conversation, so I stayed with Donnie and the rest of the Hell Hounds along with Tommy J, Nicky, and Kevin who headed towards the plane carrying their suitcases.

All together there were eleven of us on the flight. Both Kantonescu brothers, and two guys from George's chapter. I have flown I would say at least a hundred times by plane and yet I still get nervous when taking off. Shit goes wrong with a plane, it is either taking off, or landing.

And with this crew load full of Hell Hounds and Disciples, not to mention the cargo full of weed and oil, yeah until we are in the air, I will be tense.

After a couple minutes, George and Jerry got on the plane; I asked if all was good, and they said things were out-fucking-standing.

Five minutes later, you heard the engines fire up. Oscar yelled back for everyone to put on their seat belts as Air Hell Hound is about to take flight.

This made everyone hoot and holler including Tommy J and Kevin. I looked over at Jerry who nodded to me and smiled. Now I know what is going on.

All the Hounds are heading to Juneau to persuade the Disciples to patch over. I remember back in the 60s George, Jerry, and Jake spent a lot of time in Texas and they did the exact same thing.

Urban legend has it that George walked into the one bar of a club whose leadership didn't want to patch over to the Hell Hounds.

Well, George was not empty handed and he put on the bar a gym bag containing the President and the Vice President of the chapters decapitated heads. They patched over shortly afterward.

And yes, I purposely put Silverhorn and Hydes heads in a gym bag outside that same bar to put the heat on the rival Thunder Motorcycle Club. I now looked around the plane and saw a couple gym bags, interesting.

As soon as we were in the air, I relaxed. Scotty Kantonescu opened a cooler full of beer and ice and started to hand them out. I had one and then I closed my eyes and went to sleep. I was still bagged from last night's partying.

I must have been really tired as I fell asleep right away, and you know when I have a lot on my mind I dream, and these dreams are always a hidden meaning whether it be subconscious or the Sioux spirituality coming to me whether it be a good or bad.

I had this dream. I was back in Nam; I was in a fire base, and we were in the middle of a major firefight with Charlie. There was incoming mortar fire against us.

We were having our asses handed to us by our enemy. I looked over and saw the dinks now crawling under the line. I looked around to tell the guys to fire towards the fences, but they were all running away.

I got on the radio and called in an artillery barrage on that location, and no one confirmed our coordinates.

I could hear, in perfect English, my exact location being told to the approaching enemy. My own men were selling me out, but why? I look around and now see men wearing the same uniform as me pointing exactly where I am. I am in total shock and then I feel a hand on my shoulder. I turn around and it is Jake.

"Mitchell don't be a fool. They betrayed me, why not you?"

"Mitch, hey Mitch! Wake up! We are going to land. Fuck man, you are drenched in sweat, you all right?" asked Donnie.

I was in a state of shock, this dream was so fucking real. I looked around and no one was talking, staring at me. Fuck, if I had a chute, I would be bailing from this plane right now. I told Donnie a Nam nightmare, he knows what they are all about.

He nodded yes and said to buckle up as we are almost in Seattle for our refueling.

I took a deep breath, pulled back my soaked in sweat, hair and buckled up.

You replay everything about the dream, none of the soldiers who were giving me up to the enemy I recognized. Fuck, if there is a rat on this plane, it would be nice to see his face. It has to be one of the two guys with George that I have never met. Everyone else is solid, then again, I know nothing of Kevin from the Disciples.

Once we land in Juneau, if there is a row of cops waiting for us, we know the dream was a true vision.

As soon as we landed and the engines shut off, I was the first off the plane. I needed the fresh air and to stretch my feet.

It was a hot and muggy night. The air didn't cool me off, in fact, it made me more anxious.

I took my shirt off and could actually ring it out. George came up to me and asked if I was all right, as I was pretty pale looking for a half injun.

"Nightmares from Nam, George."

He at first nodded his head before saying, "I hear you have been off the heroin since your woman's death, correct?"

I showed George both my arms, he looked and said he and Val were both proud of me.

I thanked him and then walked into the little airport washroom and rinsed out my t-shirt. I threw some fresh water in my face and then headed back outside.

When we got back on the plane, I told Oscar I was going to jump in the co-pilot's chair. I didn't say why, but I didn't want to sit in the back. Totally felt like an outsider, thus, making me the easiest to be betrayed. Told him I wanted to zone out.

After about twenty minutes, we were in Canadian airspace. He told me somewhere down there are Walker's people.

I then asked him what George and Jerry talked to him about before we took off from California.

"They said they would pay me $200 a day and pay for our hotel reservations until they were ready to head home."

"You know I told Joseph I would go with him to Chicago Friday morning."

Oscar's eyes got big, "Fuck, Mitch. Sorry, man! I forgot."

I got out of the seat and motioned Donnie to the front. He could tell something was up.

"Joseph asked me to go with him to Chicago, Friday at eight, and now I hear that might not happen."

"Fuck, man. Sorry. Look, I can't tell you what is going on and I honestly don't know how long we will be here, and if shit hits the fan we need to bolt as quickly, and stealthily as possible."

"I figured out what is going on already, like Texas in '67, correct?"

Donnie smiled and nodded his head yes.

"Well, nothing personal, Donnie, but as soon as I get my cash for the weed, I am heading back to San Fran. I don't want Joseph pissed off as he has been giving me lots of free time."

"That's cool, Mitch; yeah, keep that crusty Irishman happy. All good, brother."

So, while the rest of the bikers on the plane partied, I was plotting and planning my way back home.

About twenty minutes before we landed, I went back and had a talk with Tommy J.

"Sorry to be a bummer, but as soon as we land, I have to catch a red eye back to San Fran. Something came up that I have no control over."

"Fuck, Strongbow. You are killing me. Seriously, man?"

"Sorry. My boss needs me back home. That is what Donnie and I were talking about when I called him up front."

"Shit, man! I had all these plans for us, was going to show you my cottage, do some fishing and I mean salmon the size of small whales."

"I promise you I will head back up and we will do all this."

I took a deep breath and then said, "So, as soon as we land I will need the cash for the weed and oil. You can deal with Oscar for his part of the oil."

"That's cool, I gave my word as soon as we landed, I would have the cash for you"

And my words were true; I do want to head back up and do some hunting and fishing. I think my dad would love it up here.

17

We were met by several members of the Disciples of Doom motorcycle club as we landed.

Now, with being an outsider, I watched the dynamics as the first introductions took place between the senior Hell Hounds and the leadership of the DOD.

There seemed to be some respect as each person eyed one another up and down.

Then it was time for the introduction of Oscar and me. I seemed to get a little more respect seeing as I shared the same bloodlines, and last name as Jerry.

To them, Oscar was a pilot who was not born in North America, a non-Aryan to be exact.

To be honest, I was a little worried about leaving Oscar here as I saw the little snarls from the DOD.

I took Donnie aside and addressed my concerns. Donnie assured me that he will personally guarantee Oscar's safety.

"Mitch, he will not be having any contact with any Disciples once he is dropped off at his hotel. I will be contacting him once we are ready to fly back. Now, if he gets stupid when by himself, shit, I can't stop that. All will be good."

I thanked him, tracked Oscar down and told him to enjoy Alaska and stay away from the DODs.

"Strongbow, I know those Nazi motherfuckers have no use for me, even Tommy J in prison gave me a hard time at first. Why do you think I fucked his wife so many times including in her ass? Payback is a nasty bitch, Strongbow." That actually made me laugh.

I told him I am not sure when I will be back from Chicago, but when I am, we can start to move his stuff to his new apartment.

Tommy J then approached me with a gym bag.

"Here is the remainder of the cash I owe you. I am sure this will be the first of many successful business transactions between us."

I shook his hand and gave him the business card to Pamdora's Box. I told him you never know who is listening so tell whoever answers the phone you need a custom order and say we have discussed prices already. They will ask me to verify a price and I know it will mean to contact him. I said each pound equals one t-shirt over the phone.

I then headed to the terminal to see about finding my way back home. I had a small suitcase with my clothes, a gym bag with $ 32,500 in cash and an ounce of weed tucked in every so gently between my balls and my dick. I left my handguns and knife with Oscar. So, this will be an interesting journey home.

At the terminal they said they had good news and bad news.

The good news is they have a flight leaving in an hour to Seattle and from there I will catch another flight that will take me right to San Fran.

The bad news is that the flight to San Fran from Seattle is tomorrow, so I will have an overnight layover.

Right now, I am sure if law enforcement is watching DOD they will wonder who all these other guys are with them. So, I purchased a ticket under the name Willie Hertz. Never leave home without phony identification.

Man like leaving California I wanna be in a plane with the wheels in the air.

So, I checked my suitcase, and kept the gym bag with me.

18

The restaurant was open; I grabbed a toasted western with tomato and a large black coffee. Not like I will be drifting off with all this cash with me, but you never know.

Sandwich was good; the coffee was really strong which I enjoyed.

We boarded right on time with no issues at all. I was hoping that the seat beside me was open so I could put the gym bag in the empty seat, but sure as fuck, this short, fat, bald guy in a suit that looked much older than me, was going to be sitting beside me. So, I let him take the window and I put my gym bag in the overhead compartment and took my seat.

I looked around the plane and there was no one really I deemed as a threat. A bunch of scrawny long-haired freaks. The two chicks in the aisle beside me were hotter than hell, one had to be my age, the other a couple years younger. They were dressed like they were witches, hippies, or gypsies, either way they intrigued me.

Wheels in the air and I started to relax, well maybe relaxed a little too much as suddenly that greasy breakfast and strong coffee had my sphincter at ease and ready to give birth. Fuck! Do I carry my gym bag with me to the washroom, do I trust the square beside me or the gypsy queens to watch the bag? Damn, all this hesitation had the hairs on my arms standing up. I grabbed the gym bag and pinched my butt cheeks and made a mad dash.

Man, this was close as the anus volcano erupted in full force, good thing I didn't ask a stewardess if she could do me a favor or I would be asking her for a diaper change.

On the way back, the two chicks asked if I brought my own toilet paper in the gym bag.

I laughed and said the Watergate transcripts.

So, now that the ice has been broken, which I thought I would see a lot more of in Alaska, so I asked what they were doing in Juneau.

It turns out they are in a band and are flying back to Seattle. This record producer wanted to hear them perform live.

"Actually, I know this guy Basil who opened up his own recording studio and label in San Fran."

They both raised their eyebrows and asked for SOL records.

"Yes, SOL records, I am meeting him some time next week."

Once again, the girls looked at each other in disbelief.

"We are meeting with him next Tuesday, actually."

I asked if they had a pen and paper, I gave them my home number and Pamdora's.

We did the proper introductions and then I asked if they puffed.

"We are musicians, of course we toke!"

"Have you girls ever tried Columbian weed?"

Laura the dark-haired sister said they have heard of it but never tried it.

I whispered and said, "I have an ounce on me, once we land let's smoke a joint or two."

Julie, the blonde sister, said far out, and what I was doing in Seattle. I told them catching a red eye the next morning to go home.

They asked where I was staying while in town.

"No idea, will grab a hotel."

Here I am thinking, *wishing* that they will say don't be silly. I can crash at their place and next thing you know it will be a threesome.

"One of the places we play at is in this massive hotel. We have gotten to be good friends with the owner. We can take you there and make sure you get a good deal."

And there goes my hard-on.

We talked about music for the rest of the flight. I told them about the whole Summer of Love, and Bay Area music scene that I was involved with including partying with Carlos, the Doors and my dad being Jimi Hendrix's sergeant and how I met him at Monterrey.

The guitar player and bass player took part in the conversations while the drummer stayed in his seat and slept the whole time.

Once we landed, the band parted but the girls stayed together. They told me to come with them.

An old hearse, purple in color pulls up at the front of the terminal and two guys get out, they hug the girls and introduce me to their husbands. There is no sense of jealousy coming from the guys at all. I guess with them on the road in different cities you either trust them or your marriage goes south really quickly.

The girls told him to drive me to the Balmoral hotel. They said I had some of that Columbian weed. "Groovy, let's try it," said Laura's husband.

So, I rolled us a joint as we headed to the hotel. We had enough time to smoke it, and all were impressed. Julie's husband said nice to smoke a joint and not have a seed pop in your eye. I told them no seeds but more stalks, better for making tea.

I told their hubbies that I work part time at a funeral parlor, and I really dig this old hearse. They said they use it primarily for transporting the girls' equipment.

We all walked into the hotel together, this place was built in the late 1800s. It was huge.

The girls asked for Jack the manager; they asked if he could get me a deal on a room for the night and a ride to the airport the next morning.

Jack said of course and he would throw in a free breakfast. I had to give him a credit card for the room.

Jack took it and said, "Very good, mister Willie Hertz. When you are ready, I will have the bellhop take you to your room."

Julie took out the piece of paper I gave her and looked at it once again and then raised her eyebrow. I picked up on this right away. Couldn't tell her why for obvious reasons so I nodded yes.

After they left, I went and saw Jack and asked if they had a safe in my room. He said no but they have one that customers can use and only he or the afternoon or night shift manager have the combination too.

Yeah, I plan on doing some sightseeing, so I went with him and put my gym bag in the safe.

He put a piece of seal tape on the handles and gave me a receipt.

Then the bellhop took me up to my room.

There was an old steam style radiator in the room. It was a cozy room, good vibe.

After he left, I looked at my watch and then looked outside, it was starting to rain so I laid on the bed to grab a quick twenty. I was hoping when I get up the sun will break through, and I can trip around for a bit.

That was the plan. Fuck, I woke up four hours later totally delusional. I had zero idea where I was. I sat up and looked around and nothing.

The phone then started to ring which startled the fuck right out of me. As I was reaching to pick it up things were coming back to me.

I said hello and it was Julie, she asked if I wanted to go for a coffee with her and her hubby. I had nothing else to do so I said sure. She said for me to meet them downstairs in ten. Once again, my dirty mind is thinking they want to ask if I want to do a threesome with them.

So, I throw some water in my face, a bag of weed down my pants and go downstairs.

Julie is already downstairs and comes over and gives me a hug and says thanks for meeting them. Damn right I am meeting them. I jump in the back of the hearse and her hubby thanks me as we drive over to this coffee shop.

Jim asks if I like my coffee strong. Big time I said, so he orders us a coffee.

We take a seat, and I can feel the nervous energy coming from both of them. I took a sip of the coffee while looking at them, damn strong coffee, I liked it.

Jim then said, "Curious about something…"

I told him to go ahead.

"So, is your name Mitch, or Willie?"

"Does it matter?" I asked as I took another sip of coffee and did a serious half smile.

Both looked at each other and then Julie talked.

"We both really like the weed you have. We deal with lots of people in the music industry up here, and by deal, yes, we move weed to help pay the bills. I see you on the plane with a briefcase that you are guarding with your life. The gold credit card and the way you handle yourself. I guess what I am getting at is if we wanted to buy more of this weed could you hook us up?"

Now, what would Joseph or Donnie say if they were here right now? Two total strangers asking to buy weed from me.

"And how much weed would you be asking for?"

"How much does an ounce go for on the street?"

"I am hearing fifty-five to sixty bucks"

"And how much would you sell us a pound or more for?"

Time to see what these two are all about, call it a background check via drug dealing style.

"Can I see both of your driver's licenses?"

They were a little shocked but obeyed and got them out. I asked Julie if she had a pen and a piece of paper I could borrow.

I wrote down all the info on both of them. I handed back their licenses and said, "It all depends on how much weed you buy. The more you buy the cheaper the price. How many pounds were you thinking, and everything is in kilos past a certain amount, but I can do the math for you."

"How about ten pounds?"

"You would have to come down and pick it up, too far for delivery and I only deal with people I know. Any stranger who shows up with you, I will slam the door shut in your face. So, for ten pounds it will be sixty-five hundred"

"How about six grand seeing how you live two states away?"

"Not my problem, you guys live this far away. I will do sixty-four hundred. You sell by the ounce you will make thirty-two hundred profit, not bad."

They both looked at each other, Julie nodded her head and Jim stuck out his hand to seal the business deal.

"Now, I have one more request, guys." I took out the info from their driver's license and asked them to take me to their house. Better safe the sorry.

Jim knew exactly where I was going with this, and he said no problem.

So, after we finished our cup of joe we headed over.

19

It was a really old house, but it had character.

You walk inside and you see amps, guitars and microphones stands in this huge living room that is exactly what I wanted to see.

So, I threw the bag of weed on their coffee table and told Jim to roll us a few.

We smoked a couple joints, and I asked Julie to sing a song.

She grabbed her acoustic guitar and started to belt out an original song. Man, she had killer pipes and amazing guitar playing skills. I was totally impressed, especially with it being rock.

I hung with them for a couple hours until they had to go out and meet with friends. I gave them the whole ounce except a couple joints for myself. I told them let their friends try it and you will have orders coming out your ass.

Julie said they are meeting with Basil, August 11th, so they will be in touch with me.

It was still raining, so I asked that they drive me back to the hotel.

Once inside, my gut told me it was dinner time, so I ate at the restaurant inside the hotel.

I looked outside the huge pane glass window, and it was pouring outside. Every table that was occupied had at least a couple and for the first time in a long time, I actually felt all alone.

Not even a single chick in the joint who I would ask to join me.

I looked at the chemistry of all the couples, some you could tell were madly in love with the person sitting across from them. And some were out of necessity via those two words "I Do".

I asked my server what is there to do in Seattle on a Wednesday night. He shook his head and said nothing.

Fuck. So, I paid my bill, hit the bar in the hotel that was pretty much dead. Had a couple drinks and seeing how nothing interesting came in, I went upstairs, smoked a joint. Called the receptionist for an early wake up call and stared at the ceiling until I passed out cold.

20

The next morning, I woke up delirious, hugging the pillow tight. I had a massive hard-on as I called out to Charlene in my erotic dream.

The ringing phone brought me out of my semi-slumber. It was the front desk and that dreaded early morning wake up call I asked for.

As much as I wanted to close my eyes and hoped Charlene could come back to me, I didn't want to miss my flight and have to spend another night stuck here.

So, I jumped up out of bed, hit the shower and brought imagination to life with Charlene sucking my cock.

After I blew my load, which was amazing by the way, I ran the hot water on my neck to tried and visualize where she had gone to. For once, I wish the Sioux spirituality would come through and shine the sun's beams on her, fuck I miss her, and I'm truly worried about her.

I grabbed some breakfast and then smoked a joint for the road or for the air I guess you would say. Went downstairs to grab my gym bag and asked Jack if that ride to the airport was still good to go. He said of course and had this really sexy chick drive me-where the fuck was she last night?

Flight back home was pretty smooth. At the airport I called Joseph for a ride home, but he was nowhere to be found, everyone else was in Alaska so I took a taxi home.

As I pulled up, Janine was sitting out front on Pamdora's enjoying her cuppa tea, as she calls it.

She asked where I have been. I really don't want to know

everything about my criminal activities, so I say up north. Why? She missed me?

"I miss you everyday, Mitchell. Now, that redhead was here looking for you. Sorry, can't recall her name."

Cue the stomach flip and heart flutter.

"Charlene?"

"Yes! Charlene, she popped in and asked where you were. I was honest and said I wasn't sure. That is what you want right?"

"Yeah, that is what I want. Did she say anything to you at all?"

"She said you are a hard person to get a hold of."

Man, I had so many questions, and after what Janine told me next, I had a million more after I asked how she looked.

"She looked good, she has lost some weight. One thing that I did notice is she was wearing one hell of a rock on her ring finger."

"What kind of rock and what finger?"

"Looked like an engagement ring. If it was real, someone must love her a whole lot, as I would say this ring had to be at least two to three carats, massive ring."

Holy fuck, what have you done Charlene? I felt like throwing up.

I thanked Janine and then hauled my ass upstairs to listen to my voicemails.

Messages from Rachel and Ella. Am I being punished somehow with the phantom ghost known as Charlene Borden?

I closed my eyes and replayed everything Janine said to me. I even broke out in a cold sweat as I kept hearing the words engagement ring.

This whole fucking mess makes absolutely zero sense to me. I risked my life to save hers; I have killed so she can live. We have a stupid fight, and she is engaged a couple months later.

I was sweating like a hooker in church, debating what to do next. Once again getting drunk and stoned and hearing Joseph's rants tomorrow or listening to what my dad would say, "Son, the deer won't come to you, you go and find them."

Fuck it, I got out the Mustang keys and decided to cruise the whole city. I know that was her in that Cadillac that day.

So, I fired over Emma and said out loud, time to hunt.

My gut told me I would be successful, I am so damn determined right now, total concentration and total effort giving.

I seemed to comb every inch of the city and nothing. Not going to hang around every single vacant Caddy hope she eventually goes to it.

Deep sigh as I was skunked. So, I headed to pick up my suits from the store. Tried them on to make sure, fit like a T.

I headed home and called Ella, nothing but voicemail.

So, I called Joseph who actually invited me out for dinner, a nice surprise.

Where did we go? Martins of course. Steak is my favorite meal so all good.

At dinner, Joseph gave me a run down as to what we are doing in Chicago. The Italians may be the most powerful illegal organization in the United States, but the Irish were number two. So, all of the most powerful Irish mobs meet every quarter and talk business.

I asked if Seamus was going to be there. Joseph said he was still on his honeymoon, why?

I told him I have this strange vibe we would get along really well.

Joseph laughed and said Seamus keeps a very small inner circle and I don't fit the criteria, I asked if it was because I wasn't Irish.

"No lad, you are butt ugly."

"Yeah, I will really be protecting you," my turn to laugh.

He said because we are taking a civilian flight, we can't carry weapons.

"My only concern is walking through the airport terminal, and on the plane. Sean will be driving us to the airport, he will be locked and loaded."

"Once we land, a couple of Seamus' men will pick us up at the airport. And once we get to the hotel, look under your bed, you will find your weapons."

But I *do* worry, that is my job to protect him. And lots of deaths over those diamonds. And Chicago, never been. I don't know any of these Irish gangsters.

The whole Charlene wearing a big ring was really bothering me and with Joseph owning a high-end jewelry shop, I asked if he has seen her at all lately.

"Can't say I have, lad. Why do you ask? You seem so sad when you bring up her name."

"We had a fight, not a huge fight, she went AWOL, and Janine said she dropped by to see me last week wearing this huge rock on her wedding finger."

"I can tell you still love her, Mitchell. Or is it you need proper closure?"

I had to think about this one before answering him, "I think a bit of both, Joseph."

"All good things come to those who wait, lad."

I am anything but the waiting sort of guy to be honest.

Joseph dropped me off at my place. It was still pretty early but I have a long flight tomorrow.

So, I unpacked and repacked for my flight. Packing clothes on the fly once again. Speaking of which, I wonder who Oscar is doing being solo? I am sure he is fucking some Northern chick in the ass. Will the Disciples of doom patch over? Will there be a war if they don't?

I was debating on whether to shower or not when the phone rang. My heart was beating out of my chest, fucking fate, it has to be Charlene.

It was Nyah and she was upset. I could barely understand her.

Eventually, she said she needed me to come and pick her up.

So, I grabbed the car keys and hauled ass to where she said she was. It was a restaurant in town.

I parked the car out front and went in with a 9MM down the back of my pants.

Nyah was sitting in a booth; her head was down when I said, "I am here."

As she looked up, both eyes were swollen, and not from crying.

My blood started to boil; I am thinking that asshole from her school Dave did this to her.

"Who did this to you?"

Once again, she was crying so hard, she was mumbling, and I had a really hard time understanding her.

She would try and talk and the only word I picked up on was *dad*.

Eventually I sat down right across from her. I held both her hands and told her to look up at me.

"Nyah, now nice and slow, who did this to you?"

"My dad did this."

Sean loves her and would die for her. I was totally shocked by this and asked her why he did it.

"Mitch, if I tell you why, well... then you too will be really mad at me."

"Nyah, you are very special to me, I promise I will not get mad at you."

She took a really deep breath which seemed to open up the water works once again.

I grabbed a napkin and wiped away the tears.

Eventually, Nyah composed herself and said she got busted today.

My turn to be shocked.

"How did you get busted?"

"Cops went into my locker between classes, they found a nickel bag, for personal use."

I took a long deep breath and asked, "Do you think Dave ratted you out?"

"I don't *think*, I know. As I was taking away in handcuffs, he mouthed to me, *we are even, bitch.*"

"Have no fear I will take care of him. Fucker will pay. So why did your dad hit you?"

"Because of doing drugs and not letting him know who sold me the weed."

She looked right at me, and her eyes got really big as she now grabbed my hands and said, "Don't worry Mitch, I would never sell you out. I eventually said it was Dave, fuck him."

"And where was the last time you saw your dad?"

"Right before I called you."

I have no doubts in my mind that Sean right now is on a mission and will take a blow torch to this whole kid's body before ending his life. You go Sean, torture and kill that fucking rat.

I asked Nyah if she wanted to come back to my place for a bit, she said yes, she didn't feel like going home, and being smacked again.

That put a dagger in my heart to be honest, fuck I felt really bad.

As soon as we got to my place, I made her a vodka and orange. Went into the bedroom and brought out about a dime worth of weed.

"Help yourself, babe," was my answer to the current situation.

Nyah was quiet and seemed deep in thought as she rolled a joint in between sips of her drink. After she downed the first drink, she opened up a bit more.

"Mitch, they handcuffed me and took me out in front of the whole school. Took my mug shot, fingerprinted me as if I was some mass murderer or something. Then I was locked up in this horrible cell, until my asshole dad came down and bailed me out." Nyah went into a trance and shook her head *no* the whole time.

"I have been arrested several times, hon, not a very pleasant experience at all. Fucking cops are assholes, I swear they got off on taking away your dignity."

Nyah said fucking pigs before grabbing a reefer that I rolled. She sparked up the joint and started to smoke the whole thing before she realized what she was doing, she said sorry and passed it over to me, and then she started to cry again.

I put the joint in the ashtray and hugged and comforted her.

After the second drink and three joints later, Nyah seemed to have cried herself out. She said she was really tired and could she spend the night. Of course, was my answer, she gave me a kiss on the cheek and headed to my bedroom like a zombie, poor thing.

As soon as I get home from Chicago, I am going to track this fucking rat down, take his life, and then throw him in the bay.

And as far as Sean goes, he can't hit her anymore, daughter or not. I think I am going to have a talk with Joseph and ask for advice. Seeing how Joseph was coming early in the morning I didn't stay up much later then Nyah.

I came quietly into the bedroom and saw she actually fell asleep on top of the bed fully clothed.

This might be one of the few times in my lifetime that I have a beautiful woman in my bed, and I am more interested in sleeping, then trying to fuck her.

I tried to wake her, but she was dead to the world, so I stripped down. Covered Nyah with a sheet then jumped into bed and it too didn't take me long to pass out.

My alarm as usual went off sooner than later. Nyah opened her eyes and smiled.

"Morning, beautiful. Listen, I am taking off with Joseph for a couple days. You can stay here all weekend if you wish. But don't have anyone over, hon."

She wrapped her arms around me and thanked me.

I told her to get under the covers and go back to sleep, it is really early.

She smiled and nodded yes. I then jumped in the shower and by the time I started to wash my balls, the shower curtain was pulled open and Nyah joined me. She continued to wash and stroke my cock as she necked me. I have been so horny lately and not really get a lot of action, so once Nyah went from stroking to sucking and stroking it and before I knew I was ready to cum, I let Nyah know who this, she told me to cum all over her perfect breasts.

She took the whole load; fuck she is amazing. By the time the last drop was out, she licked my load off her breasts, how fucking hot is that?

We continued the shower, cleaning each other. We dried each other off then Nyah said she was going back to bed; I gave her a nice long kiss. She started to giggle, and I asked what was so funny.

"I haven't brushed my teeth or gargled Mitch; how do you taste?"

I squinted my face that made her almost double over, she was laughing so hard.

Yeah, it was gross, but it was nice to hear her laugh.

I made a quick fried egg sandwich and coffee, polished it off when Joseph called and said he was on his way to meet him downstairs in ten.

So, like a good soldier I head downstairs with a suitcase containing my clothes and my one spare suit on a hanger. I never got onto a plane wearing a suit, a jumpsuit I guess.

Joseph's car pulls up with him in the back and Sean Quinn in the driver's seat.

What a miserable looking fuck he is. I nod to him and put my items in the trunk, and then I jump in the back with the boss.

Joseph is in a really good mood and tells me how dapper I look.

I thank him, while looking at the back of Sean's head and picture myself putting a bullet in the back of it.

Joseph asked me if I was ready to take Chicago by storm.

I didn't answer him as this rage brewing inside of me had a hold of me.

Joseph asked if I was high. "No, not at all. Deep in thought, didn't sleep very well last night."

"Has to be over a woman; they will be the death of you, lad."

"Some are worth killing over Joseph, especially when assholes hurt them."

I looked at the rear view mirror to see Sean's response and nothing; fucking caveman is too thick to figure out I am talking about him.

We pulled up to the unloading zone at the airport, Sean got out and got Joseph's stuff out of the trunk. I got my own and I zeroed in like a hawk to a snake when Joseph told Sean to be careful taking care of that matter.

Sean nodded yes, I didn't say fuck all, as I want to get away from the ape.

As we were waiting to board, I asked Joseph what was with the statement to Sean.

"Nothing for you to worry about, lad."

"Does it have to do with Nyah?"

Joseph raised an eyebrow and said maybe, and what exactly do I know.

"I know she was busted yesterday at school for having a small bag of weed, this guy Dave ratted her out. I know that fucking ape Sean smacked Nyah around."

Joseph's face went beet red, he now had anger in his voice asking how I know all this stuff.

"Nyah told me, she is sleeping at my house right now. I swear if Sean hits her again, I will empty a clip in his head."

"Now, you listen here, Mitchell Strongbow. There will be no feuds or bad blood in my crew."

"Joseph, that girl means a lot to me. She doesn't deserve to be smacked around like some whore."

"That is between a father and his daughter, heed my warning lad, stay out of it."

Joseph now grabbed a hold of my jacket with fire in his eyes and demanded to know

"Look at me right now. Are you fucking Nyah?"

"I am not answering that question, no good can come from me answering you. But I will say this. I really care for her. She means a lot to me."

"Jesus Christ, Mitchell. Of all the pussy in the bay area you have to sleep with Sean's daughter?"

"What if she was my steady girlfriend and not a piece of ass would that matter?"

"Do you love her, Mitchell? How many girls have you been with since you left prison? There was the librarian who you told me last night you still care for a hell of a lot, the bank chick, the good doctor who you say is your current and steady girlfriend. I am sure they are all special to you. If you truly care for Nyah, end whatever you have going on right now. If Sean were to get word you were sleeping with his daughter, you would be joining the guy who ratted her out in a shallow grave. Not even I could stop Sean. And this fucker the rat, he will take a couple days to die, Sean will torture him. I am willing to bet by the time we get home from Chicago he will still be alive, he will have no fingers, dick, toes, eyes, or tongue though."

"I have never been scared of any man that walks the planet, Joseph, you know that."

"Then think of Nyah, he will beat her for being with you."

"I will fucking kill him then."

"You are not killing Sean Quinn. He has been one of my closest friends, not only since being in America, but my whole life, not just as a soldier to me. I was there when Nyah was born. Mitchell, would you let your daughter sleep around with Oscar?"

"I am nowhere as bad as Oscar. I have more values than him."

"Yes, you do, but not much better, you are currently fucking two females at present moment. Sean and I have talked. If for some reason she has to do time for the weed, she will disappear as far as the USA government is concerned. Sean finds out about you two, he will send her to Russia. Think of her, not your cock."

"Joseph, I swear on Katrina with regards to Nyah, it was never about my cock."

Joseph looked deeply at me, no smile, no frown, he finally said he believed me.

We boarded the plane, and I'll say for the first part of the flight I thought about what Joseph said. I have never been able to keep my cock in my pants have I? Fuck what would Sigmund Freud think of me?

This flight showed a side of Joseph I never saw before, fear.

About an hour into the flight, the clouds became really dark, and you could see flashes of lighting off in the distance. After about twenty minutes later the turbulence started rocking the plane heavily.

Eventually the fasten seat belt sign came on. I heard Joseph mutter under his breath *Jesus Christ* and he now fumbled to get his belt on.

I asked if he needed help, his face was pure white, and he was starting to sweat.

Suddenly, the plane hit an air pocket and we started to drop; the stewardess who was helping others put their belts on was knocked to the ground after her head hit the ceiling.

She was badly hurt, bleeding from her head, a concussion was starting. I undid my belt and raced to help her, half of my steps I never touched the carpet as we were truly in the elevator from hell.

I was applying pressure to her head wound with a blanket, while another visibly shaken stewardess came towards us, and asked me to help get her fallen comrade back to her seat.

Once I did, I came back to my seat and Joseph was now frozen in fear. He couldn't speak, I told him to relax.

Believe it or not, I think I even heard Joseph praying, secretly I was dying inside of laughter.

"Joseph these pilots are used to flying in bad weather, and I am willing to bet this pilot did a tour in Nam and has been shot at. Turbulence has never caused a plane to fall apart mid-air, or crash. All will be good, boss. Listen, I want you to breathe in through your nose for a count of three, hold it for a count of three and exhale for a count of three."

Man, his breathing was really erratic, but he finally got it under control as the pilot now took us above the summer storm.

After about twenty minutes, the unfasten seat belt sign came on.

The co-pilot left the cockpit and headed for the back of the plane. Joseph said he really needed a drink now.

A couple minutes later the co-pilot and one stewardess came over and thanked me personally. I asked how she is, and they said she will need a couple stitches but will survive.

They asked if I needed anything at all. I asked for a couple drinks for my boss.

They said it was not a problem at all. Joseph thanked me for everything and said once the stewardess gets her stitches out she owes me at least a blow-job.

"Ain't that the fucking truth, Joseph!" We both started to laugh; all was good once again between us.

The rest of the flight was uneventful, and we landed at O'Hare after two. Joseph had arranged for a couple of Seamus men to pick us up at the airport. Jimmy Dolan and Aiden O'Toole.

Joseph did the introductions; fuckers don't even stick out their hands. They asked where Sean, Patrick, or Donnie were?

"They are all on assignment. Mitchell is now part of my crew. And you know what? I am glad he is here. Our plane went through a really horrific storm, the stewardess was almost knocked out cold, and the poor thing had her skull busted open. While the rest of the plane was frozen in fear and praying for their souls, Mitchell here unfastened his seatbelt, with no regard to his own safety, picked up the busted open stewardess, carried her as if she was light as a feather to her seat, fastened her seatbelt and made sure the other stewardess knew how to care for their fallen comrade. Never been so proud of him."

Holy fuck, this truly made me smile. Now Jimmy and Aiden shook my hand. They didn't say shit, nodded their heads.

They dropped us off in front of our hotel. After they drove away, Joseph asked what I thought of them. Jealous insecure fucks was my response. Joseph didn't answer me, he laughed.

We were staying at the Congress Hotel to be exact. I was in total awe as we walked in. The lobby was like no other hotel I have seen, spectacular. You could tell everything back when this was built was all about quality workmanship. It was a stunning sight to behold. This was an eight hundred plus room hotel, built in 1893. We checked in under the names Hertz for yours truly, and O'Banion for Joseph. Our rooms were on the eighth floor of the north tower.

Joseph commented how fitting we are staying on this floor, I was confused and asked why.

"Al Capone had a suite here in the thirties, lad. You know they say he haunts this hotel to this day."

"And you are here under the name O'Banion, wasn't that the name of the gang that Capone killed on Valentine's Day?"

Joseph stared at me in disbelief, "I am impressed, Mitchell. You know your history, but if I was running that crew, no way would my men be so stupid to get themselves whacked by a bunch of greasy Italians."

"I love history, Joseph. To not learn it and respect it; you are doomed to repeat it."

Joseph said to go and unpack and then we can grab a bite together.

I was staying in room 811. As soon as I walked in, I had this weird vibe as if I was being watched. Yeah, the hair on my arms went up as I checked the closet, shower, and fuck, even under the bed. Now as Joseph promised, I had 2, 9MM handguns with a couple extra clips under my bed sheets ad yes, a Fairburn Syhkes knife.

I think Joseph must have gotten into my head with this Al Capone stuff.

I put everything away, hung up my other suit and then headed to Joseph's room.

"Listen, lad. I want to go over a few things with you. For the most part, all the different crews here get together quite well, as we all hate the Italians. But there are always different packs being formed and other than Seamus' crew, I don't trust anyone. Your job is to look as intimidating as possible without beating or killing anyone. If shit does go down, do what you do best, Mitchell. Take no prisoners and if we get separated, go to this address in South Bend, it is about an hour from here."

I took the address and put it in my wallet. I then asked if there is anyone I should look out for, anyone in the past or present he views as a threat.

"Do you know the difference between a Mick and an Orangeman?"

"Yes, one is Catholic, and one is Protestant. Correct?"

"You are totally impressing me this trip, lad. Yes, you are correct. There is this Protestant from Washington, I never trusted back home or over here."

"Is his name Gerald Ford?"

This actually made him laugh, "Yes, he is a Protestant I don't trust.

No, this guy's name is "Big" Jim Malone. He is a smart ass; thinks he is a regular Don Fucking Rickles. Pay him no attention either, lad. He will say something smart to you, remember discipline unless I say so."

"Don't worry about that. By the way, where are these meetings taking place, and what do I do during them as I assume I am to wait outside. Correct?"

"It is in the actual conference room at the Hyatt hotel. They have a pretty nice bar there. Hang around there, but don't get all liquored up, lad, understood?"

"Not a problem. When are the meetings taking place?"

Joseph looked at his watch and said in less than five hours.

He took to me this pizza joint that had the thickest and best deep-dish pizza I have ever eaten. I had to have an espresso afterwards as I felt like I needed a nap. Yep, that woke me up, felt like I was doing a handful of beans.

We went back to the hotel to get cleaned up. I grabbed a shower, put on my suit, packed my two weapons and all the clips. I then knocked on Joseph's door. He answered it wearing a black pin striped suit and a fedora, black and white shoes, fuck he looked like an old school gangster. He had quite the bounce in his step. And me, I was on duty ready for anything and anybody.

We took a taxi over, and once we pulled up, I could tell the other gangsters were out front. They all had this intense, tight look on their faces.

I made sure to open the door for Joseph and let him out as a sign of respect to my boss, and I too can give a pretty damn nasty look back.

And because of actions I made sure to make eye contact with all and let them know I am one to be feared and not intimidated, I eyed all up and down and figured out who was the biggest threat.

It wasn't the bosses I worried about; it was their muscle that would be the threat.

As I am doing a visual, I am drawn to this one person who is now walking towards us with a puzzled look on his face. What was not so puzzling was the fact that he knew my name.

In a suit I didn't recognize him, but I recognized his face. It was Paul McCowell.

Paul and I served together in Special Ops and SOG.

"Jesus, Joseph, and Mary. Look at the size of you, Strongbow."

I have put on at least seventy pounds of solid muscle, with the help of steroids, where Paul has put on about almost the same size but mostly in his gut area. It appears the spuds and beers are his workout.

He gave me a hug and yes, I noticed he felt around to feel the 9MM I had in the back.

He gave Joseph the nod, as he gave us some space to talk and asked how life was treating me.

"Life is treating me better than the last time I saw you, brother. How about you?"

"I'm doing all right, working in Jim Malone's crew, you working for O'Reilly now? Where is Terek?"

I said yes, Donnie is on assignment. He asked how long have I had been working for Joseph as he hasn't seen or heard shit about me.

"I spent a deuce in San Quentin, got out a couple months ago and been working for him ever since, yourself?"

"I have been working for Jim since I came home; he treats me and pays me very well. You ever think of looking for a new boss? I will put in a good word for you."

I wanted to say death before dishonor, but I respected Paul back in Southeast Asia. But no fucking way would I ever jump ship.

"Thanks, but Joseph does the same for me. Hard to find good leadership."

Malone then called McCowell back over; we shook hands and said we will hook up for a beer before the weekend is done.

As soon as they left, Joseph asked how I knew Paul. I told him exactly. Joseph nodded his head and clenched his jaw.

"Don't trust him, Mitchell; I don't care how much dirt you ate over there."

Quite a bold statement. "I will shake with one hand and have my other hand already reaching for my 9MM."

Joseph smiled, then looked at his watch and said let's go in.

I walked with him down the hall to the elevators with my boss and a couple other Irish gangsters and their muscles.

Joseph would talk and I would watch and see the interactions.

We made our way to the elevator, pushed the button and once the door opened the elevator guy stared at me in a very non-threatening way, almost in bewilderment.

He gave me a nod with a smile and told the six of us to come in and asked what floor.

Joseph answered the penthouse and he nodded yes while still staring at me.

After about the fourth floor he asked if I was Sergeant Major Strongbow. Fuck! It has been a while since someone called me that. I answered yes I was.

He came right out and shook my hand. "You saved my life in Quang Tri province. I was in the 82nd. You and a bunch of Special Ops guys were choppered in as we were caught in a crossfire and were taking heavy casualties. You were fearless. I think you smoked a whole platoon of them by yourself. We all heard of you beforehand, but thought you were some urban myth to keep our morale up. But watching you in action was more than impressive. You were a killing machine. Listen, you need anything here let me know."

Joseph now puffed out his chest and patted me on the back and said, "That's my boy."

I asked what his name was, "Bruce Jackson"

I told him glad I could help, and yes if I need anything I know who to go see.

There were two huge bodyguards outside of the penthouse suite door.

Right off the bat I know which of the two I would take down first, both would be chest shots, and then head shots.

They nodded at everyone and knew everyone by name, but me.

Joseph stopped and said I am with him. They asked to see some identification.

My back went up, and I asked if they were fucking cops.

This seemed to piss off the one guy who went to actually grab a hold of me, fuck that, it's go time.

As he was reaching with his left arm, I moved to the right and threw really hard punches to his ribs. He hit the ground gasping for air. I then with my left hand pulled out my 9MM and jammed it into the other guy's forehead.

He went pale white as he now looked at Joseph, in fear for his life.

By now, a crowd had gathered including Francis Fitzgerald, who was the Chicago Irish mob boss who was hosting the meeting.

He said to Joseph, "What in the bloody hell is your man doing?" "It seems he has taken care of your people who are supposed to be guarding us."

He was not impressed, I asked Joseph if I should stand down.

"Thank you, Mitchell. Stand down, let them be. By the way Francis, your boys started this by asking him for his identification and then proceeded to grab him. He was defending himself, all good."

I lowered my weapon and felt a pair of eyes being burnt in the back of my head.

I turned around and staring at me was Jim Malone. Paul was beside him with a big smile on his face.

He walked over and said let's grab that beer now. I looked over at Joseph who told me to go ahead.

We jumped on the elevator together, I said to Paul, "You and Bruce were both 82nd."

I let them talk until we hit the ground floor. I have to say I am not into the hero shit, it's not who I am, or will ever be.

As we left the elevator I said, "I put those two guys down pretty easy, you think our bosses will be alright up there?"

"Fuck, Mitch. The rest of the boss's bodyguards will pull up a chair and wait in the hall with the two apes. Glad you did this so we can take off and have a beer and get caught up. Some of the so-called bodyguards up there should be let go."

We grabbed a booth so we could see everything coming at us.

A pitcher of cold draft, a couple shots of wild turkey and it was time to get caught up.

Paul, since coming home got married and has three-year-old twins at home. Cute kids if I do say so myself.

His wife is a cousin of Jim Malone and that is how he met her. Paul runs the muscle for the crew, not a bodyguard.

I told him most of my story, some things you don't tell as you don't want it used against you, almost like giving them leverage.

I told him Oscar works for Joseph now, and he and Donnie are both on assignment. He asked where the ugly Sean and Patrick Quinn were. I said back home, family issues. I really have no idea about Patrick, maybe helping Sean torture Schinn.

And that ugly ape better keep his hands to himself, or his next assignment will be figuring out how to get out from a shallow grave.

I respected what Joseph said about Paul, so I didn't tell any secrets.

The only thing I did mention was that I've known Joseph since I was a teen as my brother did business with him.

We talked mostly about the madness of Special Ops and SOG. I asked Paul if he knew Mike Battaglia, the chopper pilot.

"I know of a pretty powerful mobster with that name, any relation?"

"One in the same, I saved his life in Nam. He lives in San Fran, and we have become close friends, fuck he even dated my sister Rachel for a bit. I spent some time with Sonny and got to know him as well."

I hate people that drop names, but in our profession, you never know when it may come in handy.

"Look at you, moving up in the gangster world! That would be a good guy to save indeed, even if he is Italian."

After the first pitcher and a couple shots were downed, I had to piss.

On the way back, I see some girls sitting at a bar all dolled up and these guys in suits trying their best to pick them up.

Now, normally I would laugh to myself, and keep walking, but both my heads recognized the one blonde that kept cock-teasing me that fundraiser. Talk about being shocked.

Her baby blue eyes got huge, and her cheeks blushed as she recognized me.

My mysterious blonde's smile told me I should make my way over, and that is exactly what I did.

"Are you following me?" I said to her. She laughed and asked me the same question.

Now, the guys in the suits certainly didn't like me interrupting their so-called pick-up lame game.

I went in for a hug which was met with no resistance. I asked my blonde friend if these guys were annoying her.

"As a matter of fact, they are," she said.

I turned and said to the guys, "This is the windy city, go blow away."

The biggest guy reminded me there are three of them and only one of me.

Now, normally I would pull out my 9MM and tell him he should count again. But too many witnesses for that. So, I eyed up all three and knew to take out the biggest guy who was by far the highest threat.

Paul came up from behind the three and said, "I have seen him put many VC into body bags in Nam. Many with his own bare hands. Leave or feel his wrath. Now, I won't get involved other then to contact your next of kin, if you call the cops on him after he beats the living fuck out of each and everyone of you."

The big mouth said to his buddies, "Lets leave these whores to these assholes." Stupid people do stupid things.

I pulled him in with my left hand and with my right hand stuck my 9MM into his ribs. Paul stopped his two buddies by grabbing them really hard in the nuts.

"That is a 9MM handgun you are feeling, now I don't believe in

God after all I have seen in Nam, but you might. You wanna meet him?"

All the color left his face, he couldn't even answer but he did shake his head no in fear.

"This is your last warning to fuck-right-off."

He turned around and was quivering while walking away. I then walked up to his two buddies he left behind, showed them the 9MM discreetly in the palm of my hand, and shook my head no and growled at them. Same as their buddy their fear came to their face, and they left after Paul released his Vulcan death grip on their nuts.

My blonde female friend stared at me, as I now stared at her tits in her dress. Great sign as her nipples were sticking right out. I know she is hot for me; I am willing to bet her pussy is dripping for me right now. Time to see where things go.

I apologized to all three for the one goof's comments. They all thanked Paul and I for stepping in and defending their honor.

They offered to buy us a drink, I said how about joining us at our table, so no other creeps bother them.

All three agreed that was a good plan.

I sat across from the blonde and asked what her name was, she said Mindy. I asked if she had a last name, she smiled and said Mindy.

I shook her hand and she asked for my name, I said Mitch, she put the straw from her drink very seductively in her mouth and asked if I had a last name.

Same response as she gave, I told her my last name was Mitch. She laughed and said well played.

So, Mindy and her friends were in town for some blues festival at Soldier field.

She asked what I was doing in town, especially carrying a handgun.

"I do personal bodyguard work."

She asked if I was protecting anyone famous.

"This guy is only famous in his own mind," everyone laughed including Paul who said ain't that the truth.

Now, I noticed Mindy was wearing one hell of a wedding rock. For now, I am going to try and seduce her. If she says no, it is no. She says go; I will pound her silly.

The other girls seemed to have money, and were married, it appears that Mindy and I were the only ones at the table flirting with each other.

I have found in the past that when trying to seduce a married chick you have to give them tons of positive feedback and attention as they likely don't get it from home.

I find that unlike the dating game, it is more like the mating game, you both know what each other desired, so you go and make your move when the time is right, be the aggressor. But here is the catch 22-how solid are her friends, would they condone her actions, would they rat her out? Tis a wicked game.

But with Mindy, she was the one who took charge. She dropped her napkin on the ground, we both bent over to pick it up and while down there she whispered in my ear that she really wants to suck my cock right now.

Fuck, I can't leave the hotel as Joseph will freak. Too classy a chick to bring in the bathroom, and I really want to see my cock slide down her throat.

I smiled and shifted my eyes to meet me in the hallway.

I excused myself and said I had to make a phone call. I told Paul if Joseph comes, tell him I will be back shortly.

Two minutes later I saw Mindy get up and leave the table. Our eyes met like wolves ready to pounce on a wounded deer, you sense the animal magnetism coming from both of us.

I motioned for her to follow me. I pushed the elevator button and Bruce, who I saved in Nam appeared when the door opened.

I told him I needed a favor. He said sure anything, as he stared at Mindy's cleavage.

"I need twenty minutes alone time with my friend, can you help me?"

He smiled and said anything for the guy who saved his life.

He took us up to the seventh floor. He said the rooms at the far end were steamed cleaned today so they are empty. He gave me a master key and said to have fun.

Mindy looked at him and said, "Thanks, darling." I gave him a huge smile and a thumbs up.

Sometimes you don't need to say anything; I necked with Mindy the whole way down there all the while playing with her breasts that have been teasing me all the way from San Fran.

Mindy was rubbing my cock the whole time. I opened the door and carried her inside and laid her down on the bed. I swear she is the same height and weight as Charlene.

I then started to undo her top and once her breasts were exposed, I pulled my cock out and started to rub it and smack it on them. Mindy's beautiful ocean blue eyes lit right up, she then grabbed a hold of my cock with her painted nails and started to stroke my cock and rub it all over her breasts.

I reached down to start playing with her pussy and she said, "No, no, no, you won't like what you find."

I am thinking how many times I go to make out with a hot chick for the first time and they have their period, cursed I tell you.

So, I said thanks for the warning and started to rub her breasts as she now sat up on the edge of the bed and ordered me to drop my pants and boxers.

Mindy had a thorough look at my cock, said I had a really nice piece of meat; she gave me a wink, opened up her mouth to show her picture perfect pearly white teeth and then gently slid my cock into the back of her throat.

She started to roll her tongue around the head while playing with my balls.

Slowly but surely, she slid my cock further back into her throat until her nostrils were pressed against my stomach.

She then slowly slid her mouth back and started to stroke and suck my cock. The girl has talent; real, amazing cock-sucking talent.

I found myself drawn to her, she looked so sensual with a cock in her mouth, her makeup, eye shadow and eyes themselves all sparkled and complemented each other quite well.

Those seductive eyes seemed to light up when we made eye contact with each other.

I don't know if it was her really good at the task of sucking cock or the fact that she has driven my libido into overdrive the first time I met her and fuck even the fact I have already jerked off over her, and thought of her while screwing Ella, but I was ready to cum a lot quicker then I normally do from getting head.

I said out loud, "I am going to cum."

Mindy grabbed my ass cheeks and started to squeeze them, the pain from her nails digging into made me shoot harder, and more intense than ever before. Kudos to her, she didn't pull her head away or take my cock out of her mouth, hell no.

She swallowed me whole, every last drop. I don't know how she didn't gag as my hot load was cumming at her 200 miles per hour.

My knees almost buckled on me, and I had a major league head rush.

I looked down at her and she now kissed the end of my cock, looked up at me and said thanks.

Thanks, really? Fuck, I am the one who should be thankful. Christ that was beyond amazing.

I pulled up my pants the whole time looking at a beaming Mindy. "Your husband is one lucky bastard."

Mindy smiled and said, "Your girlfriend is just as lucky."

We both then started to laugh at the same time.

We walked down the hall hand in hand, and once the elevator door opened, I handed the key back and said thanks.

As we now exit the elevator, I ask who should go back to the table first. Mindy says she will.

I stand back and watch her walk away from me and back to the table.

Two minutes later I head back and sit at the table. No one says anything at all.

Paul looks at me and smiles. Mindy blushes as we make eye contact, and her two friends look at Mindy and then look at me. Yes, silent awkwardness.

And when I thought it couldn't get any more awkward, Joseph appears with about a dozen other people from upstairs.

He spots me and walks over to our table, looks at all the girls, zones in on Mindy, nods to her and then looks at me and raises an eyebrow.

He then heads back to the bar. Paul shakes my hand and says he better get upstairs.

Mindy asks who the guy with the crazy eyebrows was.

"That is my boss."

As soon as I mention this, it is like Joseph picks it up from halfway across the room and calls me over.

I apologize to the girls as I bluntly put it that he is a real ball buster.

Mindy starts to snicker, and her girlfriends now start to laugh.

I stand up so Joseph can see for himself that I saw his motion and asks how long they in town are for.

They said till Sunday afternoon. So, I wrote my hotel and room number on the napkin for Mindy, I gave her a wink and then headed over to see my ball busting boss.

I ask Joseph how things went upstairs; he says I certainly turned a few heads with my actions.

I asked did he catch flak as that was not my intention.

"I know it wasn't, lad. No, you made me proud. I was asked where I found you. I said I have had my eye on you since before you went to Vietnam, and that your brother and Donnie were the best of friends, and how Jerry is your cousin. All good, lad."

Joseph looked over and said, "The girls are leaving, Mitchell."

I know this is a test.

So, I look over and said, "All good, I am on the clock."

Joseph now smiled ear to ear, patted me on the shoulder and said "You are impressing the hell out of me today, great job."

He introduced me to everyone personally who seemed to be happy to shake my hand. They all sat around and got piss drunk. I stayed fairly sober as I was on the clock. I know I made a couple enemies tonight, and to be honest, I can't fucking understand a damn word they were saying. The more Joseph was around this crew of drunken Irishmen, the thicker his accent got.

In fact, I switched over to soda water as if I hear these guys babble on tomorrow while hung-over, I will put a bullet in my own head.

We ended up closing down the bar and there was talk of hitting a private club, but Joseph was beyond hammered. So, I said thanks, but he needs to sleep and asked what time they need him back tomorrow.

They said noon for lunch. I told them I would try my best with Joseph.

The doorman hailed us a taxi, Joseph would talk, smile at me and then laugh, and yep, he might as well be speaking Cantonese right now as I don't understand anything.

I had to help him in the taxi; the driver asked if we needed to take Joseph to a hotel or hospital. I told him to stick to driving a taxi, not doing stand-up comedy.

By the time we got to our hotel, Joseph was passed out cold and I couldn't wake him at all.

So, I did a fireman's carry into the lobby that drew the attention of the nighttime staff including hotel security.

I have to say they were pretty decent and brought out a wheelchair for me to put him in.

I shot them each a twenty spot and yes, Joseph will be paying me back.

I wheeled Joseph to his room. Opened the door and realized his room makes mine look like a fucking broom closet.

I checked his closet and yes, he did have several suits with him. So, I took his tie and shoes off of him. Lifted him onto the bed. Rolled him from one side to the other and got his jacket off, and eventually his pants off, and that is as far as I go.

I brought the wheelchair back downstairs and was curious if there were any calls or messages for me. They checked and said no; man, I thought for sure Mindy would have contacted me, oh well.

I asked for a ten am wake-up call and headed back to my room.

As soon as the elevator door opened on my floor, the hairs on the back of my neck went up. I listened and I could hear a mechanism being cocked, and from my past experience I would say it is the breach on a gun. Did the two hooligans I wiped the carpet with come back for revenge?

I pulled out both handguns and listened for other noises. I have to hear where they are coming from, there are so many blind spots in this older hotel.

I will be damned, couldn't hear anything, I could however smell a freshly smoked cigar, when in doubt, follow your nose.

My head was moving back and forth like a Chihuahua in the back window of a 65 Impala.

To my left nothing, to my right I saw shadows at the end of the hall moving quickly. All the training I have has told me not to pursue as it could be a trap, but my gut tells me to race after the culprits.

So, I run with both barrels in front of me and if any door opens up, I will shoot first, and deal with the carnage afterwards. I reach the end of the hallway before it goes to the left. I stop and listen and can't hear anything, other than my heart racing.

I catch my breath, do a silent count of three and then turn left with both barrels pointed down the hall and I see nothing but an emergency stairwell.

You would think I would have heard the door open, or it close, even if gently.

So, with slow silent stealth, I walk down to the fire door. It is heavy and the sign says the alarm will sound when opened.

I am not drunk, haven't smoked any dope, or done any hallucinogenic, fucked up shit though.

So, I slowly walked back to my room turning around every once in a while as I sensed I was being watched the whole way.

If someone is fucking with my head or trying my temper, they will pay with their life.

I put the key in my door and as soon as I opened it, I could faintly hear voices.

My guns are raised as I am positive, I heard *here he is, Al.*

Someone is going to die. I see nothing in the main room, so I go into the bathroom like a cop on the swat team. It is empty.

I do a front roll and point my guns under the bed and nothing there but dust bunnies.

It really takes a lot to freak me out, but guess what? Yeah, I am there. Has a fucking deathling followed me here, or did I activate one that resides in this building?

I sat on the bed and looked around my room. I have a pretty good sweat happening, so I go over and turn on the window air conditioner.

I look outside the blackness being pierced by lightning bolts dancing across the sky. Looks like a monster storm is heading towards us.

I am captivated by it, but I know all too well with this strong a vibe, stay focused.

So, I pull the chair out from the desk and wedge it against the door nice and solid.

I get undressed, hang my suit up and sit back down on top of the bed and watch the lightning show. Fuck, I wish I had a joint right now.

I start to count the time between a strike of lighting and the crackle of the thunder.

Four miles out and coming on mighty strong. Maybe too strong as a lightning strike sounds as if it hit the building. I even jumped from the bed and onto the ground as if it was an incoming artillery barrage. Once a combat soldier, always a combat soldier.

The room is in total blackness, as it seems we have lost power.

The only sound I can now hear is the sound of hail hitting the window, and air conditioner.

No power on, I might as well try and close my eyes and get some sleep.

I put one gun on the nightstand table, and the other one under my pillow, like a boy scout, always be prepared.

As I start to drift off, I am still having visions of Mindy sucking my cock, what a nice treat. Can't wait to fuck her silly. She is one of those classy chicks. Can't see her being dead in bed like Ella.

It didn't take me long to drift off and before I knew it I was dreaming, and yes, Mindy was in my dream. I was the boss on the east side of Chicago, back in the bad old days. She was my moll who I would cover with diamonds, jewels, and furs.

Mindy and I are booting around town in my Model T Ford. Eventually, we ended up at this club on the south side.

We went inside, and these huge apes tell me I have to hand over my guns. I say no, and they tell me then leave. Mindy leans in and says she will do anything to see Cab Calloway, who is the performer there tonight.

I look inside and see no threats, so I say fine, even though it isn't fine.

We go inside and take our table which with the help of a twenty spot gets us a front row seating.

Mindy is all lovey dovey and thankful. She is rubbing my cock the whole time saying she is going to fuck me silly when we get home.

She is sporting lots of cleavage in this floor length silk dress. She has a long slit up the side of her legs which I am now rubbing.

We are drinking champagne when Cab Calloway takes the stage. By now the club is packed and smoky as fuck, it is actually burning my eyes.

The band is playing a melody when Cab talks about the different celebrities in the audience, the mayor, sports figures and the most powerful man in Chicago, Al "Scarface" Capone.

Everyone including Mindy is clapping for him, everyone but me.

I have this bad feeling creeping up inside of me really fast.

Calloway now focuses on us. He says to the audience, "In the front row, Mindy and Bugs Moran." He points right at us, and the patrons now start to boo.

He sings out *Oh Oh Oh* and the audience copies his lyrics.

He then tells Al to come up with his boys as they know what to do.

I am frozen in fear as Al walks towards us with four guys carrying Tommy guns.

Capone's face is pure evil. You can tell he is soulless as he looks at me and says, "I told you this was my town and to stay away. Cab, you know what has to be done next."

Cab, with that big smile of his, chuckles, nods his head yes, and tells his orchestra to play extra loud.

His wand is moving like crazy; the band is playing so loud it is actually hurting my ears.

The four men about to execute us are faceless, defiantly I look at Capone who is now smoking a cigar and tell him, "Go fuck yourself, Italian fuck."

Capone now cracks a smile as he tells his boys to kill us both.

His eyes show no mercy or emotion, pure evil seeking revenge.

Mindy is screaming but I can't watch her, I will go to my grave as a fearless warrior growling at Capone.

The whole world slows down and I can hear the men with the weapons tightening their grips.

You hear the first round of hundreds going off, deafening to say the least. So, death isn't silent after all.

My body feels the searing heat of the bullets entering my body which is now being shaken around like a rag doll.

I start to cough from the blood filling my lungs, the smell from the lead and gunfire makes me cough at first and then I am gasping for air taking my final breaths.

I am choking in my own blood, and I still won't show any fear, fuck him.

I struggle to take my last gasp of air; I exhale and the spray of blood from my lungs paints my entire body.

To find everlasting peace I close my eyes for the last time.

I then hear this monstrous loud bang followed by a bright flash of light.

Does this signal that I have now officially passed over to the other side?

 open up my eyes hoping to see all those that have passed away in my family, when I realize I am in my hotel room in Chicago.

My sheets are soaked in sweat. The storm still has knocked out the power to the hotel, and is still raging outside, and yet I can hear music being played.

That same style of music from my dream, or nightmare is more like it.

I give my head a shake and can still hear the music really clearly. There is fuck all power in my room. So, I put on my boxers and look out in the hall and it is pitch black.

This place is fucking haunted, has to be. I go to lay back in bed, but the sheets are soaked. I go to call downstairs to see about getting a clean set and the phones are dead.

Fuck it, I grabbed a long shower and then turned the hot water off and spent a couple minutes feeling the ice-cold water shock me and bring me back to reality.

Totally refreshing and head clearing.

I stripped the sheets on my bed, flipped the mattress over and laid on the bed trying to recall the dream. Normally they mean something to me, a spiritual awakening of some sort.

You have bits and pieces come back to you, but nothing substantial. I remember Mindy being in it, Al Capone and that whole evil aura that surrounds him.

Before I knew it, I passed out cold again, this time the only thing that woke me up was the phone ringing. Looks like I survived another fucked up night.

I grabbed another shower and yes ran it ice cold to fully shake off any residual effects of last night's dream.

I called Joseph, who sounded like Capone visited him and cut his tongue out.

Funny as I was the one full of life and not hung over, and he was the hurting one.

"Come on, Joseph. Let's grab some grub, I am craving some greasy green eggs and stinky rotten ham."

He muttered something and then the phone dropped, and I heard him running then throwing up in the toilet. Violently if I do say so. Fucking love it.

Eventually, Joseph made it back to the phone, called me an asshole which made me burst out laughing.

He said he needed thirty minutes, and he would meet me downstairs in the lobby.

So, I put my suit on, packed my weapons, and headed down and grabbed a coffee and read the newspaper.

A typhoon wiped out a dam in China, thousands feared dead were the headlines. Sounds like something I would have done. And Nixon is going to be paid for an interview with David Frost. There is another lying bastard who sent thousands of young men to their graves fighting those Commies who were funded by China. Fucking crook should be lined up against the wall and shot.

Then I saw something interesting; the Bears are interested in 49er all star, middle linebacker Matt Burns as he is in the final year of his contract. There seems to be ill will coming from both Burns and the 49ers and dig this...burns is now a self-admitted, reborn Christian.

He is a great player, a tough guy, but arrogant. He likes to talk down to people and is always trying to pick up chicks and fuck them right in Popeye's. I know Jerry has had a talk with him about this. And my back still hasn't come down since I saw him with his arm around Charlene at the airport. I wonder if he is using his newfound Christianity as a way to get traded from San Fran who is projected to have a bad season.

By the time I was done with my paper, a rough looking Joseph made his way from the elevator.

He was pale, rather gaunt looking, death warmed over.

"You look rough, boss."

"Try looking out from these eyes, I don't remember too much last night."

"I put you in a wheelchair and rolled you up to your room. Tucked you in and than called it a night myself."

"Thank you, Mitchell. Let me buy you breakfast for this."

Seeing how the boss was paying, I ordered steak and eggs. He had toast and lots of coffee and water.

I asked what he thought of the storm. He said he slept through it. He then asked how I slept. I told him of the crazy dreams and all the shit I heard and saw.

He put down his coffee and smiled at first then shook his head and snickered. I asked what was so funny as I told him I was dead serious and wasn't high.

"Oh lad, I firmly believe everything you are telling me."

"So, did you book the rooms hoping Capone would tell me where he has stashed his money?"

Joseph's eyes got big, he smacked his hands together and said yes, if he comes to me again tonight can I ask him where his hidden stash is. Fucking asshole was my response. I then asked him what was on the agenda today.

"Well, lad, I have meetings from 12 till 5. Then we are going to take a boat ride to Milwaukee. These two square head brothers want to buy the diamonds. Not expecting any trouble, but these diamonds seem to draw bad luck to its owners. So, Jimmy Dolan, Aiden O'Toole and their Captain, Cashel Walsh will be joining us. After we make the deal with the German's. On the ride back, Seamus wants Dolan and O'Toole questioned to see who was behind the fuck up in Texas. Seamus believes it was either one of them, if not both. We will become the detectives, judge, and more than likely, the executioner, are you okay with this?"

I replayed what Joseph said to make sure how we are to move forward.

"I assume be nice at first, then torture, and what about Walsh? Is he going to be cool with us doing this?"

"Cashel works for Seamus, yes, he will be cool. He agrees a hundred percent someone was on the inside. These two presented the deal to Cashel, who went to Seamus. Cashel knows his head will be on the line if he doesn't back Seamus. I know you have done your fair share of getting information from the enemy. Now this is always Sean's forte. Heard he used a blowtorch in Texas."

Joseph laughed, but I am still pissed at him, fucker.

"Well, you know me, nothing like a good torturous song and dance."

I jumped on the elevator with Joseph, he told me that Cashel has a poker game set up in one of the rooms on the same floor as the meetings. Dolan and O'Toole will be playing in the game. He told me to play against them, get to know their body language. See if they give anything away. Smart idea. Joseph gave me $200 to play with, money he hopes is well spent on recon.

21

I walked down the end of the hall, the two bodyguards from yesterday, well I made them both uncomfortable, they were easy to read, hopefully Dolan and O'Toole are this easy.

Joseph went to his meeting; I went to play cards directly across the hall.

McCowell was already shuffling the cards, Dolan was to the left of him, and O'Toole beside him. All together eight bodyguards playing, with Paul playing the role of dealer.

"Strongbow, you going to jump in and play?" asked Paul.

I asked what exactly they were playing, Texas hold 'em was his response.

Now, before I even had a chance to answer, Dolan said for all to hear, while staring at his cards the whole time, "He is not one of us. Deal, Paul."

Paul looked at me, shook his head in disbelief and said to loudmouth Dolan, "James, you're a fucking idiot. Why do you think he is not one of us, cause he ain't Irish?"

Dolan didn't answer or look at Paul whose face was now turning beet red.

"I have served with this man. He is the royal fucking flush of soldiers. In fact, I am willing to bet all bets on this pot, that he would lay everyone out cold in this room, no weapon used. Just his hands and fist."

Dolan snickered at Paul's words. But what Dolan doesn't realize yet, is I will be using a weapon on him, I wanna skin this fuck alive.

I thanked Paul for his kind words, said we had a lot of fun, and killed a lot of guys. But I will sit out, supposed to be on duty anyways.

Once again, another snicker. I winked at Paul, he looked at Dolan and shook his head.

Observation is that Dolan is more of a leader than O'Toole, who almost seems scared of him. I am sure Dolan was a bully in school. Only makes eye contact when he tries to fuck your head up. He will always bluff instead of folding his hand, and then does a stupid loud laugh. Pretty sure he has no other friends in this room.

As luck would have it, today's meetings wrapped up a couple hours early. Joseph and Cashel came into the room. Now, I have never met him before, but he looked me directly in the eye, shook my hand firmly, and said Seamus personally passes along his thanks for my involvement in my last job. If the army taught be anything, it is to never accept anything without shining a light on others.

"Thank you, I had a great team that I was working with."

This comment made Cashel's smile even bigger. He then told Dolan and O'Toole they are to accompany him, Joseph, and myself as we have to move some merchandise, and Joseph has asked for help.

Dolan once again being the smart ass says, "Well according to McCowell, Strongbow is deadlier than Bruce Fucking Lee." And yes, loud stupid laugh.

Cashel got pissed, pointed his finger at Dolan and reminded him he is already on thin ice, don't push his luck.

I smiled at Dolan; he squinted his eyes at me while asking Joseph if he is getting paid.

"Oh, don't you fret Jimmy Dolan, you will be paid, you as well O'Toole."

We drove back to our hotel first so that Joseph could grab the diamonds. Up in his room I told him what went down with the whole poker fiasco.

He smiled at me, said I will have my revenge, or as I say, "There is a revenge, then there is a Strongbow revenge."

We drove down to the docks, and there waiting for us was a rusted out, and beaten up 1955 Seiner Weldcraft named the Sophie Ann.

There was a two-person crew, the Captain was Stanley Straka and his wife Lola. Both immigrants for Czechoslovakia. Both were crusty, and tough as nails.

The Sophie Ann had three gin pole gang pulleys at the rear of the boat. It would be used for recovering sunken smaller boats, or even planes. It was used as a tugboat, breaking up ice, and for us. Well, that will come in time.

Joseph seems to be friends with Stanley and Lola. I hope so, especially if this is where we will be torturing Dolan and O'Toole. Now he asked me if I have problems on boats.

"Not at all. We used PBR in special ops, a great way to get around Nam, Laos and Thailand without drawing attention. Shit, I spent a week on one, going up the Nung River into Laos looking for this renegade colonel. But that is another day, another story."

Even though we were on the water, the humidity was brutal. I asked Joseph permission to take off my suit jacket, dress shirt and go down to my tank top and dress pants.

"Fuck, Mitchell, go down to boxers and tank if you want." He yelled over to Stanley and Lola if that was all right.

Lola yelled back in her chain smokers raspy voice, "You can take off all your clothes if you want!" followed by an insane laugh, and yes, several deep smoker's coughs.

I am not sure exactly what Dolan said, but Cashel embarrassed the fuck right out of him.

"Strongbow has nothing but respect for Joseph. Something you are lacking. You better hope and pray that Seamus has an amazing, mind-blowing honeymoon. He comes back in a bad mood; I wouldn't want to be you."

I made sure only Joseph heard our conversation.

"So how is this going to go down; are Stanley and Lola okay with what we are to do?"

"They will be helping us out. After our deal with the square heads."

I had to stop Joseph, "You do realize I am half German?"

"Mitchell, you are half German, these are truly square heads. Mark my words, you will agree with me. Anyways, after we get aboard, Lola is going to ask if we want some of their homemade moonshine. Now, Dolan and O'Toole love their drink, she will have added some chloral hydrate, enough to successfully disable them, then we start our torture interrogation techniques. By the way, do you know what the drink is called we are giving them?"

I had no idea.

"Ironically, a Mickey Finn. An Irishman can't refuse a drink."

Joseph and Cashel were busy talking to each other, while Dolan and O'Toole were at the opposite end of the ship, while I was deep in thought. And yes, it was all about the females in and out of my life.

Really worried about Nyah's safety. Not really worried about her ratting me out to the cops, I have no doubts her giving up Schinn was perfect for both of us. The thought of her own Dad smacking her around really gets my blood boiling.

Charlene, another blood boiler. I am tempted to put a bullet in the back of her skull, no, fuck that. Wish she was on this boat right now. She likes threesomes, a threesome torture for info it would become, no love boat here.

And Ella, fuck. I definitely don't want to get too close with her. No way could I ever get serious with her lifestyle and inner circle.

Mindy, the mysterious blonde. I am really hoping to hear from her before we head home. Now if she was here, this boat would be rocking, and not from the waves.

Speaking of waves, as we were pulling into Milwaukee, Stanley told Joseph, don't be too long. Looks like a monster storm is headed our way. Cold blast of weather coming from Canada, mixed with the extremely high humidity here, a perfect recipe for a nautical disaster.

Every single injury I have endured so far in my relatively young life agreed a hundred percent with what Stanley said.

Cashel asked Joseph if we are expecting any issues. Joseph said there shouldn't be, but be on guard, in case. Cashel told him that goes without saying.

So, our square heads as Joseph calls them are the Fuchs, fucking triplets if you could believe that. They own a ship salvage scrapyard.

Otto, Heinrich and Max Fuchs, and God damn, they did have square heads.

Joseph was met outside by Max. He asked where his normal guys are. He said on assignment elsewhere. Max seemed nervous for whatever reason. Not to draw any unwanted attention, I looked at Cashel and raised my eyebrows as I know Max is fixated on Joseph.

Max asked us all to stay put as he went inside the office.

Cashel asked Joseph if there was a problem.

By the time Joseph had a chance to answer, Max came out with his two brothers.

Otto appeared to be the brother in charge and asked Joseph who are all these new men he brings.

Joseph once again reiterated what he told Max. Otto looks at all of us, stops at me and asks what my name is.

I am not sure if I should answer or not. I look at Joseph who now nods at me.

With the most intense look, I say Willie Hertz.

All brothers look at me and ask if I am part German.

It may have been a while, but I remember enough German "Nur diebesten teile" which means, only the good parts.

I now loosen my tie, open some buttons on my dress shirt and show them my "First SS" tattoo.

By their smile, I knew these boys were hard core Nazi's. I told them I was good friends with Helmut Fritz and was in San Quentin with him. They all start to laugh, they tell Joseph, Cashel and me to come inside for a drink. But they tell Dolan and O'Toole they are not welcome. I like these guys already.

Joseph told Otto and myself can we please do the diamond deal before they adopt me to be the 4th Fuch.

Now what happened next, totally freaked me out. Heinrich leaves and comes back two minutes later with this Hasidic Jew, we are talking the full suit, curls in his hair, hat, beard, like something right from Fiddler on the Roof. I guess money means more to him than principle working with, or for the Fuchs triplets.

He broke out his eye loop and picked up each item as if it was a baby, delicate, and with love. After the eighth piece, he stopped. Took out his eye loop, placed it on the desk and stared at Joseph, Cashel and myself. It was a pure look of hatred. Has he now figured out they were Stan's diamonds? Is he a friend of Stan's?

Joseph must have picked up what I was thinking, as he now stared back at him and asked if there was a problem.

"Yes, there is a problem, where exactly did these come from?"

Joseph snapped back at him, "No concern of yours."

Fuck, the tension was building in the room.

"I am making it my concern," he bravely barked back at Joseph.

Then I heard that one word I needed to hear, "Mitchell."

By the time Joseph said the last syllable, I already put a bullet between his eyes, and one in his chest for good measure.

Joseph and Cashel now pulled their guns on the Fuchs, as O'Toole and Dolan came rushing in with their weapons ready for the fight.

Pardon the pun, but the Fuchs were fucked. Outmanned, and out gunned in their own shop.

Now Otto was pleading with Joseph for us to lower our weapons as Yaakov is not part of their crew, he grades hot jewellery for them.

Joseph was hot, really hot. He now walked over to Yaakov slouched. Knocked his hat off. Pulled his head back by the hair, and spit in his bloody face. Then turned his attentions to the Fuchs brothers, most notably Otto.

"You and I have been doing business for about a dozen years now. Never an argument. We both know and respect how each other do business. Look at me right now in the eyes Otto Fuchs. I need to know right now. Are you and I going to have problems in future dealings with Mitchell, disposing of this nosey fuck?"

Otto looked at Joseph straight into his ice-cold blue eyes and said,

"No problems, he stuck his rat nose where it doesn't belong. Trust me, I would have done the same as your man." He now stuck out his hand. Joseph did the same, and they shook on it. Joseph said he would get rid of the body, and asked will there be a death tax for me taking the jeweler's life?

Otto shook his head no. Joseph then asked him if he still wanted to buy the diamonds, apparently, they're to die for.

Otto laughed and said of course, a deal is a deal, and yes, to die for.

Stan now walked in, saw the dead Jew on the floor, then said hi to the Fuchs brothers. They asked if he wanted a beer.

"As much as I would love to have a drink with you boys. We have a rather intense storm about 12 miles out, and approaching, fast and with a mighty punch."

Joseph got his cash, the Fuchs got their jewels, and Stan got another passenger for his boat. But this one's destination is about 3 miles below The Sophie Ann.

Yaakov's lifeless body was put in a crate. Heinrich with the help of a tow motor loaded the lifeless cargo aboard the ship.

When we set sail, I was drawn to the skies north of us. They were jet black as if the devil himself had painted the canvas with a thousand dead souls.

As soon as we left the harbor, Lola, as planned, asked who wanted to try some of her legendary pear moonshine, she said it would help us with the rough seas that are certainly to come our way.

Of course, all of us said yes. We were truly man amongst men.

Lola came back with a shot glass for each of us.

Joseph told everyone to hold on. "May your home always be too small to hold all your friends. May the cat eat you, and may the devil eat the cat. May your heart be light and happy, may your smile be big and wide, and may your pockets always have a coin or two inside!"

As I downed my shot, it burned and cleared my sinus, fuck it was strong. Did Lola give me the wrong drink after all?

We were about fifteen minutes out when the waters started to get rough, but not as rough looking as Dolan and O'Toole. Either they have a brutal case of sea sickness starting, or that Mickey Finn is starting to kick in.

Yeah, their legs were struggling keeping them upright. "O'Toole was the first one to fall down. He couldn't get back up. He reached his hand out for Dolan to hoist him up. But Dolan, fuck he fell right on top of him.

Both men now laid on their backs and stared up at ominous black clouds.

I looked at Joseph, who nodded to me. Cashel, Joseph and I now stood over them. O'Toole was now drifting in and out of consciousness. Dolan knew something wasn't right, he was starting to swear at us, his speech may have been slurred, but he knew two storms were headed his way. The one from Canada, and us three standing over him.

Joseph asked Stanley for some rope as he asked me how I am at tying knots. Boy Scouts badge was my smart ass response.

"Very well, lad, tie his feet together, and his hands behind his back , smart-ass."

Dolan now was panicking as he started to roll around, his movement was halted when Joseph kicked him in the ribs. And what was Cashel doing? Not a fucking thing. He was deep in thought. Still not sure I trust him to be honest. Any quick, or threatening moves, I will put a bullet in his head, and he can join Yaakov in the box.

As instructed, I tied up O'Toole, took away his weapon and then did the same to Dolan who by now was drifting in and out of consciousness.

After both men were bound, I asked now what. Joseph asked if I had been lifting heavy weights. I said of course why.

"Well, Mitchell, we will need all your strength. I need their legs put on the top of each gin pole. We are going to ask them questions. And when I know they are either bullshitting us or refusing to answer, they will be going face first into the lake, brought back up I am sure gasping for their lives, and for their sakes, better be telling us what went wrong in Texas."

O'Toole weighed around 200 pounds; it took every ounce of strength for me to hold him up high enough for Stanley to properly secure him in place.

Dolan had to weigh close to three hundred pounds. If I get a fucking hernia, Joseph will be paying for my surgery, pain, and suffering.

I couldn't get his feet up high enough, even with Stanley's help. It took the four of us to finally winch him in spot.

I was now drenched in sweat; this humidity is so thick. Off goes my shirt. Lola brought me up and ice-cold beer, perfect.

What was not perfect, was the intense lighting storm to the rear of the boat. It was as if Thor himself was in a drumming competition with John "Bonzo" Bonham.

As we were waiting for O'Toole and Dolan to come around, Stanley said now is the perfect time to get rid of Yaakov's body as we need to get up as much speed as possible to outrun the storm.

I never have to worry about missing gym time in my line of work. Every muscle was used once again, throwing Yaakov and his homemade coffin into the turbulent waters of Lake Michigan.

Ten minutes later, Dolan was starting to come around. If he thought he was in a nightmare being hung up by his feet, and facing the lake below, he was right, but as I watched the lightning dance across the sky, and the waves becoming more intense, perhaps he is not the only one in a nightmare.

He screamed at the top of his lungs to let him down now. He said it wasn't funny.

Sorry Dolan, to me it was funny, a 300-pound goof on a hook.

He quickly realized this was no joke when he saw O'Toole hanging by his feet.

Cashel was lead prosecutor. "A couple members of our crew killed is anything but funny. Now, one of you two are a cute hoor with the fucking Murdoch brothers. Now Mitch here, he was able to get a bit of a confession from one of the brothers before he killed him, in fact, you killed them all didn't you, Mitch?"

        "With great pride I might add. The one Murdoch mentioned both your names. Personally, I think I should slice both your throats. But Joseph said this is Seamus' final decision." And of course you have to smile when answering in such a bold statement. All part of the game.

Cashel looked at both, and asked which one conspired with the Murdoch brothers?

Dolan and O'Toole said nothing, well time for them to feel what happens when a lure goes under the water.

"Mitch, lower O'Toole."

Now, what surprised me was O'Toole not professing his innocence as I lowered him right to his belly button, face down in the water.

As I was waiting for the order to bring him back up, I was totally spellbound by the amount of lightning strikes to the rear of the boat. It was deafeningly loud, and the arc was so bright, I felt like I had a welder's flash burn.

Joseph had to come over and tap me, as I didn't hear Cashel tell me to bring him up.

Horror, nothing but horror on O'Toole's face, he couldn't even talk, he shook. Time for Dolan to get wet. He was cursing me, telling me as loud as he could how he was going to fuck me up. I blew him a kiss and lowered him in the water. That's right dummy, keep yelling at me with your big mouth open, and you will drown.

It was only the third dunk of O'Toole, when he said he would talk.

You knew that Dolan was the culprit when he was more pissed at O'Toole than me.

"Keep your mouth shut you fucking rat fink," screamed Dolan at O'Toole

Cashel told me that Dolan needs to cool off, send him into the drink.

"I will not die for that piece of shit. He treats me and my sister like crap. Jimmy owed Rob Mazzetti fifty grand for a bet that of course he lost,"

Cashel told me to bring Dolan back up above the surface. He walked towards him and said, "I told you that your gambling was a bad habit, it appears a deadly habit"

Cashel then pulled out a handgun and put a bullet in each of Dolan's kneecaps. I looked over at Joseph. Fuck, if looks could kill, Dolan would be dead already.

Dolan was screaming in pain, cursing all of us once again. This seemed to piss off Cashel even more. He went into his sock and pulled out a straight razor. Man that thing had to be as sharp as a ninja's blade as Cashel flawlessly sliced off both of Dolan's ears. I was impressed with how precise he was with his weapon.

But what Cashel did next, even turned *my* stomach, he sliced open both of Dolan's eyes.

Joseph was smiling, Lola who was now watching the torture show, had her hand over her mouth. And Stanley, he was focused on keeping us afloat and back to Chicago.

After about fifteen minutes, Cashel said, "You were a loudmouth in life, and you are a loudmouth in your final minutes of life. May the devil find your soul for ratting out members of your own crew."

And with that, Cashel finally silenced Dolan by slicing his throat.

Cashel then asked me to cut Dolan loose, and let the fucker drown.

I did as instructed, and then looked at O'Toole. His testimony in this court helped to sentence Dolan to death. I wonder if Cashel will now see O'Toole as a rat and kill him.

Guess we are going to find out as Cashel is now facing O'Toole.

"Aiden, I thank you for your honesty, Jimmy Dolan was a horrible crew member, and even worse brother-in-law to put you in the position you are in. We will let you down, and set you free, spare your life, but there are terms and conditions, understood?" said Cashel with a firm voice.

Trembling with fear, O'Toole nodded his head yes.

"This is the only story that is coming back to Boston. Jimmy was shot and killed by some asshole in a bar, a bar he went into by himself, a bar that has off track betting. This story will keep you alive, this story you will tell Mary when she loses her shit on you, as you know she will. If I hear whispers of any other story getting back to me, or any other captain, God forbid. Seamus. There will be no mercy on your life. You won't even hear the shot coming. And because we had to drag Joseph and Mitchell into our family's business, you are back on probation till further notice. If you agree to all these terms, we will let you down."

His voice was trembling and weak but was able to answer yes.

Cashel then asked me to cut him down. I said sure, but it seemed lake Michigan had other plans as a rogue wave slammed the boat so hard, all of us were knocked violently to the ground.

As I was trying to regain my senses, I saw Stanley now kneeling over Lola who has now split her head wide open. Joseph was wincing in pain as was Cashel who says he has thrown his back out.

I head straight for Joseph who has the wind knocked out of him. His eyes are huge, I tell him short breaths. After a minute he is fine and asks me to help out Cashel. But what I see next takes the air right out of my lungs, where the fuck is Aiden O'Toole?

The monsoon of rain that is pounding the boat has blurred my vision.

My stomach flips as I look up at a broken Gin Pole.

Cashel asks if I was able to get Aiden down. I said, "He is gone, must have fallen in the lake when the pole snapped."

Joseph is now on his feet and is as shocked as I am. "Are you sure, lad?"

I know better to walk towards the back of the boat, I crawl right to the edge, all I see is blackness, other than the sky lighting up.

Cashel, still lying in the same position, tells Stanley he has to turn the boat around and find Aiden.

"If I turn this boat around and try to find him in this raging storm, we will all die. I am heading to home port. My wife will need stitches to close the gash in her head. Your man is already dead by now."

Cashel told Joseph to order Stanley to turn the boat around and search for his man.

Joseph took a deep breath, kneeled beside Cashel and said he was sorry for the loss of O'Toole. But Stanley is the captain, he knows how treacherous these waters can be, he will not order him to turn around.

Cashel looked at me with intense eyes, fucking asshole, not my doing.

Eventually, he nodded his head yes. Now Stanley seemed to be worried sick about Lola. He asked if someone could look after her as he tried to get us all back to Chicago. With being in Special Ops, I am as good as a doctor when it comes to trauma inflicted wounds.

I inspected her head, yeah, she is going to have a nasty scar. Definitely has a concussion. I applied pressure with a towel to stop the bleeding. How much blood has covered my hands since Nam? How many times have I had someone die in my arms?

In hindsight I really shouldn't be thinking about death as we are stuck in the middle of a great lake, with an epic storm brewing.

The thought cleared my head when hail started to pelt the ship, and suddenly, we are talking golf size hail stones. It was even shattering the windows on the tug. But when Stanley said this doesn't look good, and picked up his maritime radio, I knew we were in trouble.

Joseph asked what the hell he was doing.

"We have a massive waterspout headed our way. And where there is one, there will be others. I want to give the coast guard our location in case we are capsized; they rescue us out of the water."

"Stanley, put down the radio. I certainly don't want the law knowing where we are."

"All respect, Joseph, but you *do* understand that a waterspout and a tornado are the exact same thing. But on the water, there is no storm cellar, or basement to seek shelter."

Joseph patted Stanley on the shoulder and said he had full confidence in him getting us safe and soundly back to Chicago.

Cashel was now starting to turn green, yeah, he will be hurling sooner than later and for yours truly? I was nervous, not going to lie, but that special forces soldier in me loved the adrenaline rush. Shit, I must have had at least a hundred missions behind enemy lines where I couldn't either call for an extract, or help.

So, I made sure that Lola was taken care of. My biggest concern was her going into shock as she was starting to shake. I asked Stanley if she was diabetic, he said no. Good, shock, I covered her with my suit jacket and tried to keep her talking.

Joseph smiled at me, Cashel, fuck he can't have anything left in his belly, and Stanley, he was focused behind the wheel.

The tug was certainly taking a beating as mother nature threw everything at us, she good.

From time-to-time, Stanley would look up at the raging storm above us and swear in his mother tongue, and sometimes, a double one finger salute.

Couple times I thought the boat was going to break in two. And yes, after this one time, my stomach flipped, ears popped, and I too was throwing up.

After about two hours or so, we could see lights coming from the shoreline. The Chicago skyline never looked so good.

After we were tied up, Joseph gave Stanley some extra cash for the broken gin pole, and for making sure we survived.

I helped Cashel to the car and as if tonight wasn't fucked up enough, well the keys were either in Dolan's, or O'Toole's pocket, which means they are at the bottom of Lake Michigan.

We ended up taking a taxi, dropped off Cashel, then Joseph and I went back to our hotel.

Joseph asked if I felt up to a night cap. I said I think my bed will be my best friend.

I asked what is planned for tomorrow. He said a road trip to South Bend.

I asked what was in South Bend.

"The Fighting Irish of Notre Dame University. You want to come along? Very spirit spiritual, lad."

"I saw enough spirits last night. If I am not needed, I will pass."

"That's fine, Mitchell. Now, we have an eight am flight Monday morning."

I nodded my head. We both checked in at the front desk and asked for messages.

Joseph at first laughed and asked who would be contacting me. Well, the clerk said I have two messages.

Joseph shook his head and said, "Let me guess, pussy right?"

I looked and one was from Paul, asking if I wanted to go out for beers tonight and the other was from Mindy telling me that her monthly friend has left, and she will be dancing her ass off at the Green Pepper lounge, unless I have other plans for her ass.

"Yes. Pussy Joseph, mighty fine pussy at that. I will talk to you at some point tomorrow."

I jumped on the elevator and pondered my dilemma between Paul and Mindy. My head and gut are certainly in no shape for drinking, but always in fine form for fucking. Mindy it is.

I grabbed a long hot shower, turned it cold once again and it certainly helped the headache.

I changed into my jeans and an Oakland Hell Hound support t-shirt.

I went downstairs and hailed a taxi to the Green Pepper lounge. It was a hopping Disco with a line up to get in.

I walked to the front where two bouncers stopped me. I said I have a fifty spot if they let me in.

They eyed me up and down and said no jeans, or gang colors allowed inside.

I was confused until I remembered what t-shirt I was wearing. I guess only in the Bay Area would this be considered an appropriate dress code.

Good thing I kept Paul's note. I looked around and saw a taxi stand a block down.

I walked five feet when I heard a female yelling my name.

I turned around and there was Mindy once again dressed to kill waving at me to come back.

She gave me this great big hug and asked where I was going.

I explained about the dress code. She tried to sweet talk the bouncers even though I told her I tried to pay my way in, like me she was unsuccessful.

So, she told me not to leave and she would be back out in two minutes.

I did as instructed and she came out with her purse in her hand and said there is a really cool jazz bar not far from here and would I join her.

"I actually really like jazz, the hottest looking chick in town asking me to join her, how can I go wrong?"

She smiled and said I was adorable. That is a first in my lifetime.

So, we walked hand in hand to Bundy's Place like two teenagers on a first date.

Swinging hands, stopping to kiss and both of us were ass grabbing each other.

And yes, she was sporting cleavage in her tight-fitting short dress.

"Baby, you have an amazing rack, so hot."

"Thanks, Mitch! I love that cock of yours, it gets me wet."

Now, this bar was an old "Speakeasy" from the twenties and as soon as we walked in, it reminded me so much of the nightmare dream I had last night.

Trust me, any excuse to get out of here and I am gone, with Mindy of course.

As the bar filled up it was half black and half white but it was weird as I didn't feel any racial tensions at all. They all seem to be relaxed, talking to each other with the main conversation being the death of Cannonball Adderley.

I sort of remember my grandpa playing him. Man, what I would give to bring him here tonight, the man loves jazz.

"Mindy, do they have any jazz festivals around us?"

"Of course they do, the Monterey Jazz Festival has been around for sixteen years now I believe."

So, I told her the whole story about how my grandpa loves jazz and I would love to take him and would she care to join us.

She smiled, grabbed a hold of my hands and reminded me she is married.

"Mitch, I really enjoyed last night, and I am sure I am going to enjoy tonight even more. But I have to play with you in the shadows and not in the light. You wouldn't want to take your girlfriend instead?"

"Ella is boring to be honest, pretty sure she won't be my girlfriend for much longer. So, does your husband give you a fair amount of time to travel and do your own thing?"

She can tell I was up to something and said sometimes and why.

"Do you consider yourself adventurous regarding the great outdoors?"

She started to laugh and judging by her nails, perfect make up and hair, not at all.

"Where do I start? Our honeymoon was in Victoria Falls, in Rhodesia. I have gone canoeing in the Amazon and did two weeks with an aboriginal tribe in Australia right in the bush. I have deep sea dived and even jumped out of a plane. Visited at least thirty different countries in the world and spent at least a week in every continent. Why do you ask, Mitch?"

This totally turned me on her being so adventurous when it came to the outdoors.

"I would love to take you to my family land in South Dakota."

She pulled me in and gave me a long kiss and when she finally let go, she said she couldn't promise but would love to go.

We talked and got to know each other a little bit more but we both seemed to be very guarded about our personal lives back home.

Mine because I am a hard-core criminal, drug dealer, contract killer and a laundry list of other things.

Hers because of her marriage which I totally respected. Now her skin was amazing, so I really had a hard time figuring out exactly how old she is.

I would say late twenties, early thirties.

The only personal question I asked was if she had any kids.

"I make a better aunt than a mom, what about yourself?"

I told her my whole story, she never understood how some woman can be so ruthless. Of course, I left out the last time I saw Tash and Katrina and I beat the taxi driver within a breath of his life.

Now my gut was a little funky so instead of beer, rye and ginger was my drink of choice. Vodka martinis for my lady.

This was my first-time hearing jazz live. They gained a new fan tonight. The bass had so much power and the guys on horns were amazing, they even had this Spanish looking chick on saxophone who could really belt out a solid sound.

Every song they played sounded better than the previous song. I was totally into this and as soon as I get home I am going to call and get the dates for the festival and take grandpa and see if Rachel wants to tag along.

After the first set, Mindy asked if I did coke. I said of course I do, why did she have some. She smiled and pulled out a little vile.

The club was jammed and there were no real places to do a line.

So, I asked her if she wanted to go back to my room.

She smiled, grabbed my cock through my jeans and said of course.

I tried to talk the bartender into making us mixed drinks to go, said he would be shot by the owner if he did.

So, we had him call us a taxi while we waited outside and made out right in front of the place.

Once we got into the back of the cab, I slid my fingers between her legs and ripped her pantyhose open right at her crotch and started to play with her pussy.

She fucking loved it, she was soaked, breathing heavy and sweetly moaning.

The taxi driver opened up the door and told us we had arrived at my hotel, didn't even have a clue. I paid him then it was a mad dash to the elevator.

I pinned Mindy against the elevator wall and pulled my cock out and rubbed it on her pussy lips. No insertion, teasing the hell out of her.

I was biting her neck, pinching her now erect nipples, she was so into this.

I once again picked her up and through her legs between my hips, her arms were around my legs as I carried her down the hall.

I managed with one arm to put the key in the hole and open up the door.

I carried her to bed, laid her down and dove my head right into her snatch, a rather meaty snatch at that.

I was pulling back on the meat while starting to finger her hard and fast. She was wetter than Lake Michigan and her pussy was making those funny noises.

I had her cumming in no time at all.

"That was incredible! oh my God, Mitch. Now get naked and get that cock of yours into my now nice and warmed up pussy."

She sat up and started to take my shirt off and her eyes got big when she saw all my scars from combat. Now when she went to reach around back, she felt one of my two handguns.

And for the first time since we met, she actually showed fear.

So, I reached around and pulled the gun out and put it on the dresser. I smiled at her and said I have one more.

I took my pants and boots off, pulled out my Sykes Fairburn knife and the other 9MM and put both on the dresser.

Mindy gave a forced smile and said, "I would be foolish to think you are a cop, correct?"

I took a deep breath, nodded my head yes, and said, "You would be absolutely one hundred percent correct."

She then smiled and said, "I grew up in Vegas, lived there until I was twenty-four. That is where I met my husband, Marvin. I met and got to know people like you, Mitch, who carried guns, a lot of them were bad people, but not all. I don't get the really bad vibe from you."

"I keep people honest and in line, Mindy. Enough said?"

She smiled, laughed and said yes, as she now started to pull down my underwear, "You know one way for me not to ask any more questions is to have my mouth full of cock, can you help me, Mitch?"

I grinned and told her to help herself and that she did. But what made it even hotter was me standing over her as she sucked my cock and played her own pussy at the same time. Total fucking turn on.

The more she yanked on her own pussy the more she moaned,

and the more I started to rough house with her breasts the vibrations coming from her mouth sent an erogenous wave right from the head of my cock and down to my balls and back up again.

Mindy then said those magical words, "Mitch, I want you to bury that huge cock of yours deep inside my pussy."

She laid on her back, spread her legs and finger motioned me.

I first started to rub the outside of her pussy with the head of my cock, after a couple minutes I started to smack her pussy. She was into it as much as I was.

Gave her a wink, and guiding my cock into her hot, wet pussy. Once I am in as far as I go, time to go to work.

I slowly start to get a body rhythm. Once we are both in sync with each other, I start to suck and bite her breasts. I look at her periodically, her facial cheeks are red, her eyes are bluer than the deepest parts of the ocean, and her sweet moans are music to my ears.

After about ten minutes, I really start to give it to her hard. I pin her arms above her head and start to bite her all over. She is so wet, I feel moisture running down my legs, so fucking hot.

After about thirty minutes I tell her I am getting ready to cum, where does she want me to cum.

"Inside me Mitch, let loose inside me."

I held back as much as I could as I wanted to shoot like a cannon, and at that I did. The contractions on my cock were so hard, my eyes were pulsating identical to every shot.

I collapsed beside Mindy while trying to slow down my heart from exploding and tried to catch my breath. Once both were achieved, I winked at her and said she was damn good.

"Mitch, I am the best you ever had. Well big guy, how long till you get hard again?"

I was pretty sober. So, I told her twenty minutes. She said perfect let's grab a shower.

One of my kinks, and chicks love this, I really enjoy lathering them up with soap, every single inch of their bodies and yes I love when they clean the outside of my body. Lord knows she certainly cleaned out anything inside my cock and balls.

We towel dried each other off, Mindy told me to go lay on the bed as she feels naked without any makeup on. So, I did as instructed.

Took her about fifteen minutes, and when she came out, she asked if I was ready to go again. I showed her I was hard and anticipating round two.

That's my big guy was her happy response as she headed towards her purse.

She had something tucked into the palm of her hand as she asked me to stand up and stay hard. Her eyes were dancing in a good way, so I trusted her.

Well, she did a first for me. She sprinkled enough coke on my cock and then neatly with her baby fingernail formed a line.

She rolled up a hundred-dollar bill and then snorted the coke right off my cock.

"FUCKING FAR OUT," was my response. She handed me the vile and said to help myself.

So, I sprinkled some powder between her breasts. I asked if she trusted me, a glazed eyed Mindy did a stoned smirk and said of course.

So, I reached around and grabbed my knife off the table. She did a gasp and stared at me now in fear as I ran the knifes razor sharp blade around her erect nipples before forming a line with the coke.

I took the hundred dollar bill out of her now sweaty palms and snorted the Nazi Marching Dust.

I let out a great big whew, fuck this was good coke. She followed the knife the whole time as I put it back on the table. I could tell she was a little freaked out.

"I told you to trust me, good girl." I went to the bottom of the bed and spread her legs and started to rub the top of her pussy with my thumb until she was ready for me to insert my rock-hard, cocaine induced cock inside of her. This time she wanted to ride me, ride me like Secretariat.

That little bit of coke she sprinkled on my cock was enough to numb it from blowing my load quickly.

After twenty minutes of fucking like maniacs we were both drenched in sweat. I had lost track at how many times Mindy said she was cumming.

Well, I know she likes a guy to take charge, so I flipped her onto her stomach and started to fuck her from behind, my turn to get rough without her telling me too.

I was smacking her ass hard and pulling on her hair asking in a firm voice if she likes it, she responded that she loved it.

Well let's see how she likes a finger in her ass. Now let's see about two fingers and me still pounding her pussy from behind.

"You like my fingers in your ass baby, you want my cock in your ass?"

She moaned out, "Yes, fuck my ass."

That's all I needed to hear.

I pulled my cock out from her pussy that was drenched in cum from her and slowly slid it into her ass. Her moans were now half pleasure and half pain.

I was now starting to get a good hard rhythm going while grabbing her ass hard, she fucking loved it and when she got on all fours and started to play with her pussy as I was fucking her ass.

All of a sudden, Mindy's blonde hair became red, total Charlene flashback to Herschel's wedding and the excitement had me building up and ready to blow my load really fast, my balls were starting to contract and my breathing told me poor Mindy's ass will be dripping cum for the next month.

Once again, I told her I am going to cum, she then started to shake and move her ass all over the place. I grabbed onto her hips and started to shoot and shoot and shoot inside of that sweet ass of hers.

My turn now to collapse and try and catch my breath as I stare up at the ceiling.

I kept reiterating out loud holy fuck, holy fuck.

Poor Mindy was now face down trying to catch her breath.

After a couple minutes she finally raises her head up, looks over at me and says, "I am going to be one sore girl for the next week, but one very happy, sore girl. Goddamn, Mitch, it has been a long time since anyone rocked me the way you did."

Once again all I could think of was with Charlene, this was a regular occurrence between us.

I echoed what she said out loud. Always make them feel more than special if you want them to come back and with Mindy, I really want her to come back.

Took me another twenty minutes till I was ready, willing, and able to go once again.

We flipped around from position to position. You are basically getting to know each other better through fucking, what a great concept and what a great lover Mindy has turned out to be.

We ended up passing out fully exhausted in each other's arms.

Before I knew it, my room phone was ringing. It was Joseph asking what type of night I had and am I feeling any better.

I look for Mindy who is gone and then look at the clock and it shows six am.

I know that Joseph seems to know a little too much about everything, so I am upfront for the most part with him.

"I met that blonde from the other night and took her to this jazz club, it was a good night."

There was silence and I told Joseph about the night he was shit faced.

"Oh O.K. I am sure she was cute, listen, change of plans. You are still heading to the airport, but you are heading somewhere else. Meet you in the diner downstairs in thirty."

I hung up the phone, did a flashback of everything that took place last night, fuck the sheets were still damp and in some spots and not from sweat.

You could smell the perfume from Mindy on my pillow, I started to get hard again.

I got up out of bed and had a little head rush. Legs were a little wobbly which is the sign of a great night of sucking and fucking, man even my abs and hips were tender.

I can only imagine how her pussy and ass must feel.

Took a nice hot shower and once again ran the water cold before getting out. I think this is going to be a new routine for me.

I packed up my clothes. Had one last sniff on the pillow and headed downstairs to meet Joseph.

Cashel was sitting at the table with Joseph having a coffee.

I am sure with whatever travel plans have changed that they involve him.

After the waitress took my order of water, coffee, juice and more water and a huge kick ass breakfast, we got down to business.

Joseph said he would like me to go to Providence, Rhode Island. My mission is to kill Ron Mazzetti.

"Why me, why not one of your own crew?" I asked.

"Everybody knows everyone up there. No one knows you. It can't be a run and gun. Mitch, you have to dispose of the body, never to be found. And most importantly, Seamus wants this guy to suffer physically before he takes his last breath. You interested, lad?" said Joseph.

"So, I assume I am doing this lone wolf?"

Cashel said the last thing anyone wants is a war if it comes back to Seamus, so yes all by myself but he would get me set up with whatever I needed.

"I will need a set of wheels, a map of where Ron lives and how to get in and out of Rhode Island if worse comes to worst. What his normal routines are, hangouts, girlfriends address, that kind of stuff.

Material wise I will need a bottle of chloroform, several pairs of gloves, ski mask, duct tape, a couple firearms as I don't want to get on a commercial flight carrying any weapons, and a Fairburn Sykes knife. And most importantly, pictures of this fuck. I don't want to be killing some poor innocent civilian."

"That is not a problem at all. Once you land, I will have one of my guys meet you at the airport," said Cashel

"You will be my one and only contact, so far we have found one rat in your group." I reminded him.

He may not have liked what I said, but it was the truth.

"So, tell me what kind of person Mazzetti is so I know what to expect from him, OCDs, left-handed, right-handed, can he handle himself and does he normally travel alone?"

"He is an ex-cop, was caught playing around with underage girls and they kicked him off the force. His cousin Vito is the head Italian in the Fratone family. Took him in as a muscle, and he worked his way up to a captain. Married but still likes the young broads which doesn't always go over well with Vito. He is always armed. Not sure what hand he is. Definite head case who likes to beat people up, but nowadays he makes sure he has muscle with him when he has to send a message, I guess he likes still getting his hands dirty but only if the odds are in his favor."

Typical cop or ex-cop sounds like a total asshole. The more they talked about him the more I thought about doing this hit for free. Who goes to parks and looks for young teens to fuck. The cops even questioned him about this fifteen-year-old girl he was fucking, she ended up going missing. Apparently, he likes to rough house them while fucking them.

When Cashel was done telling me everything, I looked at him and Joseph and said, "I am in, but I think you want him found. hear my logic. In prison, we would castrate anyone that played with kids, or jailbait. I will cut his dick off, put a pair of children's underwear and that severed dick in his mouth. This way it never comes back to you. Vito will be embarrassed, other mobsters will go after him if that dirty little death secret came out, a little war would start with the Italians. Makes Seamus gang that much stronger."

Joseph smiled and said that's my boy, always thinking.

"Cashel, not to overstep my boundaries with your crew. I think everything Mitchell said is brilliant. I strongly suggest you call Seamus and get his blessing for this type of kill."

"I too love your idea, let me phone Seamus to make sure we are on the same page."

Five minutes later Cashel came back in with this huge smile, he shook my hand and said, "Seamus loves this plan. He will arrange to have one of our men waiting for you at the Logan airport. He will be holding up a sign with your Willie Hertz name. Our guy will give you a car key, tell you where it is parked at the airport. And everything you needed equipment, and intelligence wise."

Now, the one thing that Donnie hasn't taught me is how to ask for the cash. I really would do this fuck for free, but this is my job, this job pays my bills.

So, I asked whose clock am I on right now?

"You are always on my clock Mitchell; keep all receipts and I will reimburse you once you get home. Do you have enough cash on you right now?"

I said I could use some more to be honest. So, Joseph peeled off five one-hundred-dollar bills. I asked him if he could bring my suits home. Lord knows what it took for me to finally break down and buy them.

Sadly, I never got a chance to say goodbye to Mindy, or even if she wants to stay in touch once we get back into the Bay area, I am more than down for it.

But on my flight from Chicago to Boston, that is all I could think about. If I keep Ella as my girlfriend, she opens a lot of closed doors for me, and have Mindy as a side piece, someone who keeps my sexual appetite fed, that sounds pretty perfect.

The flight was smooth, in fact, I even managed to get some much needed shut eye. Mindy certainly drained me in more ways than one.

Seamus' crew didn't let me down. As I was leaving my terminal. I see a guy holding a sign that says "Willie Hertz".

I walk over to him, let him know I am Willie Hertz. He eyes me up and down as do I right back at him. Two bravado brahma bulls staring at each other. Zero emotion, at least shown. I am wondering if he is able to take me down. Pretty sure he is thinking the same as he has asked for my identification.

Nothing but intense eye contact the whole time. Neither one of us blinks as I am getting out my wallet.

The only time he takes his eyes off me is when he verifies who I am.

He passes me the keys to the vehicle, tells me the exact parking spot, parking garage, and everything else I need to know. He says everything I asked for is in the vehicle, then he leaves. No handshake, no good luck, fuck all. Then again, I would do the same if he was coming to the Bay area to kill someone and I was handing him a set of keys. What I don't know won't come back to bite me in the ass.

Found the car. And headed to a hotel that Seamus booked for me in Pawtucket. I really don't want to stay in Providence. Low profile.

After I check in, head to my room, I sit back and start to get all the info on Mazzetti.

Mazzetti's bar was right on the main drag, no way will I be able to take him from there without drawing attention.

Now, his house is right by this body of water and near some woods that attach to an insane asylum. Now, that is fucked, and just perfect.

I was provided with several photos of him. Just like the map, I have memorized everything, scars, wrinkles and even his left eye that droops a little more than the right one.

I then checked out to see what clothes they got me, a Celtic and Bruin tank top along with a pair of shorts, a Bruins ball cap which I forgot to ask for and black track pants. Good stuff as I will fit in as a local.

Decided to get change and go for a walk into town. I want to see where everything is.

Great, I'm wearing shorts and a tank top and the only shoes I have are dress shoes. Fuck, time to go shopping for a pair of runners.

So, I put my jeans on and walked into town and found a sporting goods store.

I walked in wearing the Bruins tank top and the sales guy asked who my favorite Bruin was. Bobby Orr of course. You didn't think someone living in the Bay Area would know of him? Fuck, the whole world knows who he is.

The guys asked what I needed. I said a pair of runners, He asked what size, said thirteen.

"I will go back and check, sir."

Before he left, this Stella looking broad said she was ready to check out.

He looked at me and said, "Sorry, important customer. Yes, Mrs. Mazzetti I will meet you at the cash register."

This has to be that fucking Italian Ron's wife. She told her kids to hurry up as Daddy is expecting them at the restaurant.

The kids seem like little assholes as they are running to the front knocking over mannequins, yep, the apples don't fall far from the tree.

Once he cashed her out, he went in the back and came out with my shoes. I asked if that was Ron Mazzetti's wife and brats, he laughed and said yes.

The shoes fit nicely, so I kept them on as I know the Mazzetti family is gone out and I want to check out their house.

So, I ran back to the hotel, slipped on my shorts as I was drenched, fuck, it must be over a hundred degrees right now.

I jumped in the car and headed to 6 Presidents Drive, home of the Mazzetti's.

Judging by the size of the houses in this neighborhood crime does pay, it pays quite well.

Their house was right on the corner, which is good as I have several options of coming at him on the sly.

I then drove a couple blocks away and started to surround myself with the whole landscape.

To the south is woods, but it looks like a state-owned park, I really don't want some young kid finding him and fucking their head up for the rest of their life.

I continue on my death quest when I come to a clearing, and in that clearing, I am drawn to this gothic looking building. This has to be the insane asylum.

I decide to get a little closer as I don't need any staff seeing my dastardly deed. As soon as I crossed a little stream, I had a chill run up and down my spine. I pulled out my one 9MM as I felt I was being watched. I started to sniff, listen, and look.

I truly believe where something demonic has taken place, the soil stays contaminated. And as I look towards the hospital, I sense nothing but evil and madness.

For the next hour, my back and senses were up, but I did manage to find the perfect spot to kill Mazzetti. Time to find a place to eat, wait till the sun goes down, and come back and start digging a shallow grave.

The last thing I want is to spend another hour digging and getting dirty then heading to the airport. Just being a proactive worker.

And after the kill, if I have several hours between my flight, it would be nice to hook up with Anita. I think I will find a phone booth and see if the operator can find a phone number with her name.

22

I found a steakhouse that specializes in fresh lobster. Joseph said to keep receipts, so I had a really nice filet mignon and a lobster tail with pitcher of Sam Adams beer that I inhaled.

Went back to the motel room and crashed out on top of the bed.

I woke up and the clock said 1:11. It took me a bit to realize where the hell I was in the world and was it morning or afternoon.

I grabbed a quick shower to bring me back to life before heading back to the woods by the insane asylum.

The one item I forgot to grab was a flashlight, but we were on the cusp of a full moon. Hopefully it provides me with enough light.

I stopped about twenty feet from Mazzetti's house and wanted to see how close I could get without any light sensors going on. I walked right beside his car door, and it went off. Might be an issue, I will have to think about this one.

I then looked down at my watch and timed how far the drive would be. And how long by foot.

Three minutes by car, driving with no lights won't be a problem. Twelve minutes by foot, say fifteen as I will be carrying him.

Once again, I felt I was being watched in the woods and not by one set of eyes but several. A couple times I stopped shoveling and went into a firing position.

I wish I had a partner with me on this mission as now I am starting to see shadows, almost like an LSD trip.

Now I am starting to get a really good reputation according to

Joseph, imagine if I called Cashel and told him I am a little freaked out or spooked in the woods so can you accompany me? Yeah, not cool. Maybe the extreme heat, maybe still on a bit of a coke high, but I was thirsty. Time to find a corner store open and buy a six pack of beer. Luckily, I found one.

I don't even think the beer touched my throat.

I was still sweating really hard, so I jumped in the shower with my third beer, pounded it back in two drinks. Did the cold water only at the end, dried off and sat out front wearing a towel and the remaining three beers.

Once I saw the first glimpse of the sun starting to rise, I did my best vampire impersonation and went inside and laid on the bed till I fell asleep.

I found a place that had 24-hour breakfast, while on my third coffee; I wanted to keep an eye on the Mazzetti household, but I don't want my car to be seen too much in the neighborhood that it draws suspicion, and someone calls the cop, or he sees it and he knows something isn't right.

So, I decided to come in from the north and park at the insane asylum and walk through the woods until I am at the tree line and pardon the pun, but a view to kill for.

Driving through the parking lot and looking at the buildings you can help feel this is the perfect setting for a horror film.

I found the perfect spot and watched the targeted house. Pretty fucking boring to say the least. Looks like they have a pool as all kinds of kids left with towels around their necks.

Mazzetti came home around eight. He looks to the east when he first gets out, then west and finally north towards the woods. Looks like he might have a bad back as his movement is not fluid.

He uses a key to get in the front door, so I know that it is always locked.

Now, according to Seamus' intelligence report, he has his mob meeting tomorrow night. I wish I knew what time he is normally done.

I stuck around for another hour to see if anything else interesting happens but fuck all did. Just a bunch of mosquitoes trying to eat me. They must be attracted to the beer coming out of me. Being parched I needed another six pack of beer.

I pull up and these teenage guys are hanging around the store

"I am sure you boys like to get high. I was wondering if you could sell me a couple joints?"

They both look at each other, the one asks if I am a cop, that makes me laugh and I said, "fuck no."

Not sure who people are getting this legal advice from, and yes not the first time I have heard it. But they said I am a cop, I have to let them know seeing how they asked, it is part of the constitution.

Normally, I would tell them who I am, let them know I am associated with the Oakland Hell Hounds, but I have to keep a low profile. So I shake my head and verbally tell them that I am not a cop.

Both smile and ask if a nickel bag works. My turn to smile as I said that was perfect. Now that I have shopped outside, time to go inside and grab some beer and rolling papers.

Back at the hotel, I downed a beer straight back. Rolled up a joint and sparked it up. Fucking cheap Mexican weed, knew it was too good to be true. Well, better than nothing.

Then again, I didn't want to get fucked up, just wanted to take the edge off. That insane asylum has kind of fucked me up.

I ended up grabbing a pizza, finished the six pack and a couple more joints. You would think between the carbs and booze and weed I could shut my brain down.

Fuck, I need sleep, but I had so many scenarios running through my head about the whole approach of kidnapping, torturing and killing of Mazzetti. A single shot to the head would be so much easier, but that is not what Seamus wants.

I woke up the next morning with a spring in my step, grabbed a long shower and thought the whole time about tonight. My head was clear, and I felt confident.

I grabbed a decent breakfast. Went back to the room and cleaned my 9MM while waiting for my meal to digest.

And once that happened, I went for a long run along the shoreline of the Seekonk River. My heart racing and the sweat coming out of me was the perfect cleanse.

I went back to the hotel, did a bunch of push ups, crunches and a full body stretch out.

Another shower and then a drive to Mazzetti's bar, along the same route he would take, in case I have missed something.

I drove up to Foxborough to grab an early dinner. Something light, not too heavy, I don't need to be sluggish. I called the operator to see if there was a listing for Anita Gray in Boston. Nothing came up when I remembered her saying she was going to live with her sister for a bit.

I went back to my motel. Took a good solid nap. A hot shower and once again running scenarios through my head. Dried off and did some meditation and full body stretch out. I have to get my head totally clear of anything other than the job at hand.

Double checked my 9MM again. Made sure all the extra clips were all ready to use if need be.

Around seven I loaded up everything I brought with me and put it in the trunk of the car. I made sure not one shred of evidence showed that I was there.

I didn't bother to check out. Cops use a timeline they will put two and two together.

Put on the black track pants, the Celtic tank top, and was ready.

At twenty hundred hours I left and headed to Mazzetti's house. I still get butterflies to be honest so you box breathe on the way over.

By the time I got there, he was gone, but sometimes life or fate sends you a blessing. It was garbage night, and the Mazzetti's had all their garbage cans all by the road. Excellent.

So, I parked the car on the northeast side of the asylum on a side street. Brought with me my change of clothes and the bottle of chloroform.

I slithered through the woods like a snake waiting for his prey to arrive.

Was still hiding in the bush, but close enough if I farted, he could tell what I had on my pizza last night.

I waited till all the lights in the house went off. Just after twenty-three hundred when I walked over and gently laid his garbage cans on their sides, and strewn garbage across his grass. Italians love their grass to be perfect, like that on a golf course.

I went back into hiding and waited. Thankfully he lives on a very quiet street. Hell, no cars at all until slightly after one. This car I recognized, so I broke open the chloroform and put it on a washcloth I took from the motel.

I crouched down low and started to hustle my ass in stealth mode. I was less than ten feet from his driveway in a shrub.

He got out of the car cursing the raccoons and walked towards the mess.

I then headed to the front of his car and as soon as he bent over and complained about his aching back, I ran at him, one arm around his chest so he couldn't use his arms, and the other hand I put the washcloth over his mouth.

Very brief struggle before he hit the ground.

I picked him up and threw him over my shoulder and did the fireman's carry right to the woods. This fat fuck was well over two hundred and fifty pounds and with it being dead weight, I will ask for more cash now.

You are moving as fast as you can without falling down. My heart was pounding the whole time. Sweat was now burning my eyes. I tried to wipe it with my arms as the gloves I am wearing still have moisture from the chloroform.

We were halfway there when I dropped him to the ground and duct taped his mouth, wrists, and feet together. I was so pissed I kicked him in the ribs out of spite, fat fuck!

I caught my breath, bent down and picked him up once again. Even though he is bound he can still squirm making it difficult to move.

I eventually made it to the grave and dropped him in it. My legs and arms were shaking. Gonna feel this for the next couple days, but you know what? Mazzetti will be feeling a hell of a lot worse.

I pounded back one of the bottles of water I had in my gym bag. I jumped into the shallow grave and took his watch, rings, and wallet.

Made sure to catch my breath and had a 9MM with a silencer on it in my hand before pissing on him to wake him up.

The full moon was beaming down on him as he opened his eyes like a frightened school child from a nightmare.

He went to sit up and I fired a shot into his shoulder. That set him back into the earth really fast.

Once again, his eyes showed pure horror.

"I only want you to answer my questions by nodding your head yes or no. Understood?" His head was shaking but he nodded yes.

"I hear you like to play with schoolgirls."

He hesitated at first before shaking his head no really fast.

I picked up the shovel and speared him right in the groin with it.

Man, did he ever scream even with the duct tape covering his mouth. Yeah, this made him turn white and had his eyes rolling in his head.

Once he seemed to have refocused, I leaned in and told him, his wife and kids are dead. I killed them while he was out with his Italian pals tonight. I was told specifically to torture him, and that must be one of the worse things you can tell someone.

"Do you know why I am going to kill you?" No head movement at all, crying like a baby looking for his mama. Well, I sure as fuck ain't his mother.

Once again, I picked up the shovel and this time drove it into his right knee.

Man, I could hear his kneecap shatter. As I lifted the shovel back up, drops of blood were dripping from the spade part onto him so I decided to let the blood drip onto his face.

The moons ray almost had the droplets like some psychedelic trip.

"You are an evil person. I have a daughter; how can you stomach what you are doing to these girls and their families. I guess you don't have any feelings in that disgusting gut of yours now do you?"

Yep, drew the shovel up in the air and drove it right into his abdomen. He passed out on me now, and with how hard and far it went into him, he will bleed to death internally.

Time to get to work, real work, as I pulled his pants down, enough to look at his shriveled, anteater dick.

I pull out the knife, it is razor sharp, perfect, but what is not perfect, a reflection coming from the moon that is cascaded onto the steel blade, that someone is behind me. I jump up and spin around while doing Xs in the air. I am swinging to kill, not maim.

But it appears you can't maim or kill ghosts. There is no one around. But I know what I saw. This whole area is fucking evil, bad juju.

Almost cut my fingers off trying to castrate Mazzetti, his dick is so fucking small.

I put the children's underwear into his mouth, then his bloody severed mini sizzler dick of his in the underwear.

Wash my hands with vinegar and water, changed my clothes, can't be showing up at Logan with blood-soaked clothes. I stuff them into a gym bag. Put his jewelry in my front pocket, they have to be worth something, and his cash and driver's license in my wallet.

Joseph knows I am a loyal and thorough soldier, Seamus has never met me, but this is my fifth kill for him.

One last stop before I hit Logan. The bridge that was on the Seekonk River is where I disposed of that gym bag full of bloody sins, and the shovel.

23

I arrived at the airport after three in the morning and left the car in the parking lot with the key in the ashtray.

Walked in and I booked a flight home that had a two-hour layover in Chicago. Maybe I will get lucky, and Mindy will be on the same flight.

Had five hours to kill, pardon the pun. I was still pretty wound up from the kill and every time a cop walked by you tried your best not to draw any suspicion to yourself. Now, if three of them walk towards me then you start looking for the exits.

Thanks to a pot of coffee and the crossword book I survived till my flight was called.

Just like every single flight I didn't relax until the wheels were in the air.

By the time I got off the plane, the bar in the airport was open. A couple pitchers of draft and shots of Wild Turkey, fuck I slept the whole way back to San Francisco. The stewardess actually had to wake me before we made our final descent.

Once again, I had no clue where I was other then being on a plane. Sometimes the look in their faces is priceless.

As soon as I got into the terminal, I called Joseph to pick me up.

He showed up about twenty minutes later. Right off the bat he asked how it went.

I handed him Mazzetti's driver's license.

"Great job, Mitchell," he smiled and handed me an envelope

containing five grand cash. I gave him the watch and rings I took from him, and my receipts.

He looked at the rings and said Italians love to have signet pinkie rings.

He dropped me off, said get some sleep and either dinner tonight or tomorrow, his treat. I thanked him and said it sounded good.

As I put the key in the front door, I noticed a cops business card and written on the back was a message for me to contact him. Interesting as a million things are now racing through my brain.

I went upstairs and the place looked different, hey it looks like Oscar has moved out.

I headed to the answering machine and was really hoping that Charlene called and let me a number to call her back. No such luck, but that cop on the card did call twice. And Ella several times asking if everything was good.

I wanna find out what has been going on first before I call the cop back. I could sleep for a day, my back, legs and shoulder were starting to get stiff and sore.

So, I sat down and loaded up my pipe, put on Zappa "Hot Rats", lit the pipe and smoked every last bud.

Took the phone off the hook, headed to the bedroom and put the cash from Joseph in the safe and then laid down for a well-deserved rest.

It is true, there is no place like home.

Seemed like I just closed my eyes when I heard pounding from the door downstairs. Only two kinds of people pound a door that hard. Steroid users and cops. My gut tells me the cops are here. And they are pounding and not kicking in the door saying they have a search warrant out for me.

I went downstairs and sure as fuck two plain clothes cops were there.

Detectives Ramsey and Gibson of San Francisco homicide. They asked if they could come in or would I like to accompany them downtown for questioning.

I told them to come up and we can talk.

They both had a seat in the living room. Ramsey picked up my pipe that I forgot to put away. My face must have given that away, but he reassured me they don't care about someone who smokes weed.

"I read a report that you had a physical altercation with David Schinn a couple weeks back," said Gibson

"Yeah, but I wasn't charged, are you here now to charge me for it?"

They both looked at each other when Ramsey asked if I had any contact with Schinn since that day.

"One hundred percent zero contact. The guy is a racist and a loser, not worth taking a charge for. I am curious why two homicide cops are in my living room talking to me about him."

"Well, Strongbow, Schinn has gone missing. We are looking at person or persons who have a grudge with him or would want to hurt him."

Right off the bat I know that Sean Quinn has kidnapped, and no doubt in my mind has killed Schinn and if I know Quinn, fuck, my killing of Mazzetti will seem like child's play.

"Do you have an alibi for the past week?"

Can't say I was moving a hundred pounds of weed to Alaska, went to Chicago and killed one guy, and then headed to Boston to kill a Mafia Captain.

"I do, but I think from this point on I would rather speak with my attorney present."

"Innocent people don't need attorneys present."

"Well, I am an ex-con but you two already know that. Believe it or not, there are innocent people in prison doing time for crimes they never did. Now either charge me with something or please feel free to leave."

They both stood up and said they will be in touch, don't leave town.

Ramsey said his card was in the door for five days now. On vacation? He asked.

I told them to have a nice day and ushered with my hand where the door is.

I followed them downstairs and made sure to lock and bolt the door.

My brain was scrambling, and part of the problem is the jet lag and overall fatigue of the past week is catching up with me and kicking my ass.

Normally I would head over and ask Joseph for advice and ask what he knows. But I worry about the cops keeping a closer look on me. I have to get this cash in the bank, and will have a hard time explaining this.

Fuck, Mitch; you are over thinking everything. Go to bed but you know the brain won't shut off.

I grabbed a long shower, got changed and headed to the Drunken Leprechaun.

I took the car and kept looking in my rear view mirror the whole way.

Lucky for me, Joseph and Donnie were both sitting at the bar enjoying a drink.

Donnie looks at me and says I look like shit.

"Good seeing you too. How was Alaska?"

"I believe it will be very successful for the Hell Hounds. Joseph says everything went well for you."

"It did until two local homicide dicks paid me a visit about a missing person named David Schinn."

I looked at Joseph's face the whole time. Not a muscle moved until he took a sip from his glass.

Donnie looked at me and then Joseph and asked if he should know this name.

"No, you shouldn't. Schinn goes to school with Nyah Quinn. He deals weed. I guess he didn't like Nyah buying it from someone else and ratted her out. She was popped by the cops with a dime bag. Now, a couple weeks ago Nyah and I went out for lunch, and we pulled up to eat. Schinn is there with a couple buddies. He calls Nyah a cunt and I leave him and his buddies a bloody mess. Cops are called. I don't get charged as witnesses tell the cops they started it, and it was three guys against me. So, about an hour ago the two dicks ask where I have been as Schinn is now missing. Nyah told Sean what happened after he gave her a backhand. I will go to prison and stay solid for anything I get into with you guys. I will not go to prison for something Sean Quinn did, advice?"

Donnie nodded his head as Joseph said he had to go and make a call.

"So not only were you fucking Nyah, but you were also supplying her with the weed? You better keep a close eye on Sean," said a worried Donnie.

Joseph came out of the back and said Sean is on his way over.

"So, the cops want to know where you have been. Tell them Chicago. You have the elevator guy and the blonde you were fucking as alibis. Worse comes to worse the hotel we stayed at can confirm you were there. Nothing about Boston. Do not talk to the cops anymore without Levy present understood?"

"Not to fear, boss, I already told the cops I want a lawyer present when they want to talk to me again." Joseph said good boy and told Lauren to get me a beer and shot.

By the time I was done my second beer in walks the neanderthal Sean Quinn.

He stares at me and nods at Donnie. Joseph tells Sean to grab a beer and says for all of us to go in the back.

Donnie asks if I am packing a weapon, just what my overtired brain wants to hear. I tell him to quit fucking with me.

The three of us take a seat as Joseph remains standing.

"Sean. tell me about David Schinn."

His face went red and not with embarrassment but with anger. He growled and asked where this is coming from.

"Mitchell tells me two homicide detectives ended up at his apartment today and asking him about Schinn."

Sean looks at me and with anger in his voice asks, "What do you know about Schinn that would bring the law to your house?"

I look at Joseph for direction and he nods his head yes.

"Nyah and I went for lunch, Schinn and two buddies were there. They called Nyah a cunt, so I beat the fuck out of them. Cops were called, they took down the info."

Sean shook his head and said he is not sure how he feels about this. You could see him getting madder and madder.

I think all of us sensed this when Joseph made direct eye contact with Sean and said, "That was very honorable what you did, Mitchell. You risked going to jail for defending a friend, who happens to be a co-worker's daughter. If that was my daughter, I would be very grateful."

Sean seemed to let his emotions down for a bit and listened to what Joseph said.

"Why didn't you come to me, Strongbow, and tell me what happened?"

"I truly thought the beating I laid on Schinn would have scared him enough to back down and leave her alone. I told him I would take his life if he bothered Nyah again."

There was about a ten second delay when Sean stood up, walked towards me and stuck his hand out and thanked me.

I asked how Nyah was doing now.

"I think she is more shook up with the cops asking her if she knows about Schinn missing than the drug charge. The school has suspended her as she was arrested on school property with drugs."

Joseph told Sean if Nyah needs anything ask.

"She is a great kid. I will call in favors for her if need be."

"I won't have her do jail time. I will get her out of the country before that happens. The district attorney said she is looking at least a year in jail for this because she had drugs in school. I know he is trying to lean on me and our crew," said a frustrated Sean.

So how shitty do I feel right now? I want to go home and crawl under the covers and sleep for a week, wake up and pretend this was a bad dream.

Well, I finished off my beers, thanked the boys and excused myself and told them jet lag was kicking my ass.

Joseph walked me to my car and said, "For the sake of keeping peace, stay away from Nyah." I promised I would.

On the drive home you replay everything that was said or not said. I know in the pit of my gut Sean killed Schinn. But I really don't care other then I hoped he tortured him first.

I parked the car and walked to my door, looking both ways before putting the key in. Saw no one at all.

Bolted the door once inside, took the phone off the hook and next stop was dreamland.

I woke up the next morning with this gnaw in my gut. Everything from last night comes back even if some of it was foggy.

I look at the clock and realize I have slept almost fifteen hours. It actually hurts to get out of bed. I believe the combo of planes, fat Mazzetti and stress is making me move really slow.

I take a long hot shower and try to shake the cobwebs from my head.

I toweled off and put the phone back on the hook. It takes like two seconds, and it starts to ring. It startled the fuck right out of me.

I answer it and speak of the devil, it is Nyah. She is quite upset and phoned me from a payphone. She says she really needs to see me.

I know what Joseph said but no way can I hang up on her this upset.

She tells me where she is, and I tell her to stay put and I will come by and pick her up on the bike.

I gingerly get dressed, grab the spare helmet and head to where she is.

It is about a ten-minute drive from me at a diner.

I walk in and she comes running towards me sobbing. Patrons are looking at us, and right now, the last people I want to see us are Joseph and Sean.

So, I tell her lets go for a drive as I want to get out of the Bay Area. She wipes her cheeks and nods her head yes.

We head north to Santa Rosa. I can feel her breathing is heavy and she is very emotional.

We pull into a restaurant to talk, and for me to eat.

I order breakfast, Nyah says she has zero appetite. I come out and ask what is going on.

"My dad is sending me to Tortola to live with my Aunt Angelica. He says no daughter of his will ever see the inside of a jail cell. Mitch, this is my home."

Her eyes welled up full of tears and she could barely speak.

"The police interviewed me about Schinn. Said he is missing, and what do I know? Mitch, I know nothing. I don't know where he is."

Full breakdown this time. Good thing we are the only two patrons in here.

What do you do? I kept rubbing her back and telling her all will be good, but I know that is a huge lie, a motherfucking huge lie.

"I am going to run away, fuck my mom, fuck my dad. I hate them both right now."

"Listen, I talked to your dad last night. He doesn't want you going to prison Nyah. If you were my daughter, I would be doing the same thing. What is a year or so locked up going to accomplish? Fuck all and then you will always be known as an ex-con. No one will hire you. Fucking Schinn I don't know where he is, but I am going after him."

"That is sweet of you to say that, Mitch, but I am pretty sure my dad and uncle Joseph made sure Schinn is face down with a bullet in the back of his head already, fucking rat goof."

It was nice seeing some anger come out of her. I shrugged my shoulders and smiled. She squinted her eyes and asked where I have been.

"In Chicago with Joseph."

She asked me really, and I assured her I was.

She grabbed a hold of my hands and asked me to look her in the eye. I did as instructed and she said, "So if I was Katrina your daughter you would do the same as what my dad is doing?"

"One hundred percent I would. If Rachel lived far away, I know Kat would be taken care of. Of course, I would. I did two years in San Quentin, and I can more than handle myself, and I had several attempts on my life. You are a good kid. I would worry about your safety and treatment in prison. You wouldn't come out as the same person who is sitting across from me right now."

She started to tear up again and thanked me for being honest. Now how does she go back home and say sorry as she lost it on both parents?

"I think you should not go home alone, but me being with you would just escalate things with your dad, and I would be the next person missing. I think the best thing to do is to walk in the house with Joseph. He will calm everything down and make things right with your parents. He is your Godfather, correct?"

"Yes, he is. Will you visit me, Mitchell?"

"Of course, I will. I promise, I swear on Kat."

She smiled and said she loves me. I reached across and held her hands and told her that I loved her.

It was nice seeing her smile. I told her I would call Joseph to come and get her.

Well, it is a good thing Nyah never heard the conversation between Joseph and me.

"Joseph, its Mitchell."

"I was going to call you. Have you heard from Nyah at all?"

"Yeah, you can say that. She is with me in a diner in Santa Rosa."

"Jesus fucking Christ, Mitchell! Are you totally daft, lad? Did you not hear what I said to you last night before you left?"

"What the fuck am I supposed to do, Joseph? She calls me crying and scared shitless. Would you want to me to hang up on her? Then you'd never be able to find her. I talked to her, and she wants to you to take her home. I really don't want to talk that much on the phone. Are you coming or not cause if I take her home, it will be a bloodbath."

There was about a five second delay and some deep breaths and when Joseph finally said I was right, and he would be right over.

I went back to the table and Nyah had dug into my breakfast that arrived when I was on the phone. That is a good sign. I ordered another breakfast and told her Joseph is on his way.

Both of us had finished our breakfast and were downing our second coffee when Joseph showed up.

He gave Nyah a big smile then shot me this dirty look while he was hugging Nyah.

He sat down and had a coffee with us as Nyah told him all her fears and how I told her it was best to listen to her folks and move to Tortola.

That dirty look towards me turned into a smile after he heard the whole story.

Joseph eventually asked if Nyah was ready to leave.

"Not really, but I guess it is time for me to start a new life."

We all stood up and walked outside to Joseph's car.

Nyah looked at me with a nervous smile and said, "I guess this is it."

"For now, I promise to still be a part of your life."

I wrote down the address of Pamdora's and told her to write to me and send it there.

She gave me a really long kiss and hug goodbye, reiterated that she loved me in front of Joseph and you know what? Fuck him, I told her that I loved her back right in front of him, and yep dirty look back again.

We stared at each other as she got into Joseph's car. Once they left, I jumped on my bike and really needed to go for a long ride.

I looked north, south, west and no direction was calling to me. I thought about driving to Sacramento and seeing Rachel but she will be working and with it being a fairly new job I don't think she could bail for the day without getting in shit.

You know what I could use? A week on the reserve at the hunt camp, an escape from reality as I feel the walls are starting to close in on me.

I want to sit in a canoe, fish during the day, fire at night time and watch the stars and contemplate life. Need to refocus.

So, I head to Donnie's shop. With Joseph taking Nyah home, it would be totally irresponsible of me to take off and not let anyone know, yeah especially with the cops asking me about Schinn's disappearance.

I show up and he takes one look at me and asks if everything is alright.

I tell him everything that took place this morning. I tell him about Charlene still AWOL and I really need some serious wind down time and to shut my brain down. I tell him it has been revving in the red too much lately.

He can tell I am spinning and asks as a friend what I need to wind down, or what he can do to help.

"I will be brutally honest with you; right now, I could use either a fix of heroin or to be on the reservation getting back into myself and finding peace man. I am fucked right up, brother."

"Pussy will kill you, brother. You want to know why I stay faithful to Jeanie? That is why. Normally, I would say take off and see your grandpa as I don't ever wanna see track marks in your arms again. But Joseph wants us around this weekend, he has something lined up for us."

"Donnie, I appreciate everything Joseph does for me, and I spent the weekend with him in Chicago, torturing two guys, castrating another guy. I think I have shown my loyalty to him. I am not going to be a good soldier without some serious R&R, man."

Donnie went deep in thought then a little smile came to his face, and he said, "I hear where you are coming from, so I have an idea. Head to my property at the lake, pitch a tent, have a fire at nighttime, watch the stars and like you said, I find myself getting mellow, recharging the batteries. You are more than welcome to park your ass there. You told me how much fun you and Rachel had there fishing."

This might actually work, yeah for sure it will.

"Thanks, man; I have to slide by and get my canoe."

Donnie said that was not a problem at all, I felt that black cloud starting to clear.

I headed back to my place, grabbed some clothes, a frying pan, a fishing rod, a case of beer and a half bag of weed. Typical camping supplies indeed.

Went back to Donnie's shop and he helped me load the canoe in the truck along with everything else I would need.

He drew me a very detailed map on how to get there as I was pretty hungover the last time I was there, in fact, Rachel drove. Now the only thing he asked is that I don't leave any garbage lying around.

"Did you not see that commercial with the Indian shedding a tear because you white folks are polluting his land? That Indian is me."

Donnie laughed, shook his head, and called me an idiot.

He said to hang there and if Joseph wants me, he will come and get me; till then, he told me to go and find myself and rest and relax and get back into nature.

He said this guy he served with in the 101st has a skydiving club in Napa and Donnie uses that to clear his head. Brilliant was my answer as it made so much sense, free falling to the earth really makes you appreciate what you have to live for.

I thanked him and headed to his property on Clear Lake.

Didn't even get more than ten minutes away when I heard a siren really close, too close.

24

I looked in my side mirror and an unmarked cop car was right behind me. I quickly thought what I had on me that would get me busted.

Only weapon is my Fairburn Sykes knife. I have some weed which I am really not that concerned about as it is tucked solid between my balls and ass, aka my taint.

So, I pull over and stayed in the vehicle, I know this drill because it's happened all too often.

As I look in the mirror, I see it is detectives Ramsey and Gibson, same dicks from yesterday.

They split up and each take a side of the truck. Both have their hands inside their suit jacket pockets. Looks like Gibson is a lefty.

Ramsey approaches the driver side and asks where I am going.

"Clear Lake, why is there a law against that?"

"No law about you going there. And what do you plan on doing while you're up there?"

"I thought the canoe would be pretty obvious. Going fishing and camping for a couple days."

Next thing I know a cruiser pulls up with its lights going and two cops get out including Kurt Wilson, fuck me, I thought he was still a meter maid.

"Mitch, I won't bullshit you and I'll be honest and upfront with you. Right now, you are a suspect in the disappearance of David Schinn. I am thinking you have a canoe, go out on a lake or ocean and the body disappears for good. I would really like a quick search of your vehicle."

"Do you have a warrant?"

"Not right now but I can have one issued in thirty minutes. And we will sit here and talk until a black and white shows up with one. So can we search your vehicle?"

"Tell you what, Ramsey; If I give you permission and once you find nothing, will you let me go on my way?"

Ramsey now looked at Gibson who nodded his head yes.

"Yes, we can do that, now for our safety I am going to have you sit in the back of the black and white while we search."

"Not sure if you are aware of the history between Wilson and me. I will sit in the back as long as he is not in the cruiser and no cuffs, deal?"

Ramsey must have spotted some guilt or shock on my face as he asked what I am afraid of him finding.

I look at him and wonder how solid of a cop is he? Is he just fucking with me to get me to lower my guard? They saw some grass out the other day and didn't care. I am sure Levy would be freaking out on me about this whole conversation and me allowing the search, something tells me he is only worried about solving murders not petty crimes that will have his days off spent in court. Let's see how this goes down.

"In my right boot I have my knife I used in Special forces."

"Thanks for letting me know that; anything else, Strongbow?"

"I have a small amount of weed in my underwear."

Wilson heard this and his face started to beam with joy as he now took out his handcuffs. Fuck what have I done.

Ramsey seemed shocked at Wilson's actions. "Patrolman Wilson, did I ask you for your cuffs? No, I didn't, stand down right now. Sorry Strongbow, rookies. I am not worried about that. I will reach down and take your knife and put it in the hood of your engine. Keep your weed."

I sat in the back of the cruisers, not cuffed, and watched them take off the canoe and set it on the road. Examine it. Check out the bed of the truck and the cabin.

Only took like twenty minutes to do. Ramsey came back over and told Ramirez to let me out of the back.

He asks me if I do much fishing as my gear is pretty solid.

"Not as much as I would like to."

"You know, I was in the Korean conflict and fishing really helped me to control a lot of the demons I brought back with me. I read your service records and if that was me, I would never see shore again. I would steadily be in the canoe. If we have any more questions, when do you figure on being back?"

"I really don't know, like you said, I am getting away to relax. I am thinking should be home by the weekend, or if the weather goes for a dump, sooner."

He wished me luck and sent me on my way.

Fuck, if this cop is playing the good guy cop, he should be given an Academy Award.

I grabbed my knife off the hood, started up the truck and continued off on my journey.

How appropriate that I threw on Foghat's "Fool for the City" in the 8-track player. And I kept looking in my mirrors until I was out of the city.

I pulled into Lakeport and hit the bait and tackle shop after six. I grabbed a bucket of minnows and worms and several bags of ice which I put in the cooler and threw the case of beer in it.

Then I headed to Donnie's property. It was nice, I can tell he has been clearing away some of the trees. Nice flat land and right on top of the lake. It seemed you were in the middle of nowhere, but really not that far from civilization.

I unloaded the truck. Put the minnow can in the water. Gathered up as much wood as I could before it got too dark.

I set my tent up and then opened the cooler of beer as I broke a really good sweat. First two beers didn't even touch my throat. I was getting hungry, so I started a fire, broke out a can of beans and Spam. Scarfed them down and watched the sunset. This is exactly what I need.

By the time I had six beers and a couple joints into me, the sun and moon had done shift change.

The moon was a waxing gibbous moon. Still cascaded lots of rays but not as bright as the full moon. Yeah, the one in Providence was one of the brightest I ever saw.

I wonder if the search for Mazzetti is still going strong or do the cops not give a shit about a career criminal, pedo, and disgraced one of their own?

Guys like him I have no issues with making sure they no longer exist on the planet.

And why do I think that cop Ramsey would turn a blind eye to people like Mazzetti or his type being executed. He was a pretty cool cop. Yeah, that thought I will keep to myself, pretty damn sure no one in my crew would feel the same way.

A couple more beers, another joint I find myself staring at the moon.

I wonder if Charlene is staring up at it wondering where I am.

What did I do to make her run away and disappear? I treated her like gold. Never hit her. Never judged her for her past even though she fucked a couple screws I couldn't stand. Did I scare her away by wanting her to move in with me? She loved the idea in Reno, what the fuck happened once we got home?

A couple more beers and you really start to fuck with your head and self esteem.

Natasha, Lucy, Charlene, all three I truly loved, and they have all left me. I guess Lucy won that contest and now Nyah, who I really cared about, has moved about 5,000 miles away.

Am I cursed to never have a solid relationship? I know I have a different lifestyle but fuck, Donnie has Jeanie and Joseph has Cathy. Fuck, even that ape Sean Quinn has a decent wife.

And then there is Dr. Ella Mattina, and yes, she will let you know she is a doctor. What the fuck am I doing with her? She is not my type. I thought she was cool at first but fuck, she is a life sucker and not a cock sucker. That actually made me laugh out loud.

The booze and weed buzz has all of a sudden crept up on me, but I am fascinated by the moon, so tonight I am going to sleep under the stars, no tent.

I think I sang one verse of twinkle twinkle little star before passing out.

It was a great idea watching the stars, the sun beaming in around 04:30 in the morning, not such a great idea. I crawled back inside the tent and pulled the flap down and crashed out big time.

That lasted for only about an hour as the sun was pretty intense, and the tent with the flaps closed, was heating up really well.

So, I said fuck it, headed down to the lake and ran right in. That cooled me off and got rid of my hangover.

I went back and put some bacon and eggs over the fire and was on the lake fishing just after six.

The water was like a crystal-clear flawless sheet of glass. You could see the bottom of the lake including all the fish. At first, I didn't want to cast as I enjoyed seeing the whole world happening under my boat. I was fascinated by it. I remember watching The Incredible Mister Limpet and perhaps Don Knots had it right, and he found true love under the sea, surely to God I will find someone on land.

Once I decided to start fishing, I went deep into thought between casts.

Ella is gorgeous, great job, opens a lot of doors I never thought I would have access to, but her sex drive and lack of sexual prowess bores the living fuck right out of me.

Charlene has spoiled me. Mindy was certainly one hell of a nice treat, an unexpected treat.

So, I guess the key for any future regarding me and Ella is her ability to spread her legs and find her kink.

Well, I know she would have no problems getting drunk but will she give up her inhibitions? I am not expecting her to turn into Xavier Hollander overnight. But this flat on her back and no sucking cock has to change or we will be done sooner than later.

In fact, the more time I spent in the canoe the more I realized we are actually a shitty couple. I have always had a girl on the side but since I have been with Ella it is more than one girl on the side. If I would have been able to contact Anita while in Boston, I would have loved to see her lips around my cock or riding me.

I did Nyah and then Mindy last week, and zero guilt.

The only thing that stops me from breaking off with her and being honest about her lack of a sexual drive is old man Battaglia. These Italians love their God child like it was one of their own.

This will be a tricky tightrope I must walk. In fact, I will contact Mike Battaglia when I get home and ask for advice. Then he can tell his dad Sonny that I tried but knew in the long run things would not last between us. I am not even Italian, and the mom already has her racist thoughts about me. Good game plan.

I left the water around dinner time and had one hell of a fish fry. Nothing beats eating fish you caught yourself.

Once again, the great outdoors help to clear my head and issues. I felt so much of the stress that has been haunting and gnawing at me leaving. Fuck the cops, fuck the Italians, I now realize deep down Nyah will do fine in Tortola, and I will make sure her ape dad will be tied up with work up here and I will fly down to see her.

I only drank maybe four more beers, a couple joints, enough for a buzz and not fucked up.

I am now totally refreshed and revitalized. Life is good once again, Charlie Brown.

I decided to sleep under the stars again and embrace the fresh air.

A couple hours later, Mother Nature had other ideas as a thunder and lightning storm rolled in on me.

Hail and a lightning strike is what first woke me up. I must have thought I was back in Nam as I rolled onto my stomach and was looking for my rifle and the enemy. Once I realized it was weather related, I actually started to laugh, crazy as this sounds. I think it is a really good sign. I raced back to my tent, dried off as well as I could and then fell back asleep, thunderstorm and all.

I woke up several hours later and a small river was now flowing through the tent. The storm was still as intense as it was hours ago.

Yeah, time to bug out and head home, the skies weren't clear, but my head certainly was, thank fuck.

By the time I took down the tent and loaded up the canoe I was drenched.

I drove home wearing my shorts and no top. Double wipers all the way.

Didn't even bother to stop off at Donnie's shop. I needed a shower and to get into clean dry clothes.

I pulled the truck in the driveway and pulled the gate across and locked it shut.

As I walked up the stairs you could hear my feet swish and see the puddle of water on every step.

I headed right to the shower and spent the next twenty minutes in there under hot water.

I toweled off and headed for the answering machine. Let's see what bullshit is coming my way.

Janine called to say my rocker friends from Seattle want ten t-shirts and they will be in town this weekend. Rachel wants to know where I am and wants to hook up for a beer. George and Ruby want to hook up for beers before they head back to Texas. Oscar gave me his new phone number and said to call him when I get a chance. I wonder how long till the cops tap his phone or he starts to tap his female neighbors? Mike Battaglia tells me the old man is in town and wants to talk to me about my relationship with Ella. Whatever stress has left is starting to come back mighty fast, fuck sakes. And a very pissed off Ella, several from her, including the last one saying I drove by her two days ago with a canoe in the back of my truck. Her last words were, "If you want to end our relationship at least have the set of balls and decency to do it in person."

Double and triple fuck sakes. I think I better get on the blower to her right away. I called her home and got no answer. So, I called her office and they said she was with a patient. So, I asked that she give me a shout at home.

I purposely stay off the phone and after about an hour the phone rings and it is Ella.

"I have a couple minutes between patients. Where have you been, Mitchell?"

So, I have to come up with a lie, a lie that has some truth to it.

"I have been in Chicago. Sorry I never got a chance to tell you, it was a top priority and high risk take down. I was called in at the last minute, sorry for the no notice."

"You couldn't call me from Chicago?"

"I sat on someone the whole time. This guy was a really bad guy with lots of street smarts."

"Oh really, and do you think I have street smarts or am I some rich naive doctor as I fucking saw you drive by me a couple days ago, yep in your truck with the canoe in the back. Let me guess some big old bad catfish was your next person to bring or reel in?"

Fucking nailed like Jesus on the cross. Unlike Ella, I do have street smarts and people smarts. Once again, some truth within the lie.

"One of the guys I was working with, Chuck, well he was killed by the perp we were watching. I know Chuck from previous jobs and Vietnam, it kind of fucked me up so I needed to head to the wilderness. Donnie owns some property at Clear Lake. I had to clear my head, sorry."

I heard a faint gasp, then came the words that I knew I was safe, "Sorry Mitchell. I wish you weren't in this line of work to be honest with you."

"Thanks Ella, I am thinking of taking some time off from it. I have a few pokers in the fire for other stuff. Listen, you want to have dinner tonight?"

"My Godfather Sonny Battaglia is in town, and he is taking the family out for dinner. Mike says you have met his dad. Why don't you come along?"

"Is Mike joining you guys?"

"Yes, he is, come along and than we can go back to my place, and I can help you relax."

Fuck, maybe she is starting to realize I need her to be more aggressive as her sultry voice gave me a semi.

"Sure, thanks for the invite. Where and when and am I picking you up?"

"Martin's steakhouse as Uncle Sonny says he misses fresh lobster caught an hour ago. I will meet you there as I have some stuff to do first."

I called Mike and he asked how things were. I told him I will let him know tonight over dinner as Ella invited me. He said good as we need to talk in person about something. I said no problem and wondered what was up.

I called Rachel and got her voice mail. I can't remember the lawyer's office where she is working out of off hand. Yeah, I want to take grandpa to the Monterey Jazz Festival in September.

I called Oscar and it rang eight times before he answered it, he was out of breath. I asked if he had a chick with him. He laughed and said I know him too well. He said he would call me back.

I called Jerry at the gym and asked if George and Ruby were still in town. He said they are leaving tomorrow night. I told him I am tied up tonight but would like to see them before they leave. He said they have been hitting the gym around nine so why don't I join them and then have lunch and beers afterwards. I told him that works out well and would see him then.

I guess I better pack my gym bag in the car tonight as I'm not sure if I am going back to Ella's or she is coming here. That voice of hers still had me horny and hard.

I went downstairs to see if Janine had heard anymore from the rockers from Seattle. And yes, I still had a hard-on. Janine looked down and started to laugh and asked how happy I was to see her.

You know what, we have flirted and become close, right now I am feeling the most sexually aggressive towards her that I ever have. Fuck it, lets see where this goes and if she says no or I make her feel totally uncomfortable. This will be my last flirtation with her.

"As a teen I jerked myself off to sleep many times over thinking about the way you would practice oral sex on a Popsicle. I would still love to see your tongue playing with the head of my cock before I slide my whole eight inches down your throat."

Her face lit up and her eyes squinted but in a sexy kind of way. She smiled and walked towards me as she now undid the top two buttons of her blouse.

"So, little Mitchell Strongbow used to fantasize about me sucking his cock, did he? You ramming it down my hot throat. My tongue is swirling around the head of your cock. Me swallowing a hot load of cum. Was that your fantasy?"

God damn she totally has me at a total loss of words, I couldn't answer. I nodded yes.

She came closer, looked down at my cock, seductively had her tongue do a swirl of her lips and said, "You keep jerking off thinking of me, maybe one day I will let your fantasy come true."

I shook my head and started to laugh and called her a cockteaser. She laughed and said you know it.

Back to business as I asked when the rockers are coming in. She said their flight arrives Friday night and they want to see you and pick up the t-shirts.

She bit her lower lip and asked what the ten t-shirts really code for.

"When I flirt with you, I know you will never cross the line as you are married and have two wonderful kids, and you never want to ruin what you have. And for that very reason I feel it is in your best interest as a wife and devout mother as to why you never need to know the reason why. Have you ever saw anything illegal go on within the walls of Pamdora's?"

She took a deep breath, and said in a meek voice, no.

"I would never expose you to anything that would risk you to going to jail. Cops hate me, I am a convicted felon and if they threaten you with anything, deep down you know it is bunk. You are a good person, Janine. You do an amazing job around here and if you ever feel that coming to work bothers your soul, please let me know."

Full smile now as she came over and gave me a hug and said she loves working for me and the job.

It stopped raining so I went upstairs and grabbed the truck keys and headed for Donnie's shop to drop off the canoe. He handed me a beer and asked if I found myself.

"For the most part. Either I try and corrupt Ella sexually or end it with her, and not have her Godfather end my life."

Donnie seemed confused and asked who her Godfather was

"Sonny Battaglia who happens to be in town tonight, and has invited me out for dinner with the whole family."

Donnie started to snicker and said I sure as hell know how to pick him. "A Heathen chink, as Joseph called her, the wandering off Jew Natasha, Charlene the prison chick who did a Houdini on you, Nyah Quinn whose dad is a nutty and violent as they come, and Sonny Battaglia's Goddaughter. Charlie Manson have any exes hiding at your place right now?"

"Is that what you and Joseph do to pass the time, talk about my exes?"

"Oh, Mitchell you have to admit it is kind of funny. You better treat Ella right; you know those Italians and their family"

"I had the same exact thought process. Maybe I will get lucky tonight and he will say I am not an Italian and I should end the relationship. As long as he guarantees no harm to me if I do this. Yeah, that is exactly what I am hoping for. Ella is a dud in bed. By far one of the deadest and lest adventurous fucks in my lifetime."

"Don't tell Sonny any of this, wouldn't go over very well."

I shook my head at Donnie and asked him how stupid do you think I am. He laughed once again at me.

He then asked if I found peace at the lake. I told him I was amazed and would be interested in buying some property there.

Donnie went and got me his card. The guy's name was Patrick Price, and he was a real estate guy out of Sacramento.

I asked Donnie how he knew him and was he solid.

"I served under him in Nam. Smart guy and yes very solid guy for an officer."

"I am waiting to hear back from Rachel, maybe I will kill two birds with one stone and pop by and see him if Rachel is around."

I thanked him and he wished me good luck tonight. I laughed and said hopefully he doesn't fish me out of the bottom of Clear Lake. I will see him tomorrow morning at the gym.

I went home, was still tired from the storm interrupting my sleep last night, smoked a bowl, and crashed out.

I love the outdoors, but knowing you will wake up in a dry bed is always good.

I checked out my weed stash and I did have the ten pounds for the rockers, but I will need to order some more tomorrow.

25

I got cleaned up for the Battaglia family dinner, stopped off at the bank and put in five grand cash under the Willie Hertz account, and then headed to Martin's Steakhouse.

The smoking hot hostess asked if I had reservations with a big smile. I said yes under the name Battaglia I believe. She smiled and said to follow her. On the way over she asked if I was Mitch Strongbow? I said yes, I am, and did I know her as I looked at her name tag that said Kimberly.

"Not really other than you coming in here." She was flirting with me and any other time I would be asking what time she gets off at, taking her out for drinks, and then seeing if I can get her off sexually. But with a whole table full of Battaglia's and their muscle sitting at a table away, not cool.

Ella spotted me and then came racing over and gave me a big hug, saying she really misses me. Mike came over and shook my hand as did Ella's dad. The mom gave me the up and down stare and looked into her wine glass.

I walked over to Sonny and said it was good seeing him again.

He shook my hand, gave me a little slap on the face and said, "My sister tells me you and Ella are an item."

I answered yes sir, as Ella came in and side hugged me.

He said we will talk later about this. And yes, my mouth became dry and hard to swallow all of a sudden. Not the greatest before ordering a steak dinner.

But I did know how to get my mouth wet, beer, lots of beer.

It helped me relax and realize I have killed for Sonny, so he knows I am solid.

After dinner, Mike asked me to go outside and have a cigar with his dad. The bodyguards of course came with us and on the way out, Kimberly was giving me the look. I nodded and looked straight ahead, total discipline, but that doesn't mean I won't forget where she works.

One of the bodyguards passed out the cigars, Sonny said they were Cuban.

We lit them up and after a couple puffs Sonny asked what my intentions with Ella were. I looked at Mike who pressed his lips tightly together.

I made sure to make eye contact and said, "I really enjoy being in her company, she is a great person and fun to be around, sir."

"Yes, she is everything you said. Do you see yourself marrying her? And do you love her?"

I believe right now honesty, to a certain degree, is the right answer.

"Too early to tell. And no, I don't love her. We have different lifestyles, and I am pretty sure your sister doesn't really like me."

"You are right on both fronts; my sister calls you the half breed Nazi."

I started to snicker as did Mike and Sonny.

"Listen Mitch, I think you are a good solid citizen in the criminal world. You have never let me down. I have to agree with my sister that if things got serious, and you asked for Ella's hand in marriage, my sister would say no. She would ask me to have a word with you. I hope you appreciate the predicament I am in being her Godfather."

"I fully respect where you are coming from as I have a daughter myself and would only want the best for her. I believe that if I were to end things with her tonight she will know where this is coming from, and it will cause more grief in your family. Moms and daughters have enough of a volatile relationship. Let me end the relationship in time. I will do it with respect, but I ask for one favor and one favor only, sir."

Sonny nodded and asked what the favor was.

"I never want your sister to know that I am going to end the relationship. She will start to slam me more and more in front of Ella. It will upset Ella even more and she may become more defiant to her mom and will want to keep the relationship going at any cost including her accidentally forgetting to take her birth control. I don't want that, and I know you certainly wouldn't want that."

Sonny laughed and said I was wise young man for a half-breed Nazi.

He completely agreed with my logic. And said he will put me up for a weekend once I am no longer with Ella.

He asked if I have heard from Albert and how is he doing?

I told him I get the odd letter, but the screws watch everything. I said he and Sammy have just over four months left in San Quentin. Will be nice to see them both again.

Mike said maybe we should all head to Vegas for New Year's Eve. Ring in 1976 in Sin City. I said I was down for it.

We finished our cigars, and all came in together. On the way to the table, I am thinking to myself *Mike is a fucking hypocrite*. He went out with my sister and after a discussion in which I voiced my concerns all was good and I allowed the relationship to move ahead with my blessing. He didn't say shit outside.

And yeah, I was going to end things with Ella sooner then later, I don't like being told I have to, fucking Italians.

Ella watched me the whole time coming back to the table, she had an ear-to-ear smile on her face. She even stared at my cock and gave me a wink.

We had a couple more drinks and then Sonny said he was heading back to Vegas in the morning so when he gets up to leave the table, that means the party ends.

He gave Ella a long hug goodbye, shook my hand, and said it was good to see me again.

Ella's mom invited us back to their place for a night cap, but Ella said she wants to spend some quality time with me. Her mom looked like someone jabbed a dagger into her eye, twat.

I walked Ella to her car and asked her place or mine. She said my place as I have no neighbors that will complain about the sounds they are about to hear.

I gave her a long kiss and was shocked as she was stroking my cock through my dress pants. This is not the Ella I know. I told her to follow me to my place.

The whole drive I am thinking is she is finally loosening up now that I have been told to end it with her as I know it will be in my best interests shall we say.

I waited for Ella outside on the street and once she parked her car she got out and walked aggressively towards me.

"God, I have missed you and your cock. I have been so horny for you, Strongbow."

Seriously, what happened to sweet Ella? Then again, she was boring, I like this version.

She was grabbing my ass the whole time going up the stairs and as soon as we reached the main floor, I picked her up and started to kiss her as she straddled me.

In between long French kissing she told me to take her into the bedroom and fuck her hard.

I carried her into the bedroom and was necking the whole way.

We ripped each other's clothes off and I asked Ella did she plan on keeping her glasses on. "I have missed you so much I want to see your body, cock, and that look on your face when you ejaculate inside me."

"How about my cock sliding down your throat as I play and eat your pussy, you want that, Ella?"

She answered with a trembling voice yes. I am not going to turn down this offer so as she was flat on her back, I got myself into a push up position and targeted my cock right over her sweet lips. I so wanted to see this. I didn't start to lower my lips onto her pussy until I saw my cock go into her mouth and I don't mean the head, I mean a couple inches of meat down her throat.

She tried her best, but her inexperience showed as her hand and stroking timing was off, and her teeth were starting to do more harm than good on the head of my cock.

I did a helicopter spin and threw myself right into her. Her eyes looked huge as I pounded her with everything I had.

I kept looking at her and was asking is this what you what. At first, she nodded her head, and I would demand she talk until she finally started getting right into it.

And that totally turned me on; I would say more than anything we have ever done in the bedroom. Suffice to say my whole body was getting warm and I knew I was about to shoot a monster load and seeing at how Ella has had a sexual awakening when I was ready to cum, I pulled my cock out from her pussy and sat on top of her and started to stroke it and shoot my hot load all over her face.

Those big eyes that were watching me were now closed tight along with her lips. She was moving her head around trying to dodge my load, but I was shooting the mother loads of all orgasms. Her whole face including her glasses were covered in cum. She started to mumble while slapping me on the belly.

"Ella, what are you trying to say? Open your mouth, girl; I can't hear you."

I thought it was cute her mumbling got off me especially considering I got off on and all over her.

I lay on my back and started to laugh as Ella wiped the cum on her lips off with her hand and a disgusted look on her soaked face.

"I am glad you find humor in this," said a pissed off Ella as she was now wiping off the mess I left on her glasses.

She sighed, jumped up out of bed and went into the washroom and washed every last drop I shot on her off her face.

She came back in and said, "All you guys are the same?"

"What do you mean by that?" I could tell there was some history to her statement but what she told me had me in the red.

At first, she was hesitant until I said you have no secrets, surprised my nose didn't break though her glasses with that lie.

"Do you know who Matt Burns is?"

I nodded yes and my gut tells me I don't like where this story is going.

"He came onto me every single day at training camp."

"What do you mean? He came onto you?"

Ella stared at me, and she wasn't sure if she should proceed or not with her story.

"I promise I won't get mad or do anything stupid."

"As long as you promise not to tell my dad as he would have a heart attack. First day of training camp is complete physicals. We have to do the cough test for hernias. Burns, who now professes to have found Jesus, comes out wearing a towel. I ask him to remove the towel and he is fully hard and asks if I like what I saw."

My heart was racing as I could see that creep saying something like that. I asked what happened next.

"I told him if he ever did this kind of nonsense again, I would fail his medical."

"That's my girl, and you said everyday at camp he would come on to you, how?"

"He would ask me out for dinner and drinks. Meanwhile he was bragging to my dad how he reunited with the love of his life, converted her to this born-again religion of his, and asked her to marry him. This guy was engaged for a whole week and was still acting like some single Playboy. I actually feel sorry for his fiancée, she would be a fool not to see through him, and an even bigger one to walk down the aisle with him."

All I can think of is laying a beating on Burns. How dare he come onto Ella? that motherfucker will pay for this!

Ella could tell I was really wound up over this and she once again made me promise I will not say anything to Burns or her dad.

I nodded my head yes and said let's smoke a pipe as I have to wind down a bit.

Every exhale I pictured myself bloodying Burns, fucking goof.

We both had a pretty good buzz when Ella said she wants to talk to me about something; she seemed really bothered. So, what else has taken place while I was away?

She asked to hold my hands and look her in the eyes.

"Mitch, I am really concerned about your bounty hunting job. That could have been you who were killed. Don't you think maybe it's time for a better job that doesn't include dealing with the criminal element?"

She is so cute when she shows concern even if I am laughing on the inside.

"You don't have any patients that are ex-cons?"

"Yes, I do Mitch, but they are not shooting bullets at me."

"I appreciate your concern, baby, I truly do. Chuck got stupid and let his guard down and was killed because of it. I spent four years in the jungle and never let my guard down, I know better. And to be brutally honest with you, I couldn't handle a Monday to Friday day job. I love the rush; you do know I am an adrenaline junkie or at least that is what the shrinks at the hospital at Clark Air Force base say."

She believed everything I told her, even if she didn't like to hear it.

We went back to the bedroom and started to make out. I noticed Ella really looking at my scars really closely this time. Her eyes started to well up with tears. I hugged her and told her all is good, what doesn't kill you makes you stronger, right.

We ended up fucking one more time, but I was the only one into it.

She truly has a heart of gold, and yes it will kill me once I end our relationship.

We both got up with the alarm clock; I asked if she felt like a quickie, she said sure as long as I keep my cock away from her face, well her face turned red when I asked about her ass.

Afterwards, she made us a killer breakfast before she headed to work, and I headed to the gym.

I jumped on the bike, and as I pulled up to the gym, Jerry and

Donnie were out front talking to George and Ruby.

Hugs from the boys all the way around. Everyone seemed to be in a good mood. I guess Alaska went better than expected. But I know better than to ask, however I do expect some cash coming my way if the Disciples do patch over to the Hounds.

As we were shooting the shit, I asked Jerry if Matt Burns has been in lately.

Jerry shook his head and said, "Yeah that asshole still comes in, why?"

"Cocksucker has been coming onto Ella at training camp, he even came out wearing only a towel, dropped it and was fully hard and asked if she liked it."

Ruby asked who this goof was. I told him he plays for the 49ers.

"Sounds like there is a hole in the desert with his name on it."

Jerry said Burns has already been warned this year about being kicked out and banned from the gym for coming on to the females at the gym too strongly.

"Fuck man, you go to ban him please let me show him the door, face first of course."

What a fucking goof he is. The more I hear about him the more I want to put on a ski mask and grab a baseball bat. I'd love to break his legs and end his career sooner than later.

With all of us pumped up, we went inside, got changed and then started to work out together. Today was back and chest, a little push and pull.

I was spotting Ruby on the bench when Jerry motions for me to turn around. Well God damn if it isn't Matt Burns himself strutting into the locker room.

Fucking asshole was all the boys needed to hear as I headed to the locker room.

Weights couldn't even get me as pumped as I am right now. My brain is now joining my muscles in battle mode. He will come at me like I am a QB. Well, I played middle linebacker as well and I know what he will do.

Figures that he is looking at himself in the mirror, I am sure he hugs himself to sleep every night.

He looks up at me and he can sense I am in an aggressive mode, he straightens up and asks what's going, with a scowl on his face.

He now gets into a defensive mode body wise as he is loosening his wrists. He is not showing any fear at all.

"What's going on is you hit on my old lady, like a fucking creep, you goof."

"And who is your old lady?" he said in a defiant tone.

"Ella Mattina. You know? The doc who did your physical."

His face changed and now it showed fear as the rest of the boys entered the locker room. And the boys were not empty handed as George and Ruby had cannons in their hands.

Ruby walked towards him pointing a 357 magnum and said, "Mitch asked you a question. I strongly suggest you answer him, or I will spray your brains all over the fucking wall, and then throw your lifeless body in the bay for the sharks to feed off."

Burns has to see everyone is wearing a Hell Hound MC t-shirt and George and Ruby have different chapters on theirs.

"I am sorry, Mitch; I had no idea that was your woman. I promise it won't happen again. Please, I meant no disrespect."

He stuck his hand out in friendship. I extended my hand, and before they met, I struck him in the windpipe with two fingers.

He collapsed to the ground trying to catch his breath. I stood over him and said, "This time you got lucky, you say anything to anyone, next time I will aim one inch higher, and it will collapse your windpipe."

Ruby told him in no uncertain terms, "Just thought I would give you fair warning; I am the national enforcer for the Hell Hounds. I echo what Mitch said. You rat, or bug his woman, or any woman as far as that goes, you won't even hear the shot coming, tough guy." Now Ruby is a stocky bastard that has this dark aura around him. He intimidated me the first time I met him in Texas, and that takes a lot.

Jerry told Burns to pack up his shit as he is now barred from the gym.

All five of us escorted him out, like taking out the trash. I thanked the boys and said lunch was on me.

We finished our workouts, got showered then we all jumped on our bikes and headed to this BBQ place right off highway 1, in Sana Cruz. Best steak on a bun you will ever find. Cheap beer which was good as these boys can pound them back.

Needless to say, the customers there before us had no problems giving us a picnic table they were sitting at, as the boys were all wearing their club colors.

Most of the talk while we were eating had to do with family as George is married to Jerry's sister Val. We all told Ruby how he would love hunting on the Strongbow land this fall.

He said he would be honored to come along with us. I said Oscar can fly us up and this way we are not such a heat score.

George said no kidding. Imagine all of us taking a commercial jet and checking our hunting rifles at the desk? The FBI would have us all in interview rooms asking what we are really up to.

With everyone present and in a good mood, I decided to ask about Alaska, so I am not left off the cash train.

Ruby then had an inquisitive look on his face and asked me how solid Oscar really is.

"I served with him in Nam and did time with him in San Quentin, why?"

Ruby laughed, shook his head and said, "I don't dig the vibe I get off the guy. I did some spying on him and the fucker was banging Jovanoski's wife for fuck sakes. Can you imagine the fallout if Tommy or a Disciple found out what I did? I know he is your buddy, but I stuck a gun in his face and asked if he wanted to be buried up here."

Donnie looked at me and shook his head no in disgust.

"I think the two of them have been fucking each other for a while now. He is solid, having been in hundreds of fire fights with him. And yeah, no way would I leave him around Ella or any other female."

George said, "We might be heading back up next week. Mitch, come with us. You said you wanted to hunt and fish up here. Take Oscar with you. We will pay you to babysit him."

"I would like that. When were you guys thinking?"

Jerry said next weekend. I said that works.

The boys were heading to Los Angeles tomorrow morning and asked if I wanted to come even though it was a club run. I passed as I have the Seattle rockers coming in. Speaking of which, I have to contact Basil at SOL records and find out exactly what he needs.

We left after a couple hours. I love hanging with these guys, but no way could I join the club.

26

When I got back home, Janine came out and told me that Laura and Julie from Seattle left me the phone number of the hotel they are staying at.

So, I called them from Pamdora's. Little safer from my own phone line.

Laura answered the phone and was more than happy to hear from me. I asked if she and Julie had any plans tonight as my boss owns a bar that has live bands.

She said that was cool, it would be even better if the boys could come.

I told her that is no problem at all. I said the only problem is that I don't have enough seats for everyone. So, she asked for the address and said she will meet us there around nine.

I thanked Janine, gave her a hug, and told her to have a good weekend.

"Two sisters, Mitch; will that be a first for you?" she said laughingly.

"No, I have done several sisters, the Vigoda sisters when I was a teen, yeah, they were fun."

"Is Ella coming with you guys, and are they really rockers from Seattle?"

"Yeah, they are. They are here to sign a record deal with SOL records."

Her eyes lit up.

"Mitch, see if they can talk to the SOL people about rock and concert tees"

I looked at her and said, "I fucking love you. That is brilliant and I actually know one of the big wigs at SOL. In fact, he wants to see me about something. I think tomorrow I will show up with the band and have a meeting with Basil. I will give you a bonus if they start to use our merchandise."

Both of us were smiling, I would still love to fuck her or see my cock in her mouth, but I am glad she is the stronger one and won't let that happen.

I went upstairs and called Ella, said some friends from out of town are here and they are going to the Drunken Leprechaun and would she like to join us.

At first, she said she wanted to stay in and have a nice quiet night with me, you know dinner and drinks. Fuck that, I want to party.

So, we both sat in silence, not giving in, things will be ending soon between us. I have to do it with respect.

She spoke first, "I am not really interested in going to a loud bar tonight, it has been a really long and exhausting week. How about we do dinner and then either I will go with you for a bit, or I will come home, and you drop by after the bar. Does that work?"

"Yes, that works, what are you craving for dinner?"

"You," then she laughs, "I am craving Mandarin, sound good?"

I told her it did, and I would meet her at the restaurant.

Dinner was good as was the conversation, of course the three glasses of wine that Ella drank helped.

She asked if she would like my friends or not. I said they are in a rock band and are here to sign a deal with Summer of Love records.

She asked kind of nervously were they hippies? Like they have some plague or something.

"Rock musicians, hippies, I guess. They are decent people. Like you and I, they like their drink and pot, no needles or coke, hon, but bloodthirsty zombies living in their basement."

She laughed and said I am a zombie asshole.

I guess she had enough of a good time. She said to follow me to her place, and she would drop her car off and she would jump in mine and hit the bar with me. I was actually glad she decided to come along.

We smoked a joint on the way to the bar and Miss Mattina was in fine form, nice and mellow.

Pat and Sean Quinn were working the door. Sean gave me the nod.

I asked if anyone has been asking for me. He said yeah, they are sitting near the bar.

Still hard to ever get a true read off Sean, such a cold-hearted bastard, if I get a chance later on, I will ask if Nyah got out of the country OK.

We walked over and I introduced Ella to everyone and of course she corrected me and said for the thousandth time it was *Doctor* Ella Mattina.

As we took our seats, Christine came over and took our drink orders. Ella asked what type of wine we carry. Christine laughed and said we carry no wine.

Ella then shot me a dirty look as if I am the person who orders the booze here.

She then ordered a double vodka on the rocks while I ordered a couple pitchers of draught beer for the table.

Laura said they are meeting Basil tomorrow at noon to sign their contract. I asked if they wouldn't mind me showing up as I have some business with Basil.

Ella looked confused and asked what type of business. I told her about rock t-shirts.

Laura looked at me, raised an eyebrow and smiled. Yes, she caught on that Ella knows nothing of my weed dealing. She then whispered something to Julie who now looked at Ella and then me. Smart chicks anyways.

The band tonight was a blues band, the main guy was a well-known session player who actually played on the Howlin Wolf Sessions.

Damn, these guys were super tight. I made sure to watch all the band members from Seattle. Their faces lit up like kids on Christmas day opening up their gifts.

After the band's first set, I introduced myself as the assistant manager and asked if they wanted to go out back and smoke a joint. They said sure as did the Seattle crew and Ella. Good thing I brought a fair amount of weed with me; had a feeling it was going to be one of those nights.

Halfway through the second set Ella didn't look so good, her eyes were rolling, and she had a vacant look on her face.

I asked if she wanted to go outside and get some fresh air. She nodded her head yes, and sure as fuck as soon as she stepped outside, her knees got weak, and she bent over and started to puke. Of course, her glasses fell off and yes, she hurled on them. I am glad she puked outside rather than inside as Joseph would hear about it and I would get grief.

I kicked them off to the side and out of the pile of projectile vomit. Sean Quinn saw what was going on and asked if everything was all right.

Fuck me! Sean actually showed some concern.

"It appears the good doctor is not so good; she has had too much to drink tonight. Can you watch her for a moment while I say goodbye to my friends and get some paper towels and a bag in case, she gets sick in my car?"

Sean said no problem, she is in good hands. I stared at him for a second and not sure if I should go inside or not, he was kind of freaking me out.

But I did, I apologized and said I would see them tomorrow at noon.

Christine gave me a roll of paper towels and a brown bag for Ella.

As I came back outside, Ella looked really rough.

I thanked Sean, shook his hand, picked up the glasses with paper towels and then helped poor Ella to my car.

I was pretty buzzed myself, but not too buzzed that I didn't see a cruiser across the street watching us. My eyes were too fucked up to see the cops, but why do I have this feeling that Kurt Wilson is one of the two cops?

So, I asked Sean if he could call us a taxi, which he did.

I gave the driver a twenty to hang onto in case Ella hurled in the cab, thank God she didn't. She did, however, pass out cold against me.

I actually had to fireman carry her up the stairs as she was dead to the world.

Luckily, she is light as air as my legs were not the steadiest.

I put her in the spare bed with a bucket of water beside the bed.

Gave her a kiss on the top of her forehead then went back in the living room and checked my messages. Rachel called and invited me for dinner on Sunday. This works out well as I want to talk to that Pat Price guy about buying some land.

Tomorrow I will call both and see if I can set up some times together.

I put on some Zeppelin, sat on the couch, and rolled up a joint.

Smoked the whole doobie, and needless to say, I passed out cold right on the couch.

27

A garbage truck the next morning woke me up. It took a couple minutes to try and recall what the fuck happened for me to pass out here.

On the way to the kitchen to drink a gallon of Kool-Aid, I checked in on Ella who was snoring. I smiled and continued on my journey to quench my thirst.

I was downing the fluids as if I was in the middle of a desert. I looked at the clock in the kitchen and it was after nine. Lots of time to hook up with the Seattle crew at SOL. I poured a glass for Ella and brought in a couple aspirins.

I kissed her on the forehead, Ella really struggled to wake up and once she did, she asked where her glasses were. I said soaking in the sink.

She started to rub her forehead and asked what happened, and why she was in the guest bedroom.

I told her my fears and everything that went down last night. As soon as she said her head was pounding, I handed her the meds and the drink.

"Doctor Strongbow says take two of these and call me when you are naked."

I laughed and Ella said please no unnecessary noise.

"Get some more sleep, baby; I have some calls to make." I kissed her on the forehead and then left the room.

I called Rachel back who was finally home. I said dinner tomorrow would be great and I had an idea I wanted to talk to her about in person.

She said perfect and would see me around two, and I can have a visit with Uncle Karl and Aunt Sandy.

I then pulled out the phone number of Pat Price. I called him at his office and told him I was a good friend of Donnie Terek, and I would like to talk to him about some land purchase. Pat said he was on a tight schedule tomorrow. How does three sound? I said good. He gave me his address.

I headed back to the kitchen to make a pot of coffee and make some breakfast.

Eventually, Ella made her way into the kitchen, and she asked who I was talking to on the phone.

I told her I was headed to Sacramento tomorrow to buy some land and have dinner with Rachel.

"Well, I was kind of hoping we could have dinner with my family tomorrow."

"Sorry, but I haven't seen Rachel in a couple weeks. You know how much she means to me, right?"

"No, I respect that, Mitch. Have fun with your sister." My back was up as that is what Charlene and I had our last big fight about.

"Now how about you and I having some fun right now? So horny for you, baby."

Ella laughed and said sex is the last thing on her mind. But a cup of coffee is the first thing on her mind.

So, we sat at the table as I ate, and Ella was really deep in thought.

I asked if she was all right. She said she was really hungover. I asked if she wanted to smoke a joint. She shook her head no.

She then asked what my plans were for the day. I told I was heading to SOL records for noon. I asked if she remembered this conversation at all last night. She stared straight ahead and shook her head no.

Something had her thinking really deep. But if she doesn't want to say what, I am not going to annoy her.

I asked if she wanted to jump in the shower with me. She said no and asked if I could I drive her home.

I told her I am kind of pressed for time and my car is at the bar. I can drop her off at home and then I was going to hit SOL right afterwards on the bike.

Yeah, she didn't recall us taking a taxi back here. And I know she is not a fan of the bike, but it clears my head. She can always take a taxi home and that is exactly what she did.

Before she left, I asked if we were O.K? She answered she was not sure. She said she would call me later on.

I know I am to end this, but there is a part of me that feels a bit sad inside. I hate seeing anyone I am in a relationship feeling down.

After Ella left, I grabbed a long shower, dried off and smoked a joint. Put a quarter bag down my pants and jumped on my bike and headed for SOL records.

28

The ride was short, but it always clears my head especially with me hurting a bit this morning.

I parked my bike and asked this cute little redhead receptionist if Basil was in.

She said he was and was expecting me. I said sort of, tell him Mitch Strongbow is here to see him.

She told me to have a seat and she would call him. As I looked around the whole building had a very relaxed feel to it. No, it was a very *positive* feel. It had a 60s feel to it with all kinds of posters and records on the wall from that era, my favorite era.

After a couple minutes, Basil appeared and shook my hand and said he was sorry but today he is super busy.

"Yeah, you are signing Julie and Laura from Seattle, correct?"

Basil was shocked, he even started to laugh and asked how I knew this.

"I am Mitch Strongbow; you forget I know everything that happens in this city?"

Basil wasn't sure how to answer that, but he did have a smirk on his face, his only response was, *really?*

"No, I actually ran into the band when I was doing an overnighter in Seattle, partied with them at the Drunken Leprechaun last night."

"I hear good stuff about the bands he has in there. One of the better bars for music. Do you know the manager or owner?"

My turn for the smirk. "I actually work for the owner. I could introduce you to Joseph, that is not a problem."

Basil's receptionist called him on the phone, and he said thanks for letting me know.

"Well Mitch, it appears they are running a little late. Would you like a tour of the studio and offices?"

I said that would be great. Basil said they spent a lot of cash in having the most up to date equipment and technology in the music business.

We went into the one mixing studio, and he showed me how everything is blended together and how each instrument can be heard all by itself.

I never knew how complex it was putting an album together really was.

He said his guys on the sound and mixer boards are almost as important as the musicians themselves, he said.

We then went up to the second floor where the brains and cash flow behind SOL are. He knocked on the CEO's door and asked if she was busy, she said no come in.

Behind this big desk was this blonde doing some sort of paperwork.

As he went to introduce us the blonde's baby blue eyes got almost as big as her smile.

"Mitch Strongbow, meet Mindy Matheson." We both laughed and said we have met before.

Mindy got up and came over and gave me a big hug. She asked what brought me here.

"Basil and I have some mutual friends. Doing a tour. What an amazing place you have here."

"Thanks, Mitch. My husband and I bought into Basil's idea as we agree that Disco music quite frankly sucks."

I told her I completely agree.

Now, with Mindy being married and Basil obviously knowing her husband no way would I ever be obvious that Mindy and I have been some pretty hardcore lovers, and to be honest, I really dig what she brings to the bedroom and if she wants to keep it going, I am more than game.

Mindy's phone rang and she said, "Yes, he is here. Yes, I will let him know."

Pretty sure that call is not for me.

"Basil, the Stuart sisters are downstairs waiting for you."

"O.K thanks. Mitch, you wanna join us?"

Time to see if Mindy wants to play or not.

"I will join you in a couple minutes, I want to get caught up with Mindy."

He said sure and told Mindy we will meet in thirty minutes in the boardroom to sign the legal contracts.

As soon as Basil left, Mindy squinted her eyes and asked if this was a fluke.

"I swear on my daughter this is just a fluke, or perhaps fate."

She put her arms around my neck and said her ass hurt for days afterwards but loved every moment of us together in Chicago.

I pulled her in tight and started to neck with her while giving her ass a squeeze.

After we broke free, Mindy started to caress my cock and asked what exactly I was doing here today.

"On the tour Basil said he is looking for some muscle and someone who has access to…well…you know."

"Yes, I do know, and do you?"

"I have access to everything and anything, legal or not."

Mindy smiled and asked if I wanted to fuck her again.

"I would love to fuck you again. I have been thinking about you ever since Chicago to be honest."

"You know I am married, so we will have to be discreet. And how is your doctor girlfriend?"

"She bores me, I assume much like your husband." She laughed and said something like that.

"My husband is out of town this weekend. Do you have plans?"

"Tonight, I am free, out of town tomorrow. Why don't we go out for dinner, drinks and see how the night goes?"

"I would like that very much. I have to go downstairs and welcome our newest band from Seattle."

"Can I go downstairs with you, I actually know the Stuart sisters and the rest of the band, good solid people. I just have to tell Laura something then I have to split."

Mindy said of course I can. Fuck, she is a cool sexy chick.

I asked Laura when they are heading home. She said they have a flight Sunday night at seven. I told her to slide by my place at noon tomorrow and I will have their weed for them. She said that worked. I once again congratulated them.

I told Basil to meet me at the Drunken Leprechaun on Monday night around eight.

Then I wrote down my phone number and told Mindy to call me and that I am looking forward to seeing her tonight.

She said she would call me around four and we can make plans.
I gave her a wink and headed for home. So much shit to get ready;
weed and the cash flow for my meeting with Pat Price.

29

I went home and realized I am actually short a kilo. Fuck sakes, good thing I checked.

I have to get my Mustang. I went into Pamdora's and saw Beth in there working.

"Are you really busy right now?"

"Kind of. Why, Mitch?"

"I have to pick up my car from the Leprechaun. Do you drive stick?"

She said she did, so I asked if she could close the store for like twenty minutes. She laughed and said I was the boss.

I shook my head and said oh yeah. I asked how her music was coming along.

She said she was actually playing next Sunday night at the Leprechaun.

I smiled and she asked what was up.

"I know the manager of Summer of Love records. I am going to call him and have him check you out."

Her turn to smile, "Really, Mitch? No bullshit?"

"I was at the recording studio today actually. I promised I would help you."

She came over and gave me a big hug and said if I was a chick, she would suck my pussy right now. That was by far the funniest line I have heard in a long time.

Beth hung on tight on the ride over, man she had a nice size chest, what a waste.

She drove the Mustang back. I told her to remind me about Basil and next weekend.

I then jumped on my bike and headed to the Oakland clubhouse to see Jerry and order some more weed.

I got there in time as they were headed for some oink and doink at the San Jose club.

They tried their best to get me to come along, but I really wanted to fuck Mindy all night.

I ordered ten kilos, and I told Jerry it has to be delivered tomorrow by noon as I have people leaving town and they are new customers.

He promised one of the boys would be there before noon. He said it might be smart of me to get a safe house for dope as if the cops raid my place, I don't want to lose Pamdora's.

I thanked him and told him I would think about it, jumped on my bike, and headed home. I grabbed a long hot shower, yes the cold rinse off, and waited for Mindy's call.

Four o'clock right on the money she called. She always calls me handsome and asks what I was thinking of for tonight.

I said a nice dinner, drinks and then back to my place to work off the booze and meal.

She laughed and said it sounds like the perfect date. She said she had to go home and grab a shower, change her clothes and would be over. I told her what she had on looked amazing and she can always jump in the shower here.

There was a pause and Mindy said that will only work if I join her in the shower. I told her what kind of a host I would be if I didn't join her.

I did a quick clean up. Lit some cherry incense wicks and put a bottle of Vodka in the freezer for her. I checked out my vinyl collection of blues, note to self-get some blues on vinyl. I found one...Johnny Winter and that would be it.

Mindy arrived about twenty minutes later. She said the t-shirt store looked interesting. I said I owned it and asked her if she would like a tour.

We walked in and I introduced her to Beth. I said that she was an inspiring musician that I am going to ask Basil to listen to hear her play. Once I said who Mindy was, her eyes lit right up. All they did was talk about music and who the record label now has under contract. Never thought a lesbian would be a cock block, hmm I wonder if Mindy swings that way, if so, that would be a hot threesome.

I looked at my watch and knew Pamdora's closes in an hour and half. So, I asked Beth if she wanted to smoke a joint. I think Mindy knew I was up to something the way she looked at me, but Beth said she had plans right after work to meet her folks, and they can tell when she is high, next time she said.

Mindy said the store was really nice. I asked her where her label gets their t-shirts from. She smiled and said we can talk business later on, right now it is all about her and me in the shower.

I asked if she wanted to smoke a joint first. She looked down on the coffee table where I had a couple joints lined up, reached down, grabbed a doobie and a lighter and sparked it up. She took a couple tokes, passed it to me and said sure and then started to laugh.

As I was puffing away as she made her way to my record collection, she took out an album and put it on the record player.

She sat right on top of my lap facing me as Peter Frampton wasn't the only thing coming alive.

We were hardcore necking and groping until the joint was finished.

I then told her to put her arms around my neck. I then stood up and carried her into the bedroom and laid her on top of the bed.

"Mitch, my mouth is really parched, I need a drink, do you have any vodka?"

"I have it in the freezer, Smirnoff, how do you like it?"

She said on the rocks, same as Ella. So, I made two glasses for us and brought them to the bedroom. She asked if I stirred it. I was confused as it was on the rocks. I said no, would she like it stirred?

She told me to drop my pants and stir it with my cock. Is that fucking hot or what? I did as instructed and then Mindy took out an ice cube from the drink and put my cock in her mouth. Not the first time I have had this done. It seems all the girls who are exceptionally talented at sucking cock like to deliver this as much as I enjoy receiving this.

The burning feeling from the cold ice cube along with me horny all day didn't take long before I was shooting a hot load down Mindy's sexy throat.

Like a true champ, Mindy swallowed all of me and then polished her drink straight back.

She smiled, looked at me, and asked if I liked it. I said I loved it, and she was amazing.

"Then kiss me, Mitchell," she smiled and made the most intense eye contact. Was this a test? I thought about it and quickly realized the booze would kill any sperm and said what was left right into her belly.

So, I went in and gave her a kiss. At first it was a nice soft kiss then Mindy started to stick her tongue down my throat. Fuck it I went with her and started to run my fingers up her skirt. I could feel the heat coming from her pussy the closer I got until I started to rub her lips through her nylons. Those little soft moans drove me crazy, crazy enough I ripped her pantyhose and stuck at first two fingers into her pussy. I was thumbing the top of her pussy; she was now drenched after five minutes of this. I then added another finger and jackhammer the hell out of her cunt. I heard her have multiple orgasms as I felt her wetness roll down my forearms.

Eventually she put her hands on top of mine and said no more.

My turn to give her the seductive look. Mindy seemed astounded at first, she looked at me and said, "Holy fuck! That was amazing."

Once again, she came in for some more hard-core necking.

She then said let's order food in, and fuck and suck all night.

I love the way she thinks, I asked what she wanted to order in. She asked if I have ever eaten Indian? I started to laugh and said of course, I am half Sioux.

She then burst out laughing and said no, India the country.

Mindy asked if I trusted her. I said with my life. She asked if I like spicy food. I said I like my woman the way I like my food, spicy. She blushed, winked, and then picked up the phone and ordered our meal.

We grabbed a shower while waiting for our food to arrive. Was nice to wash and clean each other, lots of kissing. She was a sensual person indeed.

Mindy went to pay for it when the doorbell went and I said no way, she was a guest in my house.

It was like four times the price of pizza and is certainly twice as expensive as Chinese food. But I was intrigued even if it did have a funny smell to it.

I tried a bit of everything and was impressed, spicy hot which I enjoyed.

Me thinks Mindy is going to introduce me to a whole new lifestyle.

By the time we both passed out from exhaustion, I had deposited a load in her pussy, ass and down her throat one more time.

I was out for the count big time when I felt someone rocking me, I looked down and all I could see was painted nails and a massive size wedding ring.

I looked up and Mindy said someone is ringing the doorbell and pounding on the door.

My heart dropped and I thought cops for sure. So many things I can be charged for and so many different police forces.

Mindy was a little shook up by the commotion, I don't want to expose endless possibilities of criminal activities, so I told her to stay put.

I went down the stairs as quiet as I could even though my legs were shaking like Jell-O. I looked through the peephole and it was John and Scotty Kantonescu. Yeah right, my weed delivery.

I told them to come on up and I had company.

John jokingly asked if he could talk to the good doctor about getting him a prescription of anabolic steroids.

"I am sure the good doctor is home trying to sleep off a hangover, sorry brother."

I looked at the clock in the living room and it was not even eight. I asked why they were here so early, and they reminded me of the club run today and I am still invited.

I noticed both John and Scotty were not looking at me but towards my bedroom as Mindy was now coming into the living room wearing my tank top. Good thing she is short as it went below her ass cheeks.

The one thing that really struck out with me was the fact that Mindy showed no fear at all. John is one of the scariest looking intimidating guys in the club and these two were in full Hell Hound colors.

He stands over six four and weighs well over three hundred pounds; he is full of juice, so those three hundred pounds are all muscle. He has this really dark aura around him, and Mindy came right out and sat on my lap.

She looked down at the bundle of weed and said, "Breakfast is here," and then laughed. For a chick in the high society world, she fits into my world, yeah, she intrigues me to say the least.

The boys smoked a joint with us, had a screwdriver, I paid for the weed and then they were off.

Mindy asked if I wanted to grab some breakfast or go back to bed for another round. I asked why not both as I took my tank top off her.

Nothing better on a Sunday morning to have that early morning buzz, a great round of sex, and then a long hot shower together.

I asked if she wanted to jump on the back of my bike and head to this nice restaurant in San Mateo as they have the best eggs Benedict in California.

She said it sounds perfect, I asked bike or car. She said she would prefer bike, but she wore a dress here and I ripped her pantyhose.

I took a deep breath and in the bottom drawer of my dresser I pulled out a pair of Charlene's jean shorts she left here. I don't think she will be coming back for them. I handed them to Mindy and said try these on.

She did and said they fit perfectly. I had to pee and then we could hit the road.

As I came out of the washroom Mindy was looking at a 5x7 picture of Katrina and she said, "Cute kid, she has to be yours."

I thanked her and said yes. Mindy asked how often I see her.

"Never, she doesn't even know I am her dad."

Mindy shook her head and said that is sad. Then dropped it.

Before I fired up my bike I asked if she has ever been on the back of one before, she smiled and said many times and not to worry.

I jumped on the kick start, once it turned over, I told her to get on, and like Charlene her short legs made it a little awkward for her.

The whole drive there she knew when and how to lean properly and those DD tits of hers were a perfect back rest.

During breakfast, there was normal conversation, some flirting of course, and yes, Mindy performing mock oral sex on a crisp piece of sausage.

After we ate, she was drinking her coffee and I could tell something was on her mind, so I asked if everything was O.K.

"Well, I assume I will see you a lot more often at the recording studio."

"I hope so, why is that a problem?"

"No, I don't think so."

She was spooked and I think I know why.

"Look I know you are married; I would never ask you to leave your husband. But I think you are a really cool chick and I like spending time with you. If you don't want to hook up again, I will appreciate Chicago and the last eighteen hours we have spent together. I promise you I won't be annoying or make it weird."

She smiled and said she knew I wouldn't make it weird.

"Tell you what, Mitch, I too enjoy spending time with you and you really rock my world in bed. Damn you are good. My husband spends a lot of time on the road. I don't want this to sound like I am some lonely housewife using you. But I would love to call you and spend time with you. I know you have a girlfriend, so I would fully understand when you say you are tied up with her."

I pulled her in and gave her a long kiss and said, "You are a hell of a lot more fun than Ella to be honest. Yeah, this would work for me."

Her turn to pull me in and kiss me.

We stuck around for another twenty minutes before I drove her back to my place to get her vehicle. She went upstairs and gave me back Charlene's shorts for her dress. I told her if she doesn't contact me to leave a message on the answering machine for me to contact S.O.L and I will call her there.

She headed for home, and I went upstairs to wait for the Stuart sisters. Good thing Mindy left when she did as I got to the top of the stairs and my doorbell rang. I came downstairs and the whole band was present.

I told them to come on up. I broke out the beers and threw an ounce on the table and told them to help themselves.

We drank, toked and they told me they signed their contract with Summer of Love records and will be back in two weeks time to start cutting an album with them.

Julie said she has the whole weed she bought from me and is spoken for once they get back home.

John, the drummer who didn't seem to be impressed with the deal, said it would be a shame if they get caught on the plane with the weed and the dream, they have had for their whole lives is flushed down the toilet.

And then there is silence. For me that is not my problem, I respect where they are coming from, but I can't help them, or can I?

"I might know someone who can help them out and fly the dope in for you guys. But it certainly has to be worth my while."

Julie asked how much weed they would need to buy.

"If you order say a hundred pounds, I will have my one friend fly it in or I can pay someone to drive it north."

Julie asked about someone they trust with their lives to come down and pick it up.

 asked who the one person is they would trust. All of them said the same name, Eddie.

I asked what Eddie's story was. They said he is their head roadie. Said I would love him.

I respect where they are coming from, so I told them when they come back to bring Eddie. But I told them it will be Eddie and only Eddie. Cash only, no fronts.

They said that is fair. I wished them luck and said I would see them in a couple weeks.

Off they went so I grabbed an ounce for Rachel, stuffed it between my legs and headed to Uncle Karl's house.

30

On the drive over to Rachel's, my mind was racing but in a positive way.

I will launder drug money from SOL through t-shirts. Yeah, perfect way and I was pretty pumped that Mindy wants to continue what we have, the chick is amazing but having said that, she is one of the reasons I will never ever get married. I am out of town and my woman will be hooking up with some younger guy, fuck that shit. Stay single and get my rocks off and not being held accountable to anyone.

Not sure why but I love opening up my bike about a block before my aunt and uncle's house.

As I pulled up, standing on the front porch with a big smile was Rachel, that is why I opened full throttle so she could hear me coming.

I pull in the driveway and shut off the bike. Rachel walks over and says, "If it isn't my loud brother," she laughs and gives me a big hug and tells me she misses me.

I tell her, "I miss you too. Love you, sis."

She tells me she loves me and says let's grab a beer.

As we go in the house seems really quiet and I ask where everyone is. Rachel tells me they drove to Reno for the weekend, and they will be back later tonight.

I pull out the bag of weed and tell Rachel here is a gift and let's sit on the front porch and smoke a joint then.

"I remember you and Pam sending me to the store when we were younger. Is what you guys would do, get high in the house?"

I started to laugh and said yes. "Do you remember me giving you money to keep you quiet when you walked in on Lucy and me?"

She put her hand over her mouth and started to laugh. "God, I was bad for that, wasn't I?"

"You were brutal, always shaking me down for cash. Remember you would phone Tash for me, a quarter I think it was?"

She reached into her front pocket and gave me a couple quarters back and said sorry. I said what about the interest?

We both laughed about her ways of being a bratty conniving younger sister.

Now, this was excellent brother sister time.

After we smoked the joint, I asked when did Uncle Karl get a new Porsche?

Now Rachel's whole face lit up. "He didn't Mitch, that is mine, what do you think?"

"Are you serious?"

She now pulled out the keys and said dead serious.

So, we went over and had a look at her 1972 silver Targa Porsche 911. It was outstanding, in great shape for three years old, not a lot of miles.

"Listen, I have to meet this real estate guy in like an hour. Want to drive me to his place or do you want to jump on the bike? We can out for grub afterwards."

Rachel looked at my bike and said she is still having the odd nightmare about her motorcycle accident. She then asked what I was seeing a real estate guy about.

I told her the whole story and she said that sounds awesome. A place for us to fish and pitch a tent under the stars. She said sure and once I gave her the address, she said she knew exactly where his office is.

I had another beer as Rachel now switched to ginger ale.

We talked about her job and life. I asked if she was seeing anyone. She said way too busy with work. She knew of Ella, but I said it won't last the summer as I am not happy. I then asked if she heard from Tash at all. She said yes but wouldn't elaborate and because we are having such a great brother sister time I will not do or say anything to cause any tension.

Eventually, we jumped in her Porsche that she named Atticus, after Atticus Finch in To Kill a Mockingbird.

Rachel drove her Porsche like I do with Emma, or my bike, fast, really fast.

We made it to Pat's Price office in no time at all.

She asked if I wanted her to go with me, or she would grab a coffee at the corner diner and come get her when I am done.

"Sis, you are family. I have no secrets. No, come in with me."

This made her smile.

We took the elevator to the thirtieth floor where his office took up the whole floor.

Pat was president of his own real estate company that employed fourteen full time agents and clerical staff. But seeing how it was a Sunday, he was the only person around.

We walked in and I hollered for Pat. He hollered back he was on his way. When he came around the corner, I was shocked as he was wearing jeans and a Zeppelin tour t-shirt. I was truly expecting to see some square in a suit.

He stuck out his hand and introduced himself and asked if this was Mrs. Strongbow.

I laughed and said, "Sort of. This is my sister Rachel, so technically a Strongbow but Miss Strongbow."

Now, I really know my sister well and she was looking at him like a teen with a crush.

As they shook hands, they stared at each other. Fuck, did I have to break out a fire hose to bring them both out of their infatuation with each other?

I eventually had to say Pat's name twice, he apologized and said let's go to his office.

His office looked like I thought it would, very high-end furniture. He asked if we wanted a drink whether it be coffee, pop, or booze.

Rachel took a soda while Pat and I had a beer. He showed me the plots of land that were for sale at Clear Lake, and yes, there was a two-acre plot right on the water next to Donnie. I asked how much, he gave me a price, and I shook his hand and said deal. I reached in and asked if he would take a check. He said yes and did I want my lawyer to see the deed first.

I laughed and said Rachel is not only my sister, but my lawyer and handed her the deed details.

"Really? I am impressed, beauty and brains."

Oh, fuck. He now has that stupid look on his face. And of course, Rachel looks up and is starting to curl her hair around her finger.

I had to ask Rachel if everything looked good. She said yes.

Pat said he will file papers tomorrow and he can send the documents by courier, or I can slide by and pick them up.

Rachel said she can pick them up if I would like.

"Sure sis, knock yourself out."

Pat then asked where she practiced law.

"I am here in Sacramento; I work for White and Cope. Do you know them?"

"Yes, I do, a very high-end firm. I have hired them in the past. They have always either steered me in the right direction, or twice have saved my ass."

While they are flirting with each other, the big overprotective brother in me comes out. He is not wearing a wedding ring. I don't see any evidence of a wife or kid's pictures or bronzed baby boot shit in the office.

So, my back comes down a bit, I still think he might be a player though, and no matter how old or how smart Rach might be, she will always be my baby sister.

Before we go to leave, Pat apologizes and says he has some paperwork for me to fill out. Rachel volunteers to do it while Pat asks if I ride a Harley. I said yes and he said for me to follow him.

He took me to this boardroom where on the wall was a pic of him and his original business partner both on Indian motorcycles wearing their combats from Nam and green berets.

"Donnie says you were 101ˢᵗ but you went deep, Rangers, correct?"

"Rangers and SOG, I went as deep as the jungle would allow."

"Donnie says he rides with you, but you are not a Hell Hound."

"Yeah, we ride together, not into the heat score shit. And SOG taught me I don't need anyone."

He asked what I do for a living. I told him, and he asked if I ever planned on investing in real estate.

"Real estate is a great way to make cash and a great way for the government to see you making legitimate money. I would like to sit down with you and talk about it a little more."

Well, that was a calculated statement. Does he know I make money in other ways, other illegal ways? Will have to sit down with Donnie and see what gives.

"Yeah maybe, but today is not that day. I have a lot of shit to do."

"Fair enough, Mitch." I know he wanted to say something else, not sure what, and quite frankly, until I actually talk to Donnie, everything will be above board.

We went back to his office, and I told Rachel I was starving. Let's grab some grub.

Pat shook our hands and said it was a pleasure to meet us both. He took one of Rachel's business cards and said he would call her once the deed was registered, and she can bring me the documents and gave her one of his cards.

Before we left his office, Pat mentioned that he met our dad Iggy in Nam. Said he was a warrior in every sense of the word. We both thanked him; I was curious why he waited for us to leave before he told us this.

"I certainly didn't want to name drop to get your business. I wanted our first transaction to be strictly business related. Hope you both understand and forgive me for not mentioning your dad first."

That certainly impressed me, and Rach, she was all smiles.

We left and jumped into her car; she commented on what a nice guy Pat really is.

I gave her a stone face and shook my head. She laughed and said, "And cute, really cute."

I stuck two fingers in my throat and pretended to puke.

We hit this Elks Club for dinner. It had a menu of wild game on it. Nice surprise actually.

After we ordered our meals, I told Rach about the Monterey Jazz Festival in September, and I would like to invite Grandpa out to it. Ask Uncle Jack and Jerry and what she thought.

Her eyes lit right up and said that was a brilliant idea. She asked when the dates were, and I told her September 19 to 21.

"Well, the hardest thing will be getting him to leave the home and the reservation. What would we do? Grab motel rooms? As there was no way would he do the two-hour drive from San Fran to there everyday, fighting traffic and crowds and what not."

I told her that is not a problem. I will make some calls tomorrow to see about rooms. Rachel offered to throw some money in to help out with Grandpa's flight and rooms, but I said I will take care of him. Her one and only job is to convince him to come join us.

She laughed and asked why this is her job.

"Because you are the lawyer, you are used to hood winking people."

She called me an asshole, then said that maybe I was right, but only to a certain degree.

After dinner we went back to her place, and I was fighting to stay awake. Rachel asked if I was partying all night long. All I did was snicker and she shook her head and said hot date? I smiled and nodded my head yes.

"I assume not Ella either."

"You would be right once again, councillor. Good damn, you are good!"

She asked if I wanted to sleep over seeing how I was yawning my head off. At first, I said no then I realized why not. Spend the night talking to the only female who loves me as much as I love them.

We spent the majority of the night on the front porch smoking dope and telling stories about growing up as a Strongbow.

I truly sensed Mom, Dad, Jake, and Pam on the porch with us. All of them were smiling and laughing at our stories.

I spent the night, the first time I have ever crashed in this house, and I have to say it was a really cold feeling. Four walls and zero pulse.

Then again, that is exactly what Uncle Karl is like. Too business-like for me.

Mom was the complete opposite, our house growing up was so full of life, people always in and out of the house. Mom never said that we couldn't have friends drop by.

Fuck, even the bed was rock solid. Fuck, I hope Rachel never becomes stoic.

The next morning, when I woke up the house seemed even lonelier. I yelled at Rachel and no answer, it was nine. I guess she already left for work.

So, I went downstairs and made myself something to eat.

I guess all this partying and hardcore fucking has caught up with me as after I did my dishes, I sat in the living room for a couple minutes.

While trying to gain my strength I saw on the wall all these photo albums all labeled Kohler family year by year from 1932 to 1940.

Goddamn, I know nothing of my mom, the Kohler side.

I opened up the first page and there was a family portrait, but it showed five people; one adult male, one adult female, my mom, Uncle Karl and another male who was a baby, a boy I think.

Well, this appears to be a Scooby Doo Kohler mystery. I don't have a clue who he is. Maybe the rest of the pics will tell a story.

As I am going through the pictures, I never realized how beautiful my mom was as teen.

And in every family picture all of them all together they all look as if they are in the army and are all at attention.

I am totally drawn into all the pics. I find myself staring at each person and trying to get a read off each one of them.

I can tell my grandfather, the career military officer, is strict. Fuck, no smiles at all when a family portrait is taken. But there are pictures of them on vacation and it looks like they are having the times of their lives, all smiles.

Nice seeing smiles coming from my mom's face. Fuck, I miss her and every single time I hear a locomotives horn activated, I smile knowing that cocksucker Getz suffered right up till his last breath.

The more I looked through the album I became confused as to what happened to baby Kohler.

Before I knew it, I had drank a pot of coffee and Rachel was coming through the front door.

She was totally shocked that I was still here. She asked if I was all right.

Then she saw all the photo albums out.

She looked at me and said, "You really know nothing of mom's family, do you?"

I know that dad killed Grandpa Kohler during the battle of Bastogne, but I was sworn never to tell anyone.

"You are right Rach; I know fuck all. Did mom have another brother as I keep seeing this little kid getting older and older then the pics with him ended."

"That would have been your uncle Konrad. He was killed during a British air raid in 1942. You know how Grandma Kohler died, correct?"

"Mom wouldn't really talk about it. She said the advancing Russians who she hated. You hear any more than that, Rach?"

"He won't say anything, and he becomes really intense, his face goes purple and the veins in his head start to pop out."

Rach took a big breath and did a forced smile. I want to find out what happened but if he won't say shit to Rach, who he treats like his own daughter, and with me being treated like the bastard child, you know he won't say anything to me at all.

I have no doubts in my mind her death was a direct result of the Russians, no good commie bastards.

I think about little Katrina thousands of miles away and me not being able to protect her. Fucking Stan better step up that way or he will pay the piper, called me. I always have and more so then now I will make sure I am there for Rachel.

"You know, sis, anyone ever threatens you or tries to harm you in any way you call me, and I will be there faster than the speed of light."

Rach then had this really curious look on her face and said that someone I know asked her out today and she wanted to talk to me about it.

Fuck, all the guys I know are bad guys, she already went out with Mike Battaglia who is the biggest mob boss in northern California. I know I would bust her balls if it was a full patch from the Hell Hounds and I am pretty sure Jerry would kick the guy out of the club.

So, I took a big breath, had a curious smile on my face with my eyes squinted and asked who.

"Pat Price, he said he would have the documents ready on Friday and would like to take me out to dinner and we could both go over them and see if there were any issues."

"Really, Rach? is that the line he used to ask you out?" I started to laugh and now it was Rachel's turn to squint her eyes except there was no curios smile like I had, her smile was straight.

"It's dinner, Mitchell."

"That is how it starts, I know his type, good looking sly business guy."

"And your last steady, Charlene, did she play the shy librarian and kinky in bed act quite well? And, what about the good Doctor Ella? I guess she isn't that good in the sack, is she?"

Everything Rach said made sense, but I am the big brother, my job is supposed to look out for her.

Eventually after a minute I started to laugh, and Rach's face went red and asked what was so funny.

"You are bang on, yeah, I have had some interesting chicks. So, no drinks until you have read the legal shit O.K?"

"I promise you while waiting for the main entree I will go over the deed purchase."

I stuck around for another hour before heading to the Drunken Leprechaun and meeting Nigel.

I think as soon as I get there   , I really need to get a hold of Oscar and warn that horny bastard that his dick will truly be the death of him. Fuck, and Joseph thinks *I am* bad. Yeah, after what Ruby said, not good.

As I arrived, Joseph was sitting at a table with Nigel drinking a beer and sharing a laugh. Maybe this is what the English and Irish need to get along, a cold beer.

I grabbed myself one and then sat down with them.

Yeah, the whole conversation seemed to be very positive. Joseph agreed that SOL records can have certain acts perform live, and get this, they will pay Joseph instead of him paying the bands.

All and all it was a good day, Joseph thanked me as did Nigel.

Well let's hope I can continue this good luck run and Oscar is home.

God damn must be my lucky day as he picked up the phone.

He gave me directions to his new apartment and told me to drop by for a beer.

I made sure all was good with Joseph and Nigel before I bolted.

Speaking of bolts, when I made it to Oscar's door and knocked, he had to have at least five deadbolts on his door.

Once he finally had the door opened, he asked where my housewarming gift was.

I blew him a kiss and told him I have a nickel bag of weed on me, does that count?

"Of course, it counts, come in my friend," said Oscar with a big smile.

He really didn't have much furniture; fuck, he really didn't have much of anything.

Said he doesn't plan on staying in the Bay Area for more than a year. I asked why.

"I like living like a Gypsy. If you have to flee underground in a moment's notice. One less headache."

Sort of made sense, points out his loyalty in not wanting to set roots.

"Funny Oscar, as I heard a funny story about you in Alaska."

"Humor me, Strongbow; what kind of story?"

"You are still fucking Tommy J's old lady Nicky. Do you not understand the consequences of what might happen to you if you two were caught?"

Oscar shrugged his shoulders as if the consequences were not real.

"I was asked to have a talk with you, Oscar. There is stuff going on behind the scenes and you fucking Nicky could derail business deals. Please keep your dick in your pants when it comes to her."

Fuck, I sounded like one of a million lectures Joseph has had with me.

"Listen, the boys need a ride up north again. You will be paid, but this time you and I are going fishing for salmon not dipping your pole into Tommy J's wife, sound good?"

Oscar asked when, and I told him. He said that is fine, but I know Oscar, and he hates anyone telling him what he can and can't do, especially regarding pussy.

We hit one of the local bars where Oscar had made more than friends with a couple of the waitresses.

It was funny as hell watching Oscar in action, he has no grace, but chicks love him.

We flew up to Alaska later that week. Stayed five days and the whole time was spent in the wilderness. Living off the land and streams. I have never experienced anything like it in my life. I wonder if Pat Price has leads in property up here.

It is so rugged, pure, and full of wildlife. If South Dakota is a 10, this would be a 100. I truly felt so alive.

31

Once home, Rachel brought my deed, and she was glowing. Like a thirteen-year-old with her first crush. I have never seen her this happy, which was so nice to see. I think it is time for big brother to have a talk with Pat and see what his intentions are.

She told me grandpa is going to leave the sanctuary of the reservation and attend the Monterey Jazz festival with us.

All things were good, weed sales were good. Tommy J ordered two hundred kilos. Mindy and I were hooking up a couple time a week.

The only negative was the whole Ella situation. Her drinking was really getting out of control. If we had a date that night, she was already three sheets to the wind. Sex has stopped as by the time we made it back to her place or mine, she would pass right out.

And with Ella, the booze became like truth serum. She would tell me how much her mom didn't like me. How her mom thinks I am a married man as I am never home and always taking off. Fuck, Ella even said we should have a baby to kill the old witch.

32

I was at my breaking point with Ella. She totally lost her mind the night before when I reminded her once again that my grandfather was flying in later this week and my whole family was heading to the Monterey Jazz festival. And that I could not travel with her to see the 49ers open the season in Minnesota.

The last thing I want, is to see Matt Burns. Ella told me that he beat up his fiancée, and the only reason he was not charged and thrown in jail, was the 49ers owner called in all kinds of favors. I believe because this was a contract year the owner would use these favors to be used against Burns to resign with the ball club.

Inside I want to break up with her today. But my grandfather wanted to meet her, and she wanted to meet him too.

Once grandpa heads back to the reservation I will end it with her. This is sucking the life out of me.

So, on Saturday night the 49ers were hosting this big gala to introduce the team to the press, and high-end season ticket holders.

It was a tuxedo and ball gown type of night. I kept my promise to go with Ella as long as I am not at the same table with Burns.

She promised that we will be at a table with her parents and other medical staff and their spouses.

33

I was to pick up Ella at four as they had a cocktail hour before dinner and we know that is Ella's main course, not the food.

I was ready to jump in the shower when the phone rang. It was Jerry and he said he needed to see me right away.

I looked at my watch and told him I would drop by before I picked up Ella.

Jerry had a pretty serious tone in his voice. I am pretty sure if grandpa canceled Rachel would let me know. Fucking, Oscar! What the fuck did he do now. That has to be it.

So, I grabbed a long shower. Washed myself in all the right spots and not for Ella, but for Mindy as I know she will be at this gala. Her hubby will be there, but that won't stop me from finding a place for us to fuck.

I put on my tux, throw my hair in a ponytail and I have to say, what a handsome son of a bitch I am.

Jumped in the Mustang and my gut told me something was not right. All my 8-tracks are missing. All the change I keep on hand is missing. For fuck sakes someone broke into my car. And whomever it was, they were clearly an amateur as all the wires under the dash are hanging down and cut. Fuckers tried to steal the car but didn't have a clue what they were doing.

My collar on my shirt is getting really tight and as I look in the rear-view mirror, I see my face is beet red.

I will put word out on the street to find the little cocksuckers who did this. Give me their names, and I will beat them to death.

I go back upstairs and switch the car keys for the pickup truck keys. Fuck, does this look good? Me showing up to this gala in my truck?

On the drive over to Jerry's I am super stressed about tonight and what Jerry wants. So, I decided to spark up the one and only joint I packed for the road trip. Was hoping I could smoke it on the way to Ella's place, but I need to get mellow now.

About halfway there I am starting to catch a nice buzz. Tunes are cool, shoulders are dropping, a nice smile comes to my face, and a bulge in my pants thinking about Mindy and I sneaking off for a quickie.

Now what would cause me to lose that hard-on and wipe that smile off my face? A fucking cruiser being spotted in my rear-view mirror.

The next couple minutes I decide to take a different route and sure as fuck where I go, he is following.

I have maybe ten tokes left on this joint and lord knows I need every single inhale.

As I look back, I believe I see him on his radio. You know I will be red flagged.

Fate when used as a synonym means karma, fuck me.

Then everything goes into slow motion at once. My eyes pick up the cruiser's cherries being turned on. I go to flick the joint in my mouth that I am still toking when I feel myself brace for serious impact for no known visible reason, pure basic survival instinct.

An old fuck driving this huge Buick boat pulls out of the supermarket and nails the front of my truck. The joint and red-hot heater is now being seared into my tongue. I can't pull it out as I am now heading for a vehicle in incoming traffic.

Poor VW didn't stand a chance as I nailed it head on.

I don't lose consciousness, but I am stunned. Gagging on the joint that has now traveled down my windpipe. I am choking and my tongue is killing me.

All I see is steam from my radiator but I here someone yelling, "Shut off the truck and come out with your hands high!"

I know there are tons of witnesses, and the cops will not gun me down in public.

So, I yell out in not the clearest English, I am coming out as directed by him.

As promised my hands are high but as I look ahead, I see the female driver's face in the VW is covered in blood and she looks really rough.

"Officer, I think you better attend to her," with drool coming down my cheeks

"Fuck you, Strongbow! Talking as if you are injured. Hands on your truck now!"

I can't believe his hatred towards me is his whole focus right now, and how does he know exactly who I am?

I look over at the VW and see flames coming from the rear of the vehicle.

"Her car is on fire you fucking idiot!" God I sound like Elmer Fudd.

Cop does a quick look, mutters fuck and tells me to keep my hands on the truck, and if I try and run away, he will shoot me dead.

I shake my head in disgust and do as told.

A couple bystanders help him get the girl out as other cops, ambulance and fire show up.

Eventually, another cop asks me what happened. I tell him my story.

Asshole cop makes his way back and goes to pat me down and cuff me.

By now the watch commander is on scene and asks Wilson what he is doing.

"Charging him with reckless driving."

"Officer Sanford, stand down. We have several eyewitnesses saying they saw the driver of the Buick accelerate out of the parking lot. Even the Buick driver admitted to hitting the gas instead of the brake. I told Officer Lamont to charge him with careless driving."

Sanford's face went red in anger, said bullshit and walked over to my truck and started to check the cab.

I looked at the watch commander and asked what Sanford is doing now. He asked him what he was up to.

"Strongbow doesn't smoke cigarettes and yet I saw blue smoke coming from his cab."

I looked at the watch commander and shrugged my shoulders.

So, he took a walk over and asked Sanford if he found anything. He looked at me and shook his head no.

He asked if I needed an ambulance.

"I am good other then biting my tongue."

He said that after all my insurance information was taken down, I could split.

Yeah, saying I burnt it on a roach would not be cool right about now.

So now what? My truck is fucked. I have to see Jerry, but now way will he come here with all these cops around. So, I hail a taxi and head to his place.

34

On the drive over, my neck is now starting to hurt, and a headache is starting. I touch the spot on my tongue that is burnt, and it hurts like a motherfucker.

You never need to knock or ring Jerry's doorbell as his dogs let him know you are there long beforehand. Fuck, maybe I need a dog.

Jerry looks out the curtain and tells his dogs to stand down. He opens the door and asks how I got here. I tell him taxi, which is almost as puzzling as my speech.

He offers me a beer; I pass and ask for a couple aspirins which shocks him.

I asked what was so important.

"First off, I am glad you were not seriously hurt. I still think about your mom and Pam whenever I see a bad car accident. Listen, I have good news and bad news."

Jerry then passes me an envelope.

"There is five thousand dollars in it. The Disciples of Doom are patching over this weekend to the Hell Hounds. Without your help this never would have happened. Now, having said that, they will be getting their dope directly from the club, Mitch. Sorry, that is part of the Hell Hound constitution. Hope you understand."

"No, I don't understand. I was making ten grand a month off these guys. So, I really fucked myself and helped out the club. If I would have known this, I never would have introduced you to Tommy J."

I stood up, nodded to Jerry, and headed to and out the front door.

I am almost at the sidewalk when Jerry asks if I need a ride, fuck him. I keep walking.

My feet and head are killing me. I look at my watch and I am almost two hours late from picking up Ella. So, I go and call her from a phone booth.

No answer. Do I take a taxi home and call it a night, or do I go to the 49er's gala?

Pretty sure if I don't show up for the gala, she will not meet my grandfather.

So, I go into the nearest drug store, buy a bottle of aspirin, and ask if they can call me a taxi.

I wash the meds down with a soda and head to the gala.

My head was really spinning. I truly felt betrayed by Jerry. Fuck the Hell Hounds.

No more favors for him.

I pull up and the doorman asks me where my reservation is as this is a private party. Fuck, Ella has them. So, I explained to him that my girlfriend got here ahead of me, and she must have them.

The guy shakes his head, no reservation no entrance. By now, a second guy has walked over and asks what seems to be the problem.

I explained the whole car accident, missed Ella, and so on.

This guy is eyeing me up and down the whole time. I know the look he is giving me. Seen it all my life. The oh fuck, it's a low life native look.

"Sorry sir, no reservation no entrance."

I am now eyeing both of them up and am ready to knock them both out when I hear a female voice asking Roger what the problem is.

Well, if it isn't the lovely Mindy Matheson all dressed up to the nines.

"Sorry Mrs. Matheson this gentleman doesn't have his reservation on him."

"Well, he is the date of Dr. Ella Mattina. I can vouch for him."

Roger is not happy, but he says fine. As I go to walk pass Roger, he puts his hand on my chest and says, "Next time bring your reservation."

This fuck is really barking up the wrong tree. I would snap his neck in a second. Fuck, in fact I am going to wait a couple weeks and catch him when he is getting off work and jump him.

I go over and give Mindy a hug and tell her looks amazing, and then I bite her neck.

Mindy laughs and says thanks while discreetly giving my cock a little tug.

As we head to the main ballroom, she asks if everything is ok. I tell her about the car accident, and nothing about Jerry.

"Well, I am glad you were not seriously hurt. Listen, how about at eleven you meet me by the coat check, and we rip off a quickie?"

"Mindy, you know how to put a smile on my face and a bulge in my pants. Eleven it is."

I tell her she better go in first and I will wait for my hard-on to go down before I enter. She smiles ear to ear and says good plan.

I watched Mindy's sweet ass as she walked away, that was the wrong thing to do as now all I am thinking about is pounding it.

After a couple minutes I entered the room. I ask a one waiter where Dr. Mattina is sitting.

Waiter is super nice and says that happens to be one of the tables he is working.

Judging by zero plates on the table, I missed dinner. Although I have anything but an appetite.

Ella's back is to me, but her mom sees me approaching and shakes her head in disgust. What a cunt.

She calls Ella who now turns around and looks at me. She looks at her watch and does the what the fuck hand gestures.

Hell, even her dad has a disgusted look on his face.

Love the support from these fucks; yeah, we are done as soon as Ella meets grandpa.

"Sorry guys. I had a car accident."

Everyone is now shocked as my speech is all fucked up. Mr. Mattina comes over and asks did I lose consciousness as it sounds as if I had or am having a stroke.

"No sir, bit my tongue, thanks for your concern."

Ella rolled her eyes and took a glass of wine. Speaking of eyes, hers look pretty glossy. And she is slurring, fuck, maybe she is the one having a stroke, wait, no, she's just drunk as usual.

I order a double of Jack on the rocks and look around the room as it is colder than the ice in my drink.

I see the douche-bag Matt Burns milling around and being loud as usual. Patting guys on the back and hugging their woman a little too tight.

I see where Mindy and her husband are sitting. That makes me smile. Come on eleven o'clock.

Ella is not talking to me at all. She has a conversation going with everyone and anyone but me. Yeah, after I hook up with Mindy I am out of here.

I am done my second drink when this guy asks everyone to please take their seat as they are going to do the introductions of the players, coaching, and support staff. Ella gets up, does not make eye contact with me, and leaves the table with her dad who gives me this sort of frown.

I might as well be a lepper sitting here at the table.

The scouting staff is introduced first followed by the medical staff.

When Ella is introduced, I raise my glass and look over at Mindy who now does the exact same to me. My first true smile since I sat at this ice table.

Ella waits for her dad's introduction then the both of them head back to the table.

Her mom, the ice queen, gets up and hugs them both and tells them how proud she is of both of them.

I don't say shit, fuck them all. Getting drunk on their dime now.

Eventually, it is the player's turns. Start with the rookies, then the subs, then the starting defensive squad followed by the starting offensive squad.

Next are the team captains. Last, but not least, is Matt Burns. I am curious as to what kind of stunned cunt he is engaged to.

So, I watch Matt go back to his table. His fiancée stands up and my stomach flips and my heart skips a beat.

I know this silhouette, the hair, body posture. It can't be but I have to see with my own eyes.

My mouth is dry, and my heart is racing as I get up from the table and head towards Burns' table.

What the fuck! This is a nightmare. The blood now starts to rush towards my muscles, and I am ready for a blood bath as my worst fears have come true.

Burns who now stares at me and lets go of his fiancée. He gets into a fighting stance.

She now recognizes me, and her hands go to her mouth.

"Charlene, you left me for him of all people?"

She trembles and says nothing as she tears up.

Burns has a big mouth and has no shortage of words for me, "Strongbow, you sound like a fucking dumbass."

I was not there to debate him; talk is for politicians. I am a warrior.

I know he can take a punch and has one hell of a pain tolerance, let's find out how much; it's go time, tough guy.

He is still yapping and is about six inches away from me, that's it, stupid, get right in my face.

Full force I come down with a Glasgow kiss and the blood is spraying everywhere. He is stunned so I kick him in the nuts and throw an overhand right.

He goes flying backwards and smashes the table he lands on. But I am not done yet. I flashback to Ella telling me he beat up Charlene. I am going to kill him.

I go to jump on top of his knee and end his career, but I can't move. A massive lineman has a hold of my collar. Fuck him too. I give him an elbow in the nuts, step on his foot and am once again free, well at least for a second, until I am swarmed by at least a dozen players.

They tackle me to the ground and now it is my turn to take a beating. Yep, no team Strongbow players to help me.

I am a beaten and bloody mess by the time the cops show up and arrest me.

I don't remember leaving the gala, the ride to the cop shop, or even being thrown in a cell.

Dazed and confused, I finally came to and have zero idea where I am and how I got here. The only thing I know for sure is everything, and I mean everything, hurts like a bastard.

I would say for the first bit, I truly thought I was back in San Quentin. I think of Charlene and then everything sort of comes back about what went down last night.

My stomach flipped. Charlene and Matt Burns. All the shots I took last didn't hurt near as much as the pain I was feeling in my heart.

Fucking betrayed twice yesterday, once by Jerry, and by Charlene. What a fool I have turned into. No more getting serious with anyone.

I called the guard who eventually made his way down. I asked what the charges were.

"Several counts of assault, willful damage, and creating a disturbance."

"When can I get before a judge to see how much my bail is?"

"It's the weekend, son. Not till at least Monday."

I shook my head, which really hurt by the way, and asked him if I could make my one phone call, and could I see a nurse. He said I am being shipped to county lock up in about an hour's time. I can see the nurse there. And he will talk to his supervisor about my phone request.

No doubts in my mind they know of my past criminal record, so they know I am entitled to one call. They don't want me getting off all charges because of a technicality. I guess only crooked cops named Getz get that.

Now the other decision, who do I call? Normally it would be my lawyer, but I have so much on the go right now. Maybe Rachel as grandpa is landing on Tuesday; hopefully I am out to pick him up.

Jerry, fuck him. Joseph wouldn't be impressed especially if he found out I was facing charges because of Charlene.

Donnie made the most sense. He could contact Rachel and my lawyer.

I sat back down and replayed what a fucking shit day yesterday was. I managed to find humor in the fact the date was Friday the 13th.

A couple minutes later, three guards show up and say I can make my call.

Before they open the cell, they tell me to spread eagle against the wall.

They come in, handcuff, and shackle me and say to follow them. Well, yours truly has done this walk many times and it's no problem.

I take a deep breath and call Donnie's number. Lucky for me he is home.

Tell him I am in the downtown cop shop but heading to county shortly.

Ask him to contact Levy and Rachel. He asks about Joseph; I say yeah tell him it is an assault charge.

When Donnie asks who I beat up, once again another deep breath, tell him the whole story. His only response, holy fuck.

The guard says times up. I needed help getting up from a seated position.

They warned me anything stupid on my part and they will beat me senseless.

Fucking tough guys, another deep breath as I nod my head.

I didn't end up going back to my cell. I was taken down to county lock up.

Once there I saw the full extent of my facial injuries. Holy fuck I look terrible as all you can see is slits for eyes. Both are swollen, and black and blue.

The nurse asks what happened. I told her I was jumped. He performs a bunch of tests on me. Hands me a couple aspirin and tells me I will survive.

I sit in the bullpen till the walking boss has one of his goons to come and get me.

As I come into his office, he is reading my official criminal and custody record.

He eyes me and tells me to take a seat. As he reads it, his only comment is *hmm*. He puts down my file and asks who made a mess of my face.

"A bunch of 49ers," was my answer.

He shakes his head, lights up a cigar and says, "You will more than likely see a judge Monday morning. No more fighting, Strongbow, or I will have you thrown in the hole. Judging by your face, not sure if trouble follows you or you go looking for it."

"A bit of both," was my response.

He told the goon to take me up to the eighth floor. He eyed me the whole time leaving his office.

I left his office and went into the main jail, that familiar wretched smell that only a jail or prison has, came back to me.

It is a combo of body odor, piss, shit, different ethnic homemade meals, cigarettes, blood, and mold.

At least we took the elevator up to the eighth floor as no way would my legs make it.

As soon as the elevator opens on the eighth floor you can feel the tension build.

You are in fact the new meat. But I was a solid pen timer, not new meat.

I truly feel like shit, my body is battered and beaten, but you know the warrior in you is always ready for the battle if need be.

You wonder if anyone wants to make a name for them by scrapping you. Are there Thunder members or associates that want to move up the club by seeking revenge and taking out the man who killed Mutt and Cruz?

So, you go back to everything you are taught about survival, right from the old man to George Daniels' prison survival rules in San Quentin.

Your heart beats a little faster as the adrenaline is racing through you like a locomotive. My chest is stuck out, I flex my lats, I can feel my arms getting pumped and my hands start to swell.

Your senses become keener, you figure out the dynamics of the pod, and you listen to anyone giving out instructions or someone calling your name that could be friend or foe.

The screws walk me to my cell and tell me to play nice. I nod to them while looking at the douche bullpen boss.

I take a quick look at my digs for the weekend, shake my head and wonder who my celly is, as there are all kinds of Jesus shit in here, fuck!

I go out into the common area when I hear someone say, "Strongbow, you made the front page of the news you crazy fucking Indian!"

I look over to see who said it as I know the voice.

A guy sitting at the far table lowered the newspaper and said to him. Well fuck me large, it is a long haired "Mad" Bill McDowell.

I look at all the cons, look at him and give my head a shake. Fuck is he working undercover right now? Because if he is, I want no part of this. I have my gangster reputation, a very solid reputation at that.

So, I call him over so no one else can hear our conversation.

"These boys in here find out you're a cop, I can't help you, Billy. You are on your own."

"I work on the other side of the street now, same as you. More money to be made, and less bullshit to put up with."

He now touches my face and goes, "Looks like you could have used some help of your own." He then touches my arms and says, "I am impressed. I thought for sure you would be either dead by now, or in a gutter from cranking smack."

I was not in the mood to tell him the whole Lucy and San Quentin story as Charlene is part of that story.

"So, what are you doing here, Bill?"

"I was in town doing a business deal. Went out for drinks afterwards, this mouthy fuck at the bar started to make fun of my accent. I smashed the beer in my hand into his skull. Turns out he was an off-duty cop. His whole table he was with were fucking cops. My lawyer will have me out Monday morning on bail. By the way, Mitch, don't use my last name. The identification I was carrying has me as Bill Kingston."

So now I am curious, really curious. No longer a cop, business deal here.

"So, what kind of business deal?"

Bill does that devilish grin of his, he looks around to make sure no one overhears us.

"I understand you are working for Joseph O'Reilly. Heard you made quite the impression on several people in Chicago."

I was a little bit shocked, but not totally as Joseph knows about Bill, and told me he is not to be trusted.

"You heard correct."

"Do you ever do free lance work?"

"Of course, I do. Talk to me, Billy."

"Do you remember Captain Stokes from Special Ops?"

"Of course I do, I served under him with SOG."

"Well, he stayed behind after all the soldiers came home and Vietnam fell to the ruthless commies. He had all these weapons that you fucks in the CIA were selling off for dope. He contacted me and asked if me and my brothers in Belfast would be interested in them. I shipped two crates of weapons to New York, then they will be put on a freighter and shipped back home."

I see money headed my way.

"How are you getting the crates from here to New York? And are there any more shipments coming in?"

"Tractor Trailer. Why Mitch? Talk to me."

"After you get bail, you will flee the scene back to New York. You won't want to risk the cops nailing you here again as sure as fuck they will have a massive hard-on for you. I have access to a guy with a plane. I can have weapons flown to anywhere in North America. I will be your contact here, for a fee of course."

"Of course, I respect that. I wouldn't work for free so why should you?"

He stared at me and took a deep breath, then he said, "I don't want that miserable bastard Joseph O'Reilly knowing anything of what is going on, Mitch. I mean not even a sniff, or our business partnership is done, understood?"

"Fully understand. He lets me make my own earnings."

So, for the next couple hours we talked about finances, contacts, and possible spots for Oscar to land without drawing the eye of law enforcement.

He said the next shipment was due in six weeks from now. Plenty of time to make sure there were no wrinkles.

Bill asked about Natasha and Katrina. I talked about them.

His ex-wife put a restraining order on him. Like me he can't see his kid.

I asked about Louie and AJ and asked if they are still pissed at me for taking Nicky's life.

"Not sure, you will have to ask them yourself."

"And what about you?"

"All good, I would want you doing the same for me."

Most of the people on our pod knew who I was or had either heard of me or Jerry. So, everyone left me alone. I believe they could tell Bill earned the nickname "Mad" Bill for a reason and gave him space.

Now, the nurse downstairs may not have given me anything for pain relief. But fuck, the cons in here, they took care of me.

Had a nice little buzz happening when it was time for nighttime lockup.

I went into my cell and there kneeling, and praying was my celly. This older fat black guy.

What the fuck could be the worst thing this Jesus freak is in for? I was taught in San Quentin not to get into someone else's politics, but I am fucking buzzed, so I asked him.

He stopped his prayers; he had this rage come to him. "I killed a doctor that kills the unborn innocent child of God. Jesus told me to take his life."

Well fuck me ten times over, never saw that coming.

Looks like I will be sleeping with one eye open.

35

Sunday morning Levy paid a visit. I told him everything that went down. Left nothing out as I know he has told me in the past he wants no surprises in court. Best to tell him everything.

Now speaking of surprises, I felt my gut flip when he told me my so-called simple assault charge against Burns has been upgraded to attempted murder.

He said the district attorney is going to have me held without bail.

Levy believes it is Burns' way of getting even with me. Burns told the district attorney what happened at Popeye's gym, thus the upped charge.

I truly felt like a beaten mule by the time I left Levy and headed back to my pod. So many emotions running through me, the scariest part is I can't control them or what is happening in the outside world.

Bill could tell something was up when I walked back into the pod.

"Fuck, Strongbow, you look like you saw a ghost."

"Yeah, in a way I did." I told him the whole story. You could tell the wheels were turning in his head, like Jerry thinking about how I can be replaced for the weapons job.

"I will be out in time for your next shipment, Levy is an amazing lawyer. I promise I won't let you down."

Bill smiled and said good in that Irish accent of his. I have heard Joseph say the same word, exact flow and I know it is not good.

I spent the rest of the Sunday buzzing out on painkillers, I had to shut the brain down. Fuck, I should have let Ruby kill Burns.

When lights out came, I went into my cell and Rev was on his knees praying with his rosary beads out.

He looked at me and I nodded my head and got into my bunk.

Heroin, sweet, sweet heroin would be my salvation right now, you think if I asked Rev, he would pray for me to find a fix?

Surprisingly, his chants or whatever you call them, had calmed me and I was able to fall asleep pretty fast.

I woke up a little early but laid there until lights came on. I definitely needed a shower and that is where I headed. The water was soothing, helped me to clear my head and yes final minutes was pure cold water.

I forced myself to eat some oatmeal and before I knew it, the screws called for me and Bill as they were now taking us to the courthouse for our bail hearings.

He seemed pretty calm, he knows as soon as they say Bill Kingston, bail granted. Mad Bill McDowell will disappear into thin air.

We sat in the jail in the bottom of the courthouse quietly talking about our plans one more time.

Bill was called the first prisoner of all twenty or so of us. And sure as fuck he didn't come back to the cell. Good for Billy, fuck the San Francisco cops and D.A.

One by one, prisoners were taken up. Finally, we were down to under five of us when a couple of screws called my name, finally. I thought for sure I would be last and by then the judge would be miserable and wouldn't even grant Mother Teresa bail.

The two screws were quiet, and my gut told me something was up. Sure as fuck, I was taken to an interview room and the two cops that interviewed me about my assault on Schinn were waiting for me inside.

I looked at both of them and shook my head with a half smile.

They asked me to have a seat, didn't really have much of a choice.

I asked what was going on as I don't want to miss my bail hearing.

Ramsey laughed and said no way will I get bail with the combination of me being an ex-con, who I assaulted as he is a hero to many in the community, fuck they even gave him the key to the city one year. That made me almost throw up. If only they knew the real Matt Burns.

"Well, I think that is up to my lawyer and the judge, don't you?"

Both looked stoned face at me, fuck them.

"Speaking of which, I think someone should go upstairs and bring him down here."

"Strongbow, we are not looking to charge you with anything. We are looking for Nyah Quinn. She seems to have vanished on us. Concerned about her safety that is all. When was the last time you saw her?"

I laughed and when they asked what was so funny, I said, "No one would ever fuck around with Nyah as long as her dad and uncle are alive."

Both nodded their heads in agreement with me, but they asked when the last time I saw her was.

"I honestly can't remember. After the fight with Schinn she backed right off. I think I might have scared her off to be honest."

I know Sean Quinn will lose his bond money he put up for Nyah, but he won't care. I know she means the world to him, even if he is a bully and control freak.

Not sure if they believed me or not, I was curious why the sudden interest in Nyah though.

Eventually, the screws took me right up to the courtroom. Guess I was the last con to have his bail hearing.

Levy smiled at me as I sat in the prisoner's box. Sure as fuck, the D.A.'s office had upped the charges to attempted murder on Burns, assault on the other guy who fucking jumped me, and willful property damage. How does that work?

The guy from the D.A.'s office said I got out of prison for murder and am deemed a threat to society.

Levy, like me, was pissed and set the record straight. Involuntary manslaughter, and I turned myself in for those charges, did my time. After all, I am a well-respected businessman.

Judge took one look at my battered face and said bail was denied. Slammed down the gavel and said lunch.

I was taken back to the county jail where I would now be housed until I hopefully make bail, or until I am convicted, and sent back to prison.

My new housing was up on the tenth floor. I was the only one not on a list to be sent to a federal prison.

It was a rougher floor than my last one. But most pen timers want quiet, no stupid fucking games and the biggest plus, yard and gym time.

My new celly didn't have Jesus shit all over the cell. He did have a good selection of porn books and judging by all the home-made tattoos, this is not his first time being locked up and waiting to be shipped to the pen. He looked like a Gypsy with long hair and full goatee.

His name was Newton Langtree and he was in for double murder. It turns out Newton is a contract killer for the D'Angelo family in Sacramento.

I was snickering on the inside about that one. Newton seemed solid as he was ratted out by this Italian in the D'Angelo family.

No matter how solid he was, I wasn't saying shit about my connections with the Battaglia family. Especially with me killing Carm D 'Angelo and several of his men in San Quentin.

Fuck; then you get that shiver up your spine. Is it a coincidence that I share a cell with him? Has Sal finally been tipped off that I am the guy who took Carm's life, and now he wants revenge? Has he called in favors to have me finally killed?

As I know all too well, it shouldn't be, but getting away with murder in prison is fairly easy as you have way too many cons who are already convicted of murder or other violent crimes.

So, I made sure to eat with him, let Newton do all the introductions to the people he thought were solid in the pod. Quite a few knew me, or at least heard of me, and of course Jerry. He was a little shocked by how much respect I was getting from my fellow cons.

Once it was yard time, this was my time to show others what I was all about.

Pumping iron and hitting the heavy bag. My face was still tender, but my fists, feet, and arms were all ready to show off. And show, I did.

At one point I threw combos on the heavy bag like Ali and Bruce Lee themselves.

I tuned everyone out, and when I stopped to suck air, I had everyone in my pod looking at me.

What started off as me flexing my muscles turned into a vision of revenge. All I could see was Burns' face on the heavy bag. Him fucking Charlene and laughing at me locked up. I am going to kill him when I finally get out.

This is one kill that will be as slow as Getz's murder. I will make that fucker suffer; I will break every bone in his body. I will castrate him like Mazzetti, and then will bury him alive in a shallow grave.

Newton came over and said, "Fuck, Strongbow; you are one bastard I wouldn't want piss off."

I stared at him as I was still in the kill zone.

That night after dinner, Newton asked if I had ever done time before as I certainly knew how to act and behave in here. Told him I did a deuce in San Quentin. He asked who I hung out with in there.

No way could I tell him Albert and Frankie Knuckles. So, I told him Aryans, most of them have an association with the Hell Hounds.

I know that D'Angelo always used the Thunder as muscle, not sure if it is the same in Sacramento or not. He came out and asked if I was a full patch with the Hounds. That I could answer honestly. I told him no and my whole reasoning why. But you don't shun the club because you never know if being a known associate will keep me alive in here.

One thing about doing time, especially dead time is you lose track of days of the week. You worry when it is shower, grub, and yard time.

I saw Levy the next day, he talked about how the D.A is in the pocket of the owner of the 49ers. He told me to be patient as he too has powerful friends who hate the owner.

36

A couple days later the screw told me I had a visitor. You hope it is Levy and he has good news.

But when I came down to the visitation room my stomach flipped, and I truly felt like the biggest disappointment on the face of the planet.

Rachel was on the other side of the glass along with my grandfather. I felt so ashamed of myself. I totally forgot about asking him to the Monterey Pop Festival. I had to beg him to leave South Dakota and the comfort of the reservation.

He eyed me up and down in my jailhouse clothes. I could tell it bothered him as much as it bothered me seeing the look of shame on his face. I may be one of the most feared guys in this jail, but my body language right now is not showing it.

Rachel picked up the phone and asked how I was doing.

I could tell it bothered her with me being locked up once again, but she had to stay solid and strong in front of grandpa.

"You know, I am doing alright. How are you guys doing?"

"Well, we would be doing better if you were heading to Monterey with us. I hope you don't mind but I gave Pat your ticket. He will pay you for it."

I shook my head no and said, "Tell him to keep an eye on you and grandpa and that is payment enough."

The whole time when Rachel and I were talking grandpa stared at me. He wasn't rude; I know he was trying to get a vibe off me.

Eventually he asked Rachel for the phone in the middle of our conversation.

I took a deep breath and really wasn't sure what he was going to say to me.

"Rachel tells me you are in here because of a woman."

I nodded my head yes.

"And do you love this woman, Mitchell?

I again nodded to him.

"Do you think she loves you?"

"I thought she did, not sure now."

He shook his head no.

"The woman in your life brings out a demon in you, Mitchell. One that you have a hard time putting back in the cage. They confuse your heart, brain, and the smart warrior in you. One who truly loves you will have a calming effect on you; make you appreciate life and what you have. Not one who drives you to madness."

Once again, he stared at me as I nodded my head and started thinking about what he said.

"Do you know how long you are going to be incarcerated for? Are you going to miss hunt camp?"

I looked over to Rachel who discreetly shook her head no. I guess he thinks this is a dust up charge and I will be released sooner than later.

"I am not sure, I still have to see the judge, things move really slowly around here."

Then there is that moment of silence as he stares at you. He freaks me out when he does this shit as I never know if he is staring at me, or the spirit around me.

Before he stood up to leave, he said he hoped to see me at hunt camp. He said I need to get back to Mother Nature. I fully agreed with him, pretty sure the D.A doesn't echo this.

Rachel said she is going to talk to Levy and see what is going on.

Seeing her disappointed in me being back in jail really bothered me, fuck Charlene, this all comes back to you.

Over the next couple days, the disappointment in my grandfather's face was really gnawing at me. Especially on the weekend, to be specific the Monterey Pop weekend. I had a huge amount of frustration brewing inside me and I was really hoping someone in the yard would get stupid with me.

Newton, on the other hand, I found was starting to get stupid and on my nerves.

I understand shaking down the cherries for extra food or even protection money, I have been there. But to put a cigarette burn into some scared guy's family picture even after he has paid for your protection, fucking wrong in so many ways.

But he is my celly, and he will be shipped out sooner than later, so I bit my tongue.

I had several more visitors that week. Oscar, who used an alias, asked if I needed anything. I said other than a get out of jail card, the fucker must have known what I was going to ask and brought the one from the Monopoly board game. I told him I had an entertaining job offer from one of our SOG brothers. And that if I am not out in four weeks, I would give him the contact information.

Janine visited and I assured her it is business as usual in Pamdora's. make sure to pay her and Beth. If anyone from out-of-town calls, tell them I have gone fishing in the Florida Keys

Joseph showed up, he had that smug look on his face. He asked three words.

"Over a woman?"

I have no idea why he asked me when everyone in the Bay area, fuck, I would say all of North America, as me punching out Burns made national headlines.

"Yes, over a woman Joseph. You know I loved her, cut me some slack."

Joseph nodded and said he will see what he can do. I thanked him and told him to say hi to Donnie. With him being an ex-con, I knew he wasn't allowed to visit.

Ella came after the third day. It was first thing in the morning, and you could tell she had been drinking already.

All she did was bitch about how I embarrassed her and her family. I smeared her family name with the 49ers. Thankfully the owner only fired her, and not her dad.

Her rant went on for a solid twenty minutes straight. I finally interrupted her and asked if we are through, she said dam right and started to rant and ramble once again so I got up and left, fuck I would rather sit in my cell than hear her.

Now, one of the most intriguing visitors was Mindy Matheson. She was wearing a skin-tight red dress and I swear if she coughed her tits would pop right out.

She saw all that went down that night and wanted to hear my side. I told her the whole story while staring at her tits.

She thought the whole story was kind of hot, she asked if I would fight for her. I told her I would kill for her. As soon as I said that her nipples popped out.

Mindy told me she would see what she can do as she knows people in high places. I thanked her and then headed to my cell and jerked off.

Now on Saturday, exactly two weeks since the brawl took place, I had a visitor that made me mentally breakdown for the first time since Lucy's death.

A screw came and got me, said I had a visitor. As you are walking down you wonder exactly who it is, my cock and imagination was hoping for Mindy, the con in me was hoping it was Levy.

But as soon as I walked into the visitor's room I felt a change in the air; fuck, I should have listened to my gut and turned around. But I couldn't as soon as I saw who it was. Fuck me it was Charlene Borden.

A huge part of me wants to do what I did with Ella, turn around and head back to my pod. But I know deep down I need closure, so many questions I need answered. More than likely, this will be my one and only attempt to talk to her. If I do make bail, you know I want to be able to have any contact with her.

So, I head to my chair, no smile, intense eye contact. I noticed she is wearing a dress shirt that is fully done up to the neck, and you will never guess what is around her neck? A necklace, and on that necklace is a crucifix with a diamond right in the middle.

Charlene picks up the phone first, and yes, another surprise, one hell of a huge engagement ring. Has to be 2-3 carats big.

"First off Mitchell, I want you to know that I forgive you for attacking Mathew."

I actually pulled the phone away from my ear and stared at it. Is the phone fucking up, or did I hear what I think I heard?

"Should I forgive that cocksucker from stealing you from me?"

Her cheeks now matched her hair, fire red.

"You never owned me; Mathew doesn't own me. The only person that owns me is our saviour, Jesus Christ."

Once again, I pull the phone away and have a look at it, fuck this time, I even tap in on the desk.

She shot me the most stoic, cold hearted cunt face ever,

"Mitchell, it is not to late for you to devote your life, and heart to Jesus."

I was beyond fucking pissed.

"And where was your Jesus when you were being raped in San Quentin? He didn't appear out of thin air and save you; I fucking did. After everything that has happened to my family, and everything that I saw in Nam, there is no God, only the devil laughing at you. And the devil, I have seen his work firsthand, on many occasions. As have you."

"You are right, the devil walks beside us. He preys on the weak, he preys on me. But with the guidance of Reverend Wilson, yes Heather and Kurt's father, and the love of Mathew, my eyes, and my heart have been opened. I will not fear evil anymore."

Fuck me large. Reverend Wilson getting even with me? What a hypocrite. I was never a great poker player, perhaps the other players could read my face, maybe I had the twerk, or twitch that gave me away. But right now, I want to hurt Charlene so fucking bad. She ripped my heart ripped out of my chest. I fucking put my life on the line to keep her alive, I killed so she could live. I guess my eyes are finally opened, seeing her for what she truly is, a weak coward. She will always be a whore. Matt will shun her, and when he does, she will drop her pants for anyone that will give her attention. Time for me to give her some much-needed attention, attention could be an understatement.

"I was out at Herschel's place a couple weeks back. He asked where you've been. It appears you made quite the impression on several people in the porn industry. Yeah, he has quite the footage of you being gangbanged that night, sucking on pussy, basically letting everyone have their way with you. What do you think the good reverend and Matt would say, Charlene? Would make quite the scandal if it fell into certain hands. I really don't give a fuck about and your new Jesus and Matt Burns loving life. What I care about is getting out from here, and having your husband drop all charges against me. I understand the 49ers owner is putting pressure on the D.A. to make sure I get as much time as possible. What do you think the owner would say about the tapes?"

Charlene had tears rolling down her face, asking why am I doing this to her.

"Why am I doing this to you? Are you fucking serious? You are the one who went AWOL on me. I fucking asked you to move in with me, I was willing to change my lifestyle for you. I gave you my heart, I said I loved you. And San Quentin proved it."

Her whole face changed, resting cunt face now appeared.

"You wouldn't have changed your lifestyle for me, I am not that naive. Reverend Wilson, Kurt and several of his colleagues told me all about your lifestyle. They let me know you are the prime suspect in several murders in the Bay area. How you were muscle for the Hell Hounds and Joseph O'Reilly. I know your dirty little secret from inside San Quentin. I know you killed that one guy; I didn't let Detective Trower know that I covered for you when they asked if I saw anyone come through the library. That tape from Herschel's wedding gets released. I will have a long talk with Kurt Wilson and the District Attorney. I will let them know how you threatened to kill me if I ever told anyone what I know, you hear me Strongbow? You will fry in old sparky. And I will pull in every favor that I can to watch you take your last breath."

Hearing her threaten and tell a vicious lie to have my life taken, made me smile. What a phony fucking cunt she is. Jesus who?

You know, she went missing once on me, might be time for her to go missing this time for Burns.

I blew her a kiss, got up and headed back to my cell, yeah, time to plot and plan my revenge, after all, there is a revenge, then there is Strongbow revenge.

www.ingramcontent.com/pod-product-compliance
Lightning Source LLC
Chambersburg PA
CBHW020401030726
47496CB00007B/2253